THE
RIVAL CRUSOES.

"THE YOUNG RUFFIAN STRUCK HIM A VIOLENT BLOW."

1.

THE
RIVAL CRUSOES.

CHAPTER I.

A WONDERFUL ISLAND.

SOME years ago, an island suddenly appeared on the coast of Norfolk, within the jurisdiction of the corporation of the ancient and venerable town of Yarmouth.

At first it was only a sand bank.

By degrees, however, by the agglomeration of seaweed and other vegetable substances, it began to show signs of becoming valuable.

It increased also in size, and after some years was more like a verdure clad meadow than a sand bank.

As it was likely to increase yearly in importance, it was claimed by the corporation, and also by the lord of the manor.

The latter, acting with decision, built a small wooden hut on the centre of the island, and placed a man in possession.

Joe Blake was what is called a Jack-of-all-trades; a bit of a sailor, a bit of a fisherman, and something of a gardener.

Under his care the island prospered, was cultivated, and appeared likely to do well.

He made himself a garden, grew vegetables, caught fish, smoked and dried them on the bank, while, at the same time, he allowed bathers and pic-nic parties to enjoy themselves on the level meadow and pleasant strand.

The corporation brought an action against the lord of the manor to decide whose property it was.

But law was slow in those days, and the matter remained undecided for years.

In the meantime persons of all ranks enjoyed its fragrant breezes.

One of the favourite frequenters of the island was Ned Summers, a youth of about fourteen.

His grandfather was an admiral on the retired list, and had but one idea of Ned's future.

He was to be a sailor.

He was studying for his profession, and fortunately for him one of his favourite occupations was swimming.

He could already make his way from the mainland to Joe Blake's hut; and from this man he received many a useful hint.

The old sailor doted on him, and told him many wild and exciting narratives of the sea, always so attractive to the Boys of England.

At length it became necessary for him to leave Yarmouth to go through the preliminaries required before he could join his ship.

He had dined with his grandfather—his father was away on a foreign station—and then made up his mind to pay one last visit to Joe.

The day had been fine, but for several hours the sea-gulls and curlews, which hovered around, had been flying more and more inshore, while the bright blue of the firmament was chequered to windward by those mazy feathery streaks called mare's tails.

A storm had been brewing for hours, and when Ned Summers reached the denes in front of the island, the strong east wind became a tempestuous blast; by the time he reached the shore it had become a furious hurricane, roaring, shrieking, howling, and bellowing.

"A bad night for Joe, sir," said one of the men, who were looking out seaward.

Ned Summers peered in the direction of the island, but the boiling billows so foamed and tumbled against the leaden sky that he could make out nothing.

"I should like to fetch him off," said Ned, with a meaning glance towards the men.

"Can't be done, sir," replied one; "no boat of ours would live."

Ned thrust his hands in his pockets, a habit of his when occupied in meditation, and still gazed in the direction of the island.

Suddenly he caught sight of a faint glimmer of a light.

The old man was probably about to make some signal to them.

Next instant the flare of a torch was seen, and then the hut of the guardian of the island was in a flame.

He had evidently done it on purpose.

"Something wrong, I'm sure," said Ned Summers, throwing off his jacket. "I shall swim."

The men declared that it was simply madness, and would only render his own death a certainty.

"Joe Blake shall not perish!" cried the brave boy, resolutely.

The men spoke in whispers, and after some minutes, decided that they would put out to the number of eight, with Ned to steer, in order to save the worthy old fisherman.

Sailors, especially English sailors, do not like being outdone by a boy.

The boat was soon run into the boiling waves, and manned by four pair of stout oars.

The sea, however, ran so high, with the wind off shore, that a thin, but strong line was made fast to the bows of the boat, so that once they turned towards land the men might aid them by hauling in the slack.

The waves broke like thunder on the shore, and had any of the wives or children of the boatmen been by, they would never have been allowed to start on their humane but perilous enterprise.

In a few minutes they were lost to sight in the tossing billows.

Ned stood up with the tiller in his hand.

For a few minutes he could make out something like a glow, but the fierce impetuosity of the wind soon destroyed the burning hut, and they had nothing to guide them.

No island was to be seen, nothing but the white waste of waters.

The men looked wonderingly around.

Joe Blake and his island home had, to all appearance, vanished!

Suddenly, however, the water seemed to get smoother, and the old fisherman was seen lashed to a beam.

In a moment he was detached from this extempore raft, and hauled in the boat insensible.

The men then gave a ringing cheer, and turned towards the land.

Though the rope, which those on land began at once to haul in, was neither very thick nor very strong, it still served the purpose of guiding them directly towards the land, which was completely invisible, for to the fury of the blast was now added torrents of rain, which rendered everything, beyond a few yards, completely undiscernible.

Ned did all he could to keep his boat in a steady course, but, with such waves tumbling in, it was all but impossible.

Presently, however, he made out the dark outline of the shore, and saw the men ready to assist them.

Every time the waves receded they rushed in to meet the boat, and at last, tossed on a billow heavier and more powerful than ordinary, it sped with great force and vehemence upon the sand, and, ere it could be drawn back by the strength of the undertow, was dragged up high and dry.

Old Joe Blake was insensible, but evidently alive.

He was carried to an inn, put in a warm bed, and taken every possible care of.

Ned, after promising a handsome reward to the men, went home, where the news had, however, preceded him, and where, though he got a lecture from his mother and grandfather, he also received every kindness.

Next day, when the wind abated,

the wondering population of Yarmouth turned out to see the strange island.

It had ceased to exist.

The sea which had yielded it up, had swallowed it completely, and no trace of it was ever seen again.

It is said that the jury were about to retire to consider their verdict when the astonishing news reached Norwich, where the case between the lord of the manor and the corporation of Yarmouth was being tried.*

The case was abandoned, but the incident was long remembered by the friends of the young and gallant lad.

---

* Historical. The law suit lasted some time. The Yar, from which the ancient town took its name, was continually changing its mouth, until science and engineering succeeded in enclosing it in due bounds.—*Palmer's History of Yarmouth.*

CHAPTER II.

THE WRECK ASHORE.

THE news of this gallant exploit, which was noised over the whole town and county, preceded Ned Summers' arrival on board the ship to which he was appointed.

The admiral took care to let the captain know of it; he mentioned the circumstances to his officers, through whom it was made common property of in the ship.

Ned Summers was now midshipman on board a sea-going vessel—a frigate bound for the Indian seas.

His courage, his courtesy, and manliness, at once made him a great favourite.

Some of the usual practical jokes were played upon him, and then this persecution, more and more discouraged in the navy, wholly ceased.

He had one enemy, however.

On board ship, as in most schools, there is generally a bully, who is also in most cases very much of a coward.

The officers of the " Sultana " formed no exception.

One Samuel Petworth, a midshipman of one year's more standing than Ned, took a dislike to him from the first.

He tried at first to tyrannise over him, but as Ned was perfectly well able to take care of himself, this he found useless.

One of those pitched battles, which are winked at, if not allowed, settled the question of strength and science in Ned's favour.

Sam then resolved to bide his time in the hope of catching his rival napping.

In vain.

Ned did his duty strictly, was attentive and respectful to his officers, and had therefore nothing to fear.

Sam fumed with rage, and in proportion as Ned Summers gave him no provocation, and was even inclined to be civil to him, did his hate increase.

The vessel having called in several ports, took its way at length to the southward.

For several weeks the weather was all that could be desired; but, after a dead calm, near the line, suddenly changed and blew with extreme violence.

Every precaution, however, was taken, and though the fresh breeze soon increased to a gale and the sea was very heavy— so bad as to compel them to keep under close-reefed main-topsail and reefed foresail—the gallant ship bore herself admirably.

For several days the storm not abating, and the dense cloudiness of the sky preventing observations, the captain grew very uneasy.

Fortunately, after a week's duration, the weather cleared, and the vessel was found to be in sight of land, both high and wooded, though no one could say what land it was.

A boat was ordered to go ashore in search of water, fresh provisions, and any fruit or vegetables which might be found.

It was also the duty of the officer in command to discover what land it was.

As the long boat was sent with a large crew, two midshipmen were allowed to accompany the second lieutenant in command.

These happened to be Ned Summers and Samuel Petworth.

The ship did not anchor, simply lying to, with the fore-topsails aback, and the boat's crew received strict injunctions not to waste any time more than was necessary.

Ned was delighted.

Much as he liked the sea, much as he was attached to his profession, he could not but feel considerable pleasure in the prospect of a run on shore.

He was, moreover, allowed a gun and ammunition, which added to the zest of the adventure.

As they approached the shore and entered a bay, or mouth of a river, they soon became aware of the tropical character of the climate.

The shore was covered with trees, leaving scarcely any landing places.

As, however, they advanced higher up, rocks were discovered, as well as a fine sandy beach, and, what was better than all, a sparkling cascade of water.

"Pull away, my hearties!" cried the lieutenant, and, in a few minutes more, the bows of the boat grated on the sand.

It was a very beautiful spot, but, above all, the bright, fresh water was welcome, and the empty casks being rolled on the beach, the men at once prepared for the task.

The lieutenant looked grimly at the two boys, who were leaning on their guns.

"I am afraid," he said, "to let you loose on this island. There is no knowing what damage you may do. Well, don't shoot an elephant, as it is too big, nor a paroquet, because it is no use; anything else we shall be glad of."

"All right, sir."

"If you see any natives, be cautious, and fall back. There are more savages than white men about here, I expect," he added, and turned to his duty.

Now Ned would gladly have joined Samuel in an expedition, but that worthy, as soon as the officer's eye was no longer upon him, scowled furiously at his companion, and turned away.

With a shake of the head, and a light laugh, Ned went in the opposite direction.

He soon found that the island, though so wonderfully rich in vegetation on the side towards the sea, was very varied as he advanced into the interior.

There were stunted grass, low bushes, and small fields and rocks, on the summit of which he fancied he could see something moving.

At first he was inclined to believe that what he had discovered was the track of human beings, but his keen, quick and sportsman-like instinct soon indicated to him that it was something of the goat species.

With a wildly beating heart he now made up his mind to a day's shooting— this was game worthy of being pursued.

The rocks were rude and difficult to climb, but he was resolved to use caution.

Clasping his gun firmly with the left hand he contrived to haul himself upward by means of roots and bushes, until at last he reached a jagged summit, from which he could look back from whence he came, and gaze also on a narrow valley beneath him.

The goats had fled from the summit and were all in the valley below, prepared, he knew not which, for defence or flight.

The descent was steeper than the ascent, and yet Ned, who was one of those who like not giving up an attempt, determined to do his best.

At his own end of the valley was a small wood, and this he determined to reach.

Lying down on all fours, he surveyed the path before him.

It was difficult, but possible; and without letting go his gun, he commenced to descend.

Slowly, but safely he reached the bottom, taking little care as to how he was to get back, and at length was securely landed on level ground.

The goats were about forty feet from him, browsing the scanty herbage of the valley.

Every now and then they would look up, and then continue their occupation.

Something told the animals there was danger, though they did not actually see the hunter.

Taking a few minutes to gain breath, Ned selected the finest and fattest of the herd, and fired.

The echoes reverberated sharp and ringing in that narrow and confined valley.

When the smoke cleared away, not even the spoil selected was to be seen.

Ned stood amazed and bewildered, and half inclined to rub his eyes.

Pushing forward, however, to where the whole body of goats had stood, he saw by the marks of blood that his shot had not been ineffectual.

Bounding in pursuit, and loading as he went, he soon descried the flock ascending a steep hillside at no great distance, but too far for him to reach.

In the rear was the wounded animal dragging himself along with great difficulty.

Several of the other goats sniffed around him.

Excited to the utmost, Ned followed, after loading his gun.

The goats were bounding from crag to crag and shelf to shelf of the rocks, in evident terror, while every moment the laggard was losing strength.

At length he suddenly fell upon his side, and, when the young midshipman came up to him, he found that he was dead.

In the first excitement and delight of the victory, all idea of the animal's sufferings were forgotten.

Ned, having assured himself that the animal was quite dead, looked about him to see how to leave the valley.

He was determined not to leave his trophy behind.

Tying the animal's legs together and throwing it on his back, Ned began the ascent of the hillside.

It was steep, rugged, and, loaded as he was, the task was very arduous.

Still he persevered, and at length was near the summit.

Below him was a small cluster of live oaks; above, one of those trees with its roots overhanging the summit of the cliff.

Ned grasped at this, and as he did so, caught sight of the villanous countenance of Samuel Petworth leaning over and grinning at him.

"I've got the best of it here," said the young ruffian, and struck him a violent blow on the head.

CHAPTER III.

HARD AGROUND.

WHEN Ned Summers came to his senses it was quite dark, that pitch darkness of the tropics when neither sun, moon, nor stars are anywhere visible.

He was in intense pain.

Every bone in his body ached, and when he strove to rise he soon found that one ankle was broken or sprained.

Dead silence everywhere!

The morning and evening hum of the forest in hot climates was over.

With a deep groan Ned fell back.

He was parched with thirst, and though he had his bottle or gourd of water by his side, it was quite empty.

What had happened?

He had a most confused recollection.

His head appeared not to be as clear as it should have been.

Then, with lightning rapidity, it all flashed across him; the storm, the landing, the chase, and finally the cowardly assault by Samuel Petworth.

He knew that worthy disliked him, but did not know he hated him with such virulence.

Then he recollected that Samuel had been once punished on his evidence, for what appeared very like theft, and threatened with dismissal from the service.

That accounted for all.

Now the terrible question arose as to how he was to drag himself to the ship; the boat was in all probability gone before now.

At this instant a loud boom fell upon his ears.

They were firing signal guns to warn him that the search was either over or would recommence in the morning.

Satisfied with this, Ned Summers whispered a silent prayer, and again fell off into a heavy slumber.

When he again attempted to move, the pain was even acuter than before, especially in the case of his ankle.

It was day, however, and he could look around.

Near him was his gun, and the goat which had cost him so dear.

All, however, was silent; no human cries, no firing of guns, nothing to give him hope.

Something must be done, or he would perish there where he lay.

With a great effort he contrived to rise, but found that he could not walk.

Then, for the first time, an utter sense of loneliness and despair fell upon his soul.

The ship people had given him up; supposed him lost, or destroyed by the natives who probably abounded on an island of such extent.

At all events, some effort must be made to save his life.

In his pocket was a flint and steel, such as boys in those days generally had about them, and a knife.

Around were heaps of dry wood ready to burn like tinder.

Crawling about on his hands and knees, he collected a pile, and, as fast as he could, set fire to it.

It burned rapidly, but being very dry, made scarcely any smoke.

The sight of the embers put an idea into his head; and drawing the goat to him, he cut several slices of the best part, which, being tolerably full of gravy, and only done on the outside, gave him at once relief from hunger and thirst.

Then he waited with more patience for whatever might be going to happen.

But night came again, and still there was no relief.

That night Ned Summers was feverish in the extreme, and had odd and curious dreams; but towards morning rose with a determination not to lie there and die like a dog.

His ankle, from rest, was considerably better, while the bruises over his body were less severe.

The remains of the goat he secured on a bough, with very little prospect of ever seeing it again, and then slowly began his journey.

The valley appeared to descend beyond the grove of live oaks; and he thought he would try this way.

It was easier, the sward was soft and pleasant, and soon he saw the wished-for opening.

The valley debouched upon a kind of lake, which, in his present state, he thought the most beautiful sight he had ever seen.

As soon as he came to its banks—it was only a pool—he cast off his shoes, and bathed his foot.

Finding the water neither too cold nor too hot, he soon undressed, and indulged in a thorough swim.

The effect was magical.

His whole system appeared renovated, his energies seemed to return, and himself feel altogether a different being.

Still, when he continued his route, he had to walk slowly and with extreme care.

Following the outlet of the little lake, he soon reached a small river, which, of course, led towards that where he had left his companions.

He contrived, by continual rests, by seeking the occasional shade of a tree, to come in sight at last of the open sea.

The ship was gone!

As he feared, he was abandoned in this wild and desolate region, without a friend, without means of existence, without hope of escape!

He had just eight charges of powder for all ammunition, he had the clothes he stood in, and, unless he became a feeder on roots, herbs, and perhaps fruits, he knew not what would become of him.

It was no comfort to him that he was placed in a romantic and exciting position.

Ned wanted to distinguish himself in his profession, and not in contests with savages and wild beasts.

His heart fell wholly within him.

Had he even known where he was, it might have given him some hope, as, if in the track of ships, he would probably be rescued.

Then came the reflection as to why he had been abandoned without a thorough search of the island.

He knew the captain and officers too well, he thought, to think they would lightly abandon him.

Suddenly the thought occurred to his mind that perhaps he had lain insensible a day and a night; but as this was a matter impossible to be decided, he dismissed it from his mind.

The future, not the past, must be thought of.

The first matter to be taken into consideration was some sort of a home.

Like everyone else placed in similar circumstances, this he determined should be near the sea, as the human mind is so constituted that hope scarcely ever deserts it

From that position he would see every passing ship.

The next thought was for food and clothing.

Of vegetable food he would probably have more than enough.

Then came the consideration, was the island, for such he believed it to be, inhabited by any wild and savage beasts, or, worse still, by venomous snakes?

The very idea made him shudder and look round for a site whereon to make something of a hut.

How was it to be done?

His clasp knife was neither large enough nor strong enough to avail him.

The matter was therefore hopeless, while in his present weak state exertion was neither agreeable nor possible.

Very downcast and miserable, Ned seated himself on the banks of the sea, to reflect.

Presently, however, he found the heat in that position too great, and rising, prepared to retreat to the shade of some lofty trees.

As he did so, he once more gazed out towards the sea.

It was low water, and the sight of some shells exciting his curiosity, he waded out a little way through the pools, and brought ashore a number of oysters.

They were a very coarse specimen, but they were fat and nutritious.

They afforded Ned a hearty meal under the trees, and this finished, he indulged in the siesta or afternoon nap so essential in hot countries.

When he awoke he was much restored, and his ankle, which he had bound with a neckerchief, was much less painful.

He looked around him.

There were many trees at hand in which he might pass the night, but they were too high for him to climb.

Something else must be thought of.

Looking inland he saw at no great distance a line of rocks, and hoping that here he might discover a temporary retreat, he slowly took his way in that direction.

The ground was smooth, the grass pleasant, the trees, though scattered, gave an agreeable shade.

When, however, he reached the rocks, they proved to be arid and steep, covered only by a rough and prickly cactus.

Ned, nothing daunted, moved slowly along, hoping to find some hollow, or cavern, or fissure, where he might pass the night.

Nor were his hopes doomed wholly to be disappointed.

He had not gone far when he noticed one of the rocks to project over a kind of hollow, which was, however, choked by prickly and other plants so completely as to leave in doubt how far the hollow extended.

Ned scarcely hesitated.

Dry grass, fallen boughs, and inflammable materials of all kinds lay round about.

In a few minutes a respectable pile was collected; and, striking a light, he cast a torch into the midst.

A dense smoke arose, which drove him back some distance, followed by flames which wavered for a few minutes and then burnt steadily.

When the fire was over, Ned advanced, and saw clearly that there was a cavern beyond, but could not enter because of the heat on the threshold.

He drew back accordingly and determined to wait awhile.

At length the ashes ceased to smoulder, and, taking up the bough of a tree, he swept them on one side.

Then, lighting this bough, which was dry and inflammable, he proceeded to examine his discovery.

It was a small, dark, and gloomy cavern, with a very narrow entrance, and not a fissure by which light or air could enter.

It was likely to prove a good hiding-place and a shelter in wet weather, but nothing else.

However this may be, Ned was compelled to make it his abiding place for that occasion, as he could not go any further.

Fortunately he had discovered very many fruits as he moved slowly along, but did not venture to try any save a wild strawberry and a kind of acorn which proved very sweet.

He had his water bottle, without which, in such a climate, no sailor ever lands.

A few boughs and some dry grass made him a comfortable bed, on which, utterly exhausted and worn out, he lay down, soon after sundown, his loaded gun close beside him and his bold heart not without fear of what would turn up next.

But the night passed without further adventure, though once or twice Ned was startled by singular noises.

Somebody or something appeared to be moving about at no great distance.

When, however, he peered out, nothing was to be seen.

Leaving his gun at half cock close to his hand, he contrived to doze through the night, while awaiting the morning with painful anxiety.

Was his mysterious visitor a man or a beast?

CHAPTER IV.

NED FURTHER EXPLORES HIS TERRITORIES.

WHEN the young midshipman woke in the deep gloom of that cavern, it was with a very confused idea as to where he was.

For a moment he thought that he had been placed in the dark and close cockpit for punishment.

Two minutes after, he sincerely wished he had, as memory came back with its inexorable review of the past.

Crawling out of the cavern, he determined to try a journey through the locality on which he had been cast, in the hope of discovering whether it really was an island or *terra firma*.

This promised to be an arduous task, and could not be undertaken without water and provisions.

He had noticed when bathing that the stream was full of fish, but until he could devise a hook or line, or make a net such as he had seen the Yarmouth old men and women work at, this knowledge was of little use.

Then it flashed across his mind that he could be content if he only had Joe Blake for his companion.

What wonders those two might perform!

Well, he was not with him, and all speculation on that point was useless.

Ned, keeping to the southward, along the line of rocks, was not long before he came to another stream, which, as a celebrated translator once said, was very *poisonous*.*

He determined to cross it, and found that he could do so without swimming.

It was remarkably clear, running over a pebbly bed, and showing thus clearly its great wealth. But in vain.

Ned Summers had no means of catching the swiftly-gliding fish, so he passed on to the other shore.

Here he lay down for a brief repose, and had scarcely done so when he started up with a wild expression in his eyes.

He glanced around with terror?

His gun was eagerly clutched.

Then, stealing into some bushes, he listened with the deepest attention.

There was nothing to be heard but the soughing of the wind.

What, then, had alarmed him?

A powerful smell of cooked meat.

Under any other circumstances this certainly would not have alarmed him, but in the position in which he was placed it simply indicated the presence of men, therefore of enemies.

Ned crawled slowly on hands and knees in the direction of the odour, for, hearing no voices, he suspected no danger.

Presently he halted again.

He was in sight of the expected camp.

It was deserted!

There was a kind of circular hollow, in the centre of which still smouldered the remains of a large fire.

All around were scattered bones, which, recollecting certain passages in the stories of Indians in that quarter of the world made Ned shudder.

Advancing nearer, however, and convincing himself that no human beings were near, he soon satisfied himself that the food was quite orthodox.

It was chiefly goat, and several quarters of roast or grilled kid hung temptingly under the leafy boughs of a tree.

---

* An English scholar of experience, in translating a book of French travels, gravely informed his readers that a certain river was very poisonous—translating by this word *poissoneux*, full of fish.

Ned Summers was sufficiently hungry to help himself to a quarter of kid, which he at once retreated into a thicket with, and eagerly devoured.

At every mouthful his appetite appeared to increase.

Still he kept his ears open, as, if his theft were discovered, he would be surely pursued and punished.

As soon, therefore, as he had finished his meal, he clutched his gun and prepared to continue his journey.

A lofty hill had been noticed by him while crossing the stream, and towards this he determined at once to make his way.

The presence of inhabitants on the island was a discovery of sufficient importance to require reflection.

Ned knew well that different tribes along that coast bore very different characters; some were savage and brutal to the last degree, delighting in torture and rapine, while others were kindly and hospitable.

In the former case all he had to do was to hide himself until his escape could be effected; in the latter, the natives might be induced to assist him.

While thus communing with himself, Ned was ascending a grassy slope leading to the summit of a rock which looked down upon a small and pleasant plain on the banks of the stream he had just left.

No sooner did he reach the summit, than he fell flat on his face, in a state of considerable alarm and terror.

Not a hundred yards from him were some twenty of the wildest and most savage-looking men he had ever seen, engaged in the somewhat singular pastime of dancing round a large, upright post.

They were partially naked, but wore very fine head dresses of feathers, while round their waists were richly ornamented petticoats.

As they danced their cries were most hideous and terrifying.

At first Ned Summers thought they were merely taking some sort of gymnastic exercise, but presently he became aware that something was tied to the post.

At that distance he could scarcely make out, but, after some minutes, he saw it was a man.

And, what pained him more than all, a white man.

He was, however, whatever might be his wishes, helpless to aid.

True, these men were armed only with spears, bows, and arrows, which were piled up close at hand, while he had a gun and a small supply of ammunition; but they were twenty tall and powerful men, while he was only a boy.

Presently the circle was broken up, and the men, after seating themselves to obtain breath, took each his supply of arms.

The prisoner hung apparently lifeless at the stake, his head hanging on his bosom.

After a few minutes he was untied, supplied with some drink, and then allowed to sink to the ground, where he lay like a log.

The savages then took up positions round him in a circle, only much larger than when they were dancing.

Each clutched his lance, cast his bow and quiver on his shoulders, and waited.

Presently the wretched prisoner rose and looked around, helplessly.

Then one advanced and gave him something to drink.

This infused life into the unfortunate being, who was evidently given to understand that he had to run the gauntlet.

Was it merely for the wanton amusement of the ruthless savages, or did they intend to sacrifice him?

Ned could give no opinion, all he could do was to lie still, a helpless spectator.

The savages, brandishing their lances, and uttering most horrid cries, formed in two lines.

The helpless being, nearly naked, stood as if spellbound, until one of the more brutal of the inhuman gang pricked him savagely with his spear.

Then, with an awful yell of anguish, that went to the heart of Ned Summers, he bounded in a direction that would bring him almost to the foot of the rock.

It was evident the savages intended allowing him full law; for not one threw his lance, waiting until he had a good start.

The fugitive made for the wood, where, probably he hoped to conceal himself.

Away came the Indians, their lances quivering in their hands like Arab jerrids.

One or two of the fleetest were coming up fast and appeared ready to throw.

The fugitive increased his bounds, looking around, above, everywhere for shelter.

Ned had great difficulty in restraining a cry of horror and amazement.

In the wretched prisoner he had recognised his fellow midshipman, Samuel Petworth!

Retribution had come upon him already; and, while he had escaped *his* malice, the other was in the jaws of death.

One of the youths, with uplifted spear, was close upon him and prepared to strike a fatal and deadly blow.

Regardless of consequences, Ned Summers took aim and fired.

The young savage fell prone upon his face, the other Indians stood still alarmed and amazed, while the fugitive in the confusion disappeared in the forest.

Ned took occasion to act in a similar manner, descending from his eminence as rapidly as possible, and skulking into the first thicket that offered itself to his view.

CHAPTER V.

A NIGHT OF PERILS.

NED, as soon as he had gained a temporary retreat, began to think.

The presence of Samuel Petworth appeared to explain the departure of the ship.

Doubtless the savages had attacked the boat's crew, and driven them off, while Samuel had been taken prisoner by them.

The captain must have believed our hero included in the same wretched fate, and hence the departure of the vessel.

But what was he to do now? The island was evidently inhabited, and the fact of his having fired a shot would inform them that a white man or men were free among them.

The position, under these circumstances, became perilous in the extreme.

It was no longer possible to fire a gun even to kill a goat or flying game, while to make a bow and arrows was clearly beyond his means at present.

Escape from immediate danger was, however, the one thing needful now.

Ned found, on examination, that what he had taken for a thicket was one huge tree on the edge of a kind of morass.

In this morass grew other trees, the roots of which were chiefly out of water, and could be easily reached one from the other.

Expecting every minute to be discovered in his present retreat, Ned having recovered his breath and a certain amount of equanimity of mind, determined to put the morass between himself and his pursuers.

Keeping firm hold of his gun, his shot bag, and powder horn, with his water bottle and a remnant of roast kid in his wallet, he grasped the bough of a tree and drew himself on to the nearest root.

He at once recognised the danger of his position.

The roots were slimy and slippery, and evidently, in certain seasons, wholly covered with water.

Still danger was behind, and safety, to all appearance, in advance.

He used extreme caution; he clung to the overhanging boughs of what he afterwards knew to be the mangrove, never trusting to the roots wholly, and, in this way reached, with infinite trouble, a small island.

His hands were so lacerated, his whole frame so weary with the great exertion he had made, that here he determined to halt awhile.

The more that night was coming, and in these latitudes there is no twilight.

The spot where he stopped was a small hillock surrounded by water, with one gnarled trunk in the centre.

Ned seated himself, and bathed at once his hands and feet.

Then he lay down.

Many minutes had not elapsed before he bounded with horror to his feet.

The swamp was salt, was tidal, swarmed with alligators, and the water was rising!

"REGARDLESS OF CONSEQUENCES, NED SUMMERS FIRED."

The situation was simply horrible.

From one awful death he had escaped to suffer one even more terrible.

The alligator, though feeding mostly on fish, like the Egyptian crocodile, does not disdain man.

Its voracious appetite, sharp teeth, and powerful jaws make it a terrible foe.

As the water rose, Ned had heard something in the distance in motion, which, on reflection, he had no difficulty in making out to be some large monster.

His own reflections and the peculiar motion of the tail at once explained the mystery.

This slimy, muddy, half-salt, half-fresh morass—fresh at low, salt at high water, was the home of the alligator.

Ned was not easily frightened, but here was a contingency for which he had not bargained.

Being wholly ignorant as to how high the water reached, Ned looked about him.

The tree was huge in bulk, gnarled and knotted, but not high.

He made a grasp at a branch, and hauled himself up.

He was out of reach of the hideous reptiles below, but he could not lie down.

The branches were thick, and closely intertwined with pendant plants.

What was to be done?

Pass a sleepless night he could not.

He must climb higher up.

With great exertion he did so, and at length got to where several boughs separated.

It was a hard bed; but it was safer than below, and Ned determined to remain.

With a silent, but heartfelt prayer, he lay down, and courted sleep.

In vain.

The blowing of the huge monsters, the splashing of their tails, the different strange noises of the night, for a long time kept him awake.

At length fatigue overcame him, and a nightmare kind of slumber followed.

It did not last long.

He was startled from his uneasy rest by an awful cry.

It was light, and Ned could see without being seen.

Samuel Petworth had evidently been discovered by the savages, and was fleeing again.

He, too, had taken to the morass, but without the precautions which Ned had observed.

He thought it merely soft ground, and at the first step he took floundered in the deep mud.

It was in consequence of a fearful discovery he then made that Samuel Petworth gave the wild and penetrating shriek that so startled Ned.

As he touched the bottom something suddenly moved.

He knew at once what it was—an alligator at rest!

He clasped the root of a tree, and, shivering with cold, even on that hot day, he reached the support of the tree in time.

The animal, assaulted in his own element, began scourging the water with his tail.*

Samuel, terrified in the extreme, clasped the tree round the trunk and tried to climb.

He was either too weak or not accustomed to the exercise.

Suddenly he ceased, and crouched at the foot of the mangrove in an agony of terror.

The Indians had heard his cry and were on the edge of the morass in an instant.

They were six in number, and armed, as usual, with bows, arrows, and lances.

Every man peered keenly about, but none saw him.

Probably they believed themselves to have been mistaken.

They at all events retreated.

Samuel Petworth, the most abject, the most wretched-looking being Ned had ever seen, naked save a pair of drawers, his teeth chattering, took a survey of the morass.

It was nearly low water.

In the daylight this made the place doubly horrible, as all about in the mud and reeds could be seen the hideous monsters.

* "Though they are often speedy, and on occasions can be lashed to a furious pitch of excitement, bellowing with fury and whirling round until they churn the water into a white foam with their movements, these reptiles are usually very sluggish and indolent, and will remain many hours without moving in the least."—WOOD.

Some lay like logs, with their terrible snouts in the air.

Fear of the savages, however, overcame every other consideration.

Looking back for the stoutest trees, for the roots which were highest out of water, the unhappy being, victim to his own bad passions, leaped from tree to tree and root to root, with the dexterity of an Alpine climber.

In so doing he came near to where Ned was concealed.

Touched by compassion, the generous youth was about to invite him on to his island, when a loud and taunting cry announced that the savages had outwitted him and were in full pursuit.

Samuel Petworth nearly fell headlong into the water.

He stood bewildered, and as if lost.

Ned had been studying the geography of the place with a view to his own escape.

He could see one dry causeway towards the land.

"Samuel Petworth," he said.

The other stood shivering and trembling with excessive fear.

He, however, made no answer.

"'Tis I—Ned Summers, who speaks."

"Oh, Ned!"

"There is no time for words. Just by the fallen tree to your left is a path.

Keep to high ground and you are safe. Make haste."

Samuel needed not twice telling.

He was in that awful state of mind that he was quite prepared to believe in the supernatural.

His terror was only augmented.

Obeying, however, the advice given him, he followed the path at a rapid rate, and disappeared.

The Indians, in a body, followed, and then Ned thought it was time to take care of himself.

Lowering himself slowly from the tree, he made no delay.

His path was already chosen.

He meant to follow directly in the track of the savages.

This was easily done, and at the end of twenty minutes he too had emerged from Alligator Morass, sincerely desirous of never seeing its hideous purlieus again, under any circustances.

There remained the consideration as to what he was to do.

Wandering about the woods without an object, while the howling savages were about, was not a wise proceeding for him.

Still, in this dangerous position of his, the question of food and drink always arose.

He could not do without it.

CHAPTER VI.

NED MAKES A DISCOVERY.

AFTER going through a considerable amount of mental calculation, and several times almost despairing of a wise decision, Ned Summers determined on seeking the most dense thicket on the borders of the fresh-water stream, and there abiding until the savages took their departure.

Having no tents, no women, and no children, they could certainly not abide in that particular spot.

His selection of the stream was because of the imperative necessity for water.

Treading with extreme care, scarcely venturing to put his feet to the ground, avoiding above all to touch small dry sticks, which would be sure to betray his

presence, Ned also listened with all his ears.

Every now and then he believed he heard a kind of view halloo.

The fugitive was leading them a terrible dance.

Still there would be very little hope for him, and much as Ned regretted it, under the circumstances he had to think of himself.

Samuel deserved no sympathy.

With this idea he rapidly crossed the kind of wooded meadow he had fallen upon, and taking an oblique direction from the pursuers and the pursued, reached the river.

It was here bordered with trees on both

.es, leaving ample room for him to walk.

Being neither muddy nor slimy there were no alligators.

The fish were, as usual, abundant.

This, however, was of no moment now.

A secure and comfortable hiding-place was what he required.

Still he advanced slowly and guardedly.

The river grew narrower, the trees taller, arching overhead, and the way more difficult.

Presently he had to crawl under the creeping plants, and thus reached a snug and pleasant little bay, formed by the winding of the river.

His eyes then lit up with sudden animation and delight.

A small fleet of canoes lay moored, that is, drawn up on a small sandy beach.

They were unguarded, and the paddles were all leaning against a tree.

Ned took careful stock of the whole scene, and, making sure that no one was visible, examined the boats.

They contained fishing spears, nets, and some rude hooks and lines.

Ned's heart bounded with delight.

He was in a savage country.

His hand was against every man, and every man's hand was against him.

Securing the best-looking of the canoes, he appropriated a due supply of nets, a spear, some hooks and lines, and taking a paddle from the heap, he then put out.

His course was up the river.

He was well aware that he would be looked for below, and in consequence was determined to outwit the enemy.

The river was still thoroughly navigable, and he easily impelled along his boat.

Joe Blake had taught him the peculiar way of urging forward a canoe.

It is easy enough after one lesson.

Ned moved along slowly and methodically, looking to the right and the left.

At last he saw a kind of small stream, falling into the larger one, and at once determined to follow it up.

It was sluggish and completely covered, roofed in by vegetation.

It was narrow too, and partially overgrown by reeds.

Ned urged his canoe up its course, and current being slow, easily made his way to a small open pool of clear water, where he determined to rest.

The discomfited Indians, on discovering the loss of their canoe, would probably go down stream in chase.

It was a problematical question if they returned at all.

All he had to do was to keep still.

To his delight, the boat contained some bait, which he immediately put on his hook.

He then lowered it into the pond.

It literally swarmed with fish, and Ned took as many as he required.

When he had filled the bows of his boat, he could not help chuckling.

What was the use of raw fish?

Fire was a luxury he dared not indulge in at present.

Raw fish was out of the question.

And yet Ned well knew how many had been compelled to live on it for an indefinite time.

He consoled himself with a deep drink of water, drew his boat under a tree, the boughs of a tree that trailed its long boughs in the water, and waited.

Not for long.

A loud, wailing cry apprised him that the loss of the boat was discovered.

It also made him aware that the water-camp of the Indians was close at hand.

The river, winding in every direction, had deceived him.

Then came a loud jabbering, quarrelling in a variety of shrill voices, and then the whole died away.

They were in pursuit.

Ned remained still until all signs of the savages had ceased, and then again came forth; he had resolved to cross the pond and reconnoitre.

It was quite certain the Indians had gone the other way.

The pool was narrow enough, and Ned was soon on the other side, where, secreting his canoe as best he might, he trod the shore.

His intention was to strike for the bay whence the Indians had taken their boats, and see if they had made a final departure.

The camp was soon reached and surveyed.

It appeared wholly empty.

Every boat was gone, every living creature had fled!

Ned stepped into the open space, and at once saw that he was mistaken.

Bound hand and foot, a martyr to the insects and flies which haunt these waters, lay Samuel Petworth on the ground.

He had again been captured, and was to be made a victim to the savages.

Ned drew his knife and approached him.

The wretch opened his eyes.

Never had Ned seen such a change in any human being.

Firmly believing that his fellow midshipman was about to take a dastardly revenge, Petworth gasped some words for mercy.

Ned smiled contemptuously.

"I came to save you," he said; "at all events to give you a chance of safety."

And he cut his cord.

Then he turned away.

"Take me with you. I will be your slave," muttered Samuel.

"I cannot carry you," said Ned, drily; "if you can follow, do so."

And, giving him a drink of water, he turned away, and again disappeared in the forest.

He would have shown more generosity, but it appeared to him that to take his would-be murderer with him would be to ensure the capture of both.

While he was wholly free he might still be able to assist Samuel Petworth, but if both were taken, they must inevitably perish.

Samuel followed him with his eyes with such a malicious scowl, that, had he seen it, he must have felt very uneasy.

As it was, he walked away, hoping that his messmate, with all his faults, would escape from the Indians, and making up his mind to aid him if possible.

He returned to the pool, concealed all signs of his boat having touched the shore, and pushed off.

Once more he drew the canoe under the deep shadow of the tree, and waited the course of events.

Not for very long.

Towards dark he plainly heard steps on the opposite shore.

He sat upright in his boat, with his gun upon his knees.

He never moved—scarcely breathed.

Presently he ventured to move a bough, and to look across the water.

At first he saw nothing, and fancied it must have been the sound of some animal moving.

Again steps were heard.

Keenly scrutinising the whole shore, he saw the countenance of Samuel Petworth fixed upon his hiding-place with a cold and sarcastic expression of countenance.

He was about to speak, when the other smiled a perfectly demoniacal smile, and, shaking his fist at the place where his old messmate was hid, retreated towards the water-camp.

Samuel Petworth had discovered his hiding-place, and was about to curry favour with the savages by betraying him.

CHAPTER VII.

DIAMOND CUT DIAMOND.

IT was quite clear to Ned Summers that his treacherous comrade, Samuel Petworth, whose grovelling nature could neither understand nor bear to recognise his more generous and high-minded character, was about to curry favour with the copper-coloured Indians by betraying him into their hands.

There was no time to lose.

He was determined, on no account, to part with his capture, the many uses of which he had already pictured to himself.

Apart from other probable advantages, in case of a ship being seen in the offing, it might enable him to escape.

To remain where he was a minute more would have been fatal.

Urging his prize canoe, therefore, along by means of the boughs above his head, he was soon again in the open water.

With a sense of desperation impelling him onward, he advanced upward.

The fact that the stream moved the other way appeared to indicate some channel, however narrow.

For some little time he proceeded unmolested, but then the stream began to narrow, and the boughs of the trees on the opposite banks to interlace one with another.

The boat presently, small as it was, could scarcely float.

Leaving all his treasures inside, Ned got out and waded.

The light canoe at once resumed its buoyancy, and came slowly after him.

Once or twice even then its progress was checked by snags.

At length, after some minutes of slow progress, there was no bottom but actual slush, along which it could scarcely move.

Tugging desperately, Ned made a last effort, which hurled him headlong into deep water, and sent the boat flying to some distance ahead of where he had plunged.

Wholly unencumbered, Ned soon righted himself, and swam after the boat, which he drove before him until he once more reached a shallow.

Here he paused for a moment or two to look about him.

He was in a hole.

On both sides rose steep and rugged rocks, covered by creeping plants.

Between meandered the stream.

The place was dark from overhanging trees on the summit.

His gaze was rapid and keen in search of a hiding-place.

Under one of the tallest of the rocks was a completely dark hole, before which hung a mass of heavy, creeping plants.

To this Ned Summers swam, and saw that he could thrust his canoe therein completely out of sight.

He did so, and then wading forth, with his gun in his hand, drew the leaves slightly together, thus wholly concealing the orifice.

Then he bethought himself of his own safety, and looked upward.

The rocks were rather steep, and, moreover, would leave too clear and evident a trail.

He advanced, therefore, a little further, wading, and was soon checked by a falling wall of verdure.

He clutched some of the creeping plants which grew downward from a huge trunk that lay across the gully.

It bore his weight.

Slinging his gun on his back, he drew himself up slowly.

Once or twice the treacherous plants appeared about to give way under his weight.

He, however, clutched at others, and, at last, in this way, reached the summit, where he lay panting and exhausted on the tree.

It was wide, and gave ample room for him to conceal himself.

But the broken creepers would certainly betray him, and as soon, therefore, as he recovered his breath, he pressed forward in the direction of the rock on which the upper part of the fallen tree rested.

Scarcely had he moved when he heard a noise at no great distance.

Looking down, without moving, he saw eight Indians in the act of launching a boat which they had carried over the portage.

They were soon in the canoe and in the act of crossing the pool.

They, too, looked keenly on every side.

Nothing attracted their attention, however, until they were again obliged to leave their boat.

Then the broken creepers, the fallen leaves, betrayed at once the route he had taken.

"Ugh!" muttered one, pointing upward, exactly at the spot where he had landed.

The whole party began to examine the means of ascent, and evidently to discuss what was to be done.

Ned did not wait to make himself master of their decision.

In his present position he was helpless, lying flat on his stomach.

He moved gently, almost imperceptibly, forward, and writhing like a snake, made his way slowly to the summit of the rock.

He was determined to defend his life to the last gasp.

He had, however, only seven bullets and seven charges of powder remaining.

The rock at length was only about four feet distant.

He had, in fact, almost reached it, when a low cry from beneath proclaimed him discovered.

But he had in a minute more reached the rock, and could act.

Gazing down, he smiled grimly at the spectacle which presented itself.

A tall Indian, a perfect giant, stood

bolt upright, with his hands upon his stalwart hips.

On his shoulders was a second savage, who, in this way, could almost touch the cross beam.

Still he wanted some inches.

A short conversation ensued, after which the giant put up his hands.

The lighter Indian smiled approvingly, and then stepped upon them as readily as if they had been the most solid of supports.

By this means he was at last enabled to grasp the beam.

Ned Summers frowned darkly.

These men were seeking his life, and every instinct of self-preservation told him to defend his existence as best he might.

If they gained the beam a hand-to-hand encounter must follow.

The Indian warrior was now about to hoist himself up.

Quick as lightning Ned fired at the one below.

With a fearful yell he fell backward, splashing up the water on every side.

The young man swung wildly in the air, holding on by the frail creepers.

Next instant he fell to the bottom of the gully, overcome with terror.

Ned, with a wildly beating heart—to him this mortal conflict was painful and humiliating—turned to go.

If he possibly could he would avoid further bloodshed.

The way was hard enough.

The summits of the rocks were jagged and pointed, the trees grew close together, the underbrush was thick and difficult to affront, being interlaced like a mat.

In many places Ned was compelled to crawl leaving everywhere a broad trail.

That it would be followed up he knew only too well.

The principal thing to be done was to get away as far as possible.

Half-an-hour elapsed, and though he listened with the deepest and most profound attention, nothing came to his ear.

At length the dense underwood ceased, and he found himself in a kind of table-land, with no other growth but that of small trees.

With a sigh of relief, he walked upright.

Where should he flee was the next matter for consideration.

To hide in one of these trees was futile in the extreme, as the power of the Indians to follow up a trail is notorious.

Nothing but cunning would in any way serve his purpose.

He moved slowly along, his gun cocked and ready for action.

Presently the slow rustle of moving water attracted his attention.

He was close to a river.

Turning round a small tuft of trees, he saw before him what he had no doubt was the main stream where he had captured the canoe.

It was wide, but extremely shallow, and flowed over a golden, gravelly bed.

There was an opportunity to hide this path he had taken, of which he readily availed himself.

Water leaves no trail.

The flowing stream was pleasant and cool, and was welcome, indeed, to one fatigued and exhausted as he was.

Scarcely, however, was he half way across, when a guttural cry proclaimed that his pursuers were already coming after him.

With one glance behind, Ned Summers darted off, hoping to escape the Indians by sheer force of muscle and resolution.

An almost hopeless task.

CHAPTER VIII.

STARVING AMID PLENTY.

THE opposite bank of the river consisted first of an open plain dotted with trees, and then of a slope covered with a rough collection of trees and bushes.

Ned began well.

The cold water had refreshed him

thoroughly, and he bounded on like a deer.

The whooping and yelling savages came, however, behind at their long loping pace, which they can keep up without fatigue for so long a time.

As is, however, always the case, one was far ahead of the others.

He was well known to be the fleetest runner of his tribe.

He was armed exclusively with a bright tomahawk.

His bounds were fearful, and a very few minutes after Ned Summers began to ascend the hill, in the hope of finding some spot where he might stand at bay, the wiry youth was close behind him.

Ned Summers clutched his gun ready for action.

His blood was up, and yet to kill a comparatively unarmed man was entirely repugnant to his feelings.

Escape from them, however, he would at any price.

Besides his gun, he had only his midshipman's dirk, which was of no avail against a tomahawk.

He would club his gun, and meet his foe with only that weapon.

With this view he uncocked the weapon, and, turning suddenly, faced his enemy just as he reached the top of a small hill.

The Indian, without thought or reflection, cast his tomahawk at him, so startled was he at the sudden act.

At the same instant Ned stepped on one side, and as the Indian leaped on a small platform close to him, thrust forward his gun and tripped him up.

The Indian, taken by surprise, rolled over the edge of the hill, nor could stop his career until checked by some trees.

When his companions came up they found the crest-fallen youth searching in the brushwood for his tomahawk.

Ned Summers was, of course, nowhere to be seen.

Indians, however, are not easily baffled, and the whole party were soon again searching for the lost trail.

Fortunately for him he had kept on the crest of the hill, which was hard rock, without tree, grass, or even the smallest floweret to take the impression of his foot.

Running for his life—he cared not how he expended his breath for awhile—he succeeded in getting out of sight of the Indians.

He then necessarily slackened his pace, for he was faint and weary.

He now again took his way in the direction of the stream, which he hoped to cross and seek refuge in some of the most arid and rugged rocks on the seashore, where the Indians would be least likely to seek him.

The winding course of the stream was easily made out, and walking as well as he could, Ned at last reached its banks, here narrower and steeper than before.

The water, too, was much deeper, and yet not too deep for him to wade in.

Being clear and pellucid, it was sure to be free from dangerous vermin.

Ned stepped in, and finding himself breast high, had to carry his ammunition on his head in order not to spoil it.

In this way he finally succeeded in reaching the other side, where the vegetation was dense in the extreme.

A number of trees lay prone on the ground, the relics of a recent storm, and two or three bold and resolute men might easily have made an extempore fort, and held it against an army of savages.

Ned Summers was, however, quite alone in the world.

The only country within reach was his bitter and reckless foe.

But dangerous as is delay, he was obliged to seek repose for awhile.

His eye, however, was kept upon the river all the time, while his gun lay close to his hand.

Not the slightest show of mercy would the Indians show him if taken.

He was determined, therefore, to escape or perish in the attempt.

At the end of half-an-hour he again rose, took a refreshing drink of water, and prepared to depart on his way once more.

Not a sound was to be heard, save the singing of the birds on every tree; even this was companionship, however, and cheered him for nearly half-an-hour, when once more his progress was checked by mere physical exhaustion.

He was now, in fact, so faint as to be scarcely able to crawl.

Want of food was telling on him.

Nothing eatable, even fruit or berry, was to be seen, and he bent his weary, almost hopeless way despairing and utterly heart-broken.

He was compelled at every step almost to pause.

Had the triumphant Indians come up

now, he must, indeed, have surrendered at discretion.

His way was along the banks of the sparkling river as far as he could approach it. What would he not have given for some of the numerous fish which he had seen glancing quickly away as he crossed, to deep holes and places under cover?

Once he thought in desperation of returning to where he had concealed the canoe.

But he feared that spot would be watched more than any other.

No! he must find some place to hide his weary body and pass the night. Even repose might restore something of his animal vigour.

The thickets became denser and denser as he advanced, until at length, when sundown fell with its sudden darkness on the scene, he could scarcely make head at all.

He accordingly moved further away from the banks of the river, and again emerged upon a kind of meadow, or prairie.

As he did so, something ran away through the grass, which he, at the moment, believed to be a bird.

If he could have only caught it.

As he felt just then raw flesh would, by no means, have frightened him.

Suddenly he trod upon something that crushed under his feet.

He had stumbled over a nest of eggs of tolerable size, and the parent animal had fled at his approach.

With a prayer of thanksgiving he greedily devoured several.

Though raw, they were certainly most delicious. Ned felt at once revived and hopeful, nor did he finish his meal until he had swallowed the last egg out of the nest.

His discovery, which, in the excited state of his feelings he looked upon as little less than providential, aroused him to hope and renewed energy.

Glancing on every side, and aware that in the darkness the Indians could not follow his trail, he skirted the wood for some little time, feeling quite another man, or perhaps we should rather say boy.

He was now seeking for a tree in which to pass the night.

But some had too lofty trunks, some were too small, while others were without the necessary branches to help him to the higher parts.

And so he advanced, utterly unaware of where he was going.

Presently, however, he saw what had some appearance of a rude path through the forest.

At all events a narrow fissure between the trees and green wall of undergrowth appeared before him.

It was very winding in its character, and as he advanced had all the appearance of a complete labyrinth.

Once or twice he fancied he came back to a place he had seen before.

This, however, he argued with himself, must be the effect of imagination.

Taking particular notice, however, as he progressed, he endeavoured in the gloom to study the locality.

Suddenly he found himself in a small clearing, overshadowed by one huge and widely-spreading tree.

There was apparently no further path to be seen.

Ned suddenly paused, and listened with all his ears.

He certainly heard a footstep—a footstep close at hand.

He drew himself up in the darkest corner of the open space, and again waited.

Silence again.

He was, however, sure of not having been mistaken. Whether human being or beast of the forest Ned could not make out, but something living he had heard.

Again.

His heart throbbing wildly, he clutched his gun and waited.

A slow, cautious, stealthy footstep was decidedly approaching.

The deadly weapon was cocked ready for use, and then a figure stepped forth into the open space before the tree.

It was human, and that was all Ned could make out, though rather dwarfish.

The form was concealed by a rough costume; such as was worn by some of the Indian women—a tunic, and loose trousers, and plaited reed hat.

At all events, he, Ned Summers, fancied he had nothing to fear, and stepped out into the clearing.

The creature whatever or whoever it

was, gave a startled, unintelligible cry, and bounded wildly into the thicket.

At the same moment a rush of other footsteps was heard, and poor, hunted Ned, taking the way by which the strange apparition had fled, found himself again in a thick and almost impassable forest.

The footsteps then ceased as if by magic, and Ned Summers knew that the enemy were listening keenly.

He determined, therefore, to be as cunning as themselves, and stepped onwards slowly and deliberately.

It was a terrible and almost fatal dilemma; but life is dear, and Ned Summers knew that nothing but patience and the most consummate art could save him from his inveterate and savage enemies.

They appeared on this occasion, however, very soon to give up the chase, for as he got further and further into the gloomy wood, all signs of them ceased.

At length Nature asserted its rights, and finding a large and comfortable tree, and securing himself as best he might, the hunted youth prepared to sleep.

He was, as it happened, fortunate enough to find repose, and, despite his desperate situation, he slept until the dawn without being disturbed by man or beast.

CHAPTER IX.

A WONDERFUL ESCAPE.

WHEN Ned Summers awoke, the wood was still.

Nothing was to be heard but the pleasant song of the myriad song birds, the wild shrill cries of the little green parrots, and the thousand strange and shrill sounds which fill the forest in uninhabited places.

The tree into which he had climbed was of enormous size.

He was secreted in the lower and more leafy branches.

Clambering upward, he never stopped until he was high up as the branches would bear him.

He now had a splendid view.

The sea spread itself like a mirror before him at no great distance.

To the right was a green hill, one mass of vegetation.

To the left was the river where Ned Summers had already passed through so many dangerous adventures.

Below was the leafy and undulating green forest.

All this, however, told him nothing, and he slowly descended.

Unfortunately, man is so constituted that the having a tolerable supper over night in no way compensates for the want of a breakfast in the morning.

Ned Summers was hungry again, and, as it happened, very hungry.

He reflected with grim doubt on the chances of a breakfast.

But the island where the roast pheasants and pigs run about crying "Come eat me," remains yet to be discovered.

At all events, which was just the same, it was unknown to our hero.

He reached the lowest bough, and, before he alighted, took a keen survey around.

He could neither see nor hear anything to create doubt or alarm.

After some hesitation he glided to the ground and stood erect on the sward below. Still no sign.

He could now make out no path; not the remotest trail to guide him.

He must advance, therefore, completely at hap-hazard.

Taking advantage of a tree at some distance, which gave him a vista to guide him, he advanced in a straight line.

In a forest this is a good plan.

Fix your eyes on a tree, and never leave it until you reach it.

Then, with your back to this tree, fix your eyes on another, and, in all probability, the person lost in the woods will go in a tolerably straight line.

Ned tried it, and never once swerved from his course.

In this way he got to the edge of the wood, where a few sweet acorns assuaged the first rage of furious hunger.

"Was this to last for ever?" was his sad and weary reflection while munching his frugal repast.

While he was still eating, he heard a loud and triumphant cry, and saw Samuel Petworth, nearly naked, distinguishable only from the savages by his whiter skin, come rushing in his direction.

The others were at no great distance behind the wretched young midshipman.

He had no choice left but to re-enter the wood and strive to conceal himself within its gloomy and dark haunts.

He was becoming strangely savage.

What had he done that he should be hunted thus, and by one, too, whom he had never injured?

It was really enough to make him murderously inclined.

Samuel Petworth, as he expected, had tried to curry favour with the Indians by betraying him.

He had perseveringly dogged his footsteps, and at last succeeded, somehow, in discovering his retreat.

After this he returned to the lair of the savages.

He was, to a certain extent, quite free, but would not escape.

He had neither the courage of Ned Summers, nor was he armed, while his own evil nature prevented him from having any belief in the generosity of others.

Had he trusted Ned Summers, all might, perhaps, have been well for both of them.

But this he could not make up his mind to do.

So he sat down upon the bank until the discomfited Indians returned from their abortive chase.

His being at liberty amazed them much.

At first they were disposed to be aggressive, but, after a time, they thought better of it.

Samuel clearly made signs that he was ready to guide them to the hiding-place of the being that had stolen the canoe and freed himself.

This satisfied the savages, and, for the time, they were kind, even jocular.

They presently, in high good humour, dressed him up like one of themselves.

In this guise he accompanied them, and was present when our young hero shot and wounded the giant savage.

The huge Indian, however, was not killed upon this occasion, but he was unable to go any further, and remained, therefore, with the boat.

The rest, without troubling themselves to clamber to the top of the beam, took a way well known to them, by which to circumvent the fugitive and waylay him as he advanced.

He was, however, too quick for them, and though a kind of instinct guided them in the right direction, they could not capture him that night.

How he escaped they could not even attempt to imagine.

They simply took up their post under trees and slept until morn.

As soon as they had risen and partaken of a frugal breakfast, they again started in chase of the much-coveted white man.

Samuel was fortunate enough to be the first to see him, which raised him much in the estimation of the savage people.

They at once distributed themselves over the wood, which was by no means of large extent, and determined to examine it, even tree by tree, until they found him.

Samuel Petworth, who had every reason to fear Ned Summers more than anybody, kept alongside a tall and powerful Indian.

He himself was wholly unarmed.

His gun had been taken from him, and lay in the bottom of one of the canoes.

But though they made a regular *battue* of the wood, and peered under every bush, and shot arrows up trees, and examined every hole and corner, they made no discovery.

Ned seemed to have escaped in some strange and mysterious manner.

The discomfited Indians at last collected together and consulted.

They were evidently very far from being in a good humour, and Samuel Petworth thought once or twice that they cast rather strange glances at himself.

He was in a state of no slight perturbation, for, as he well knew, the temper of savages is very uneven.

Should they not find the much-coveted captive, they might turn round and vent their spite and rage upon him.

Sam's teeth began to chatter, and he looked round for some loophole of escape from the wrath and fury of the savages.

As he did so, his face brightened up, and he gave a kind of view-halloo.

"THE HUGE TRUNK, WITH SOME OF THE INDIANS, FELL INTO THE ABYSS."

At a considerable distance he had caught sight of Ned Summers creeping low and carefully behind some bushes.

The Indians followed the direction of his hand, and, though they could see nothing, made a rush.

Samuel was compelled to follow them.

He was sure it was Ned, but if the Indians did not find him, they might think it a mere trick to deceive them.

Yes, there he was, running down another slope towards a still narrower part of the river.

He bounded vigorously and desperately the moment he knew himself discovered.

What could be his hope?

No one could say.

However that may be, he continued his course until he reached the banks, when he turned round and presented his loaded weapon at his foes.

All stopped their headlong course, Samuel Petworth the first—he, in fact, cowering abjectly behind the others.

Then Ned, with a loud cry of triumph, disappeared.

Away bounded the pursuers, satisfied that he had leaped into the river.

They soon, however, found themselves completely mistaken.

A large trunk of a tree had fallen over the river, and just touched the other side, which served Ned as a bridge.

He was only about half across when the whole party came up.

But how was this?

A black-looking savage animal preceded him on the tree.

Ned reached the other side, and again turned.

The Indians, after the first check caused by surprise, swarmed on the trunk, eager to follow in his track.

Ned Summers laughed aloud, stooped, and exerting his utmost strength, hurled trunk, Indians, and all into the yawning abyss below.

Then, with a loud and hopeful cry, he fled once more, without waiting to see what steps would be taken by those who were hunting him even unto the death.

CHAPTER X.

A FOUR-FOOTED FRIEND.

WHEN Ned Summers made his last desperate dash into the dark and gloomy wood, in his endeavour to escape from the savages at any price, he ran for some time with unabated vigour.

Flight was his only chance, and yet, with so many to hunt him up, what chance had he of ultimate escape?

Unless something almost miraculous occurred he must be taken.

Still he was determined never to give in while life lasted.

As these thoughts passed rapidly through his mind, he was suddenly startled by a strange and wholly unexpected sound close at hand.

He halted and looked round just as a huge black animal came leaping forth from the bushes.

He instantly levelled his gun and took steady aim at the brute.

It still advanced, however, and, just as he was about to fire, he recognised a large Newfoundland dog, with a brass collar round his throat.

The animal's manner was rather suspicious than unfriendly.

Suddenly, as the youth removed his gun from the charge, it halted close to Ned, and smelt him all round.

Ned did not move, but spoke kindly to the animal, which, as if satisfied with the inspection, gave a low growl, and, turning round, appeared to wish to lead him in a direction opposite to that whence his enemies were coming.

What could this mean?

No harm any way; for, doubtless, this noble animal was owned by some castaway, belonging, at all events, to a civilized nation.

The dog, once aware that the other partially understood him, trotted on at a good pace, bringing him directly to the bridge, which, by a bold and thoughtful impulse, Ned had subsequently cast into the water.

He knew, however, that this was but a respite, as those daring savages would find a way to cross, while they were never known to give up a trail once they were on the scent.

He, however, for the present, trusted wholly to the dog, which took him forward now at a more leisurely pace, *with his nose to the ground.*

Who or what was he following?

This, of course, was to him a mystery.

The dog, meanwhile, kept straight on, neither turning to the right nor the left, until he reached a small, but dense thicket.

Casting one glance at Ned, the intelligent animal darted under some bushes.

The bewildered youth followed, to find himself at the foot of a perpendicular cliff, in a kind of hole, apparently without any outlet.

The dog stood still, wagging his tail, and looking vastly cunning and intelligent.

Ned was utterly nonplussed.

Then the sound of a voice, an English voice, pleasant and homely, fell upon his delighted and gratified ears.

"You are English, and in danger?" said the unexpected speaker.

"I am both," faintly ejaculated Ned.

"And my secret is my own. If I assist you, you will take no advantage of the discovery?" continued the other, speaking from above.

"On my honour as a British sailor," was Ned's hearty response.

"Come, Carlo," said the voice.

Then the dog, which hitherto had remained quiescent, turned to the right, and began ascending a narrow ledge, imperceptible at first sight, but quite a path when discovered.

Ned, after a careful examination of the difficulties, hesitated no longer, but began his ascent.

He had but to walk steadily, look upward and keep his left hand close to the rock.

Presently he reached a narrow level ledge, like a landing.

The dog stood still.

Next instant a ladder fell down from above, a ladder of ropes and wood.

Ned required no invitation, but clambered up, wild with excitement and curiosity.

Well might he be surprised at the sight which presented itself.

He was on a rocky shelf half way up a hill, and on this shelf stood a youth about his own age, as far as he could judge, habited in a strange costume.

He was shorter, but slightly stouter than himself, as far as his habiliments allowed him to make out.

His countenance, regular, handsome, and English, was quite brown from exposure.

A tunic of goat skin, tolerably decently made, loose trousers, as baggy as a Turk's, gaiters and rough shoes completed the lower man, while his head was surmounted by a slouched hat of reed and skin.

In his hand was a light, useful, double-barrelled gun, his belt held pistols, and from his side hung a sword something like a midshipman's dirk.

"You are certainly having a good look at me," said this singular personage, half merrily, half pettishly.

"Well, one does not meet a friend on such a deserted place as this every day," replied Ned; "let me first thank you for your kindness."

"You are a countryman and in distress," was the quiet reply. "My dog found you out last night, but the savages were too close for me to risk discovery by communicating with you before this morning."

"Where is the dog?" suddenly asked Ned.

"He will be here directly," said the stranger, smiling; "in the meantime, let me introduce you to my fortress."

Ned looked open-mouthed at a small stockade of wattled boughs and stakes.

The strange youth stepped within, and introduced him to a small but neat chamber.

There were some rude stools, a coarse table, several guns, as well as a very fair supply of useful utensils.

"This is my sitting-room," said the youth, "and this my pantry."

As he spoke he opened a wattle door separating a hollow in the rock from the room.

Several lumps of goat's flesh, with some coarse cakes, were then brought forth, with a gourd of water.

"You must be hungry," said the stranger; "if so, eat at once."

Ned was not likely to refuse, being indeed utterly faint and exhausted.

While he was eating, the dog came panting in and lay at their feet.

Ned threw him a bone which he took up readily enough.

"How could he get up here?" continued our hero, still continuing his meal.

"You know nothing of the mysteries of this place as yet," replied the other, with a smile.

Suddenly the dog gave a low growl.

The stranger started, looked uneasy, and then spoke in a low tone.

"Your enemies have followed you. But they will scarcely find us," he went on, "if they do, life is sweet, and you must fight. I will load."

And, with this singular remark, the stranger led the way into the open air.

Ned Summers, without any hesitation, peered over the rock.

The savages were at its foot, looking round and about, everywhere but upwards.

They were evidently exasperated to the last degree at the dance he had led them; and their glaring eye-balls and savage words sufficiently indicated their murderous intentions.

From where he stood, Ned Summers, properly provided with arms and ammunition, could have killed the whole party; but then they were not alone on the island, while, to commit such wholesale slaughter was very much against his feelings and principles.

Besides, to betray the retreat of his young friend, unless compelled to do so, would be both foolish and unjust in the extreme.

The savages examined the grassy sward, surveyed every step of ground, and finally, as if convinced the white man had given them the slip, turned round and retreated by the way they had come.

The youths watched them until they were out of sight, and then turned into the hut to make better acquaintance with each other.

CHAPTER XI.

THE WRECK.

HENRY THORNTON, as the youth described himself, was born in India, of English parents, and had been sent home for the benefit of his health and for purposes of education.

A fearful storm came, carrying away the topmasts and opening the seams of the vessel so much that she every moment threatened to founder.

Captain and crew knew that she was, to a certain extent, doomed.

The long-boat, which was very large and serviceable, was first amply provisioned, and to this all who could find room in it betook themselves.

The pinnace, however, had also been prepared in case of accidents.

The boy, for some reason which he did not explain, and which will appear at a future time, was below in his state-room when the last passenger entered the long-boat.

When he came on deck he was alone with his faithful dog, which gambolled around him unconscious of danger.

The position was an awful one.

Alone on board a sinking ship, what could a mere child like Henry Thornton do?

Wait and pray.

His despair at first was something terrible; but, when he found the vessel, though rolling and pitching fearfully, gave no immediate sign of sinking, he forced himself to something like resignation.

The storm was clearly breaking.

If the ship weathered the gale, probably the crew would return and navigate it into port.

Comforted somewhat by this hopeful reflection, he searched for food for himself and his companion.

This found, they ate a hearty meal, and, Nature asserting her rights, he slept.

When he awoke, he was surprised to find the ship almost quiescent.

Rushing on deck, he found the storm had ceased, and a dead calm taken its place.

His first glance was for the horizon.

Not a speck of land could he see.

The boats, too, had disappeared.

They had, then, utterly deserted him.

In an agony of such anguish as a gently nurtured child might be expected to feel, cast thus upon his own resources, he threw himself on the deck and wept bitterly.

After a time, however, hope and the love of life prevailed.

The ship might, at all events, float for many days, and would probably be seen by some other vessel.

He rose to his feet and again glanced round the horizon.

A hazy line in the distance was undoubtedly some kind of land.

His heart bounded; but how was he to reach it?

Suddenly a startling and thrilling sound attracted his attention.

Something was beating against the counter.

He looked over the side.

It was the pinnace, furnished and provisioned for a voyage, even to a small mast and sail.

Henry Thornton's resolve was come to at once.

Certain premonitory symptoms, a sighing and soughing in the interior of the merchantman, warned him that the vessel's days were numbered, and that, at the end of a certain time, she must break up.

He collected everything useful that lay to his hand—some biscuits, some cooked meat, several bottles of wine, the captain's guns, some ammunition, knives, spoons, and other useful utensils, and lowered them into the boat.

It was somewhere about midday when he himself, with a wildly-beating heart, descended into the pinnace.

The dog bounded after him without the slightest hesitation.

The animal seemed aware that some great change was about to take place.

A gentle, balmy breeze just ruffled the surface of the waters.

The youthful castaway was able to hoist the sail, and, being a tolerable sailor by this time, headed at once for the land.

He was very grave, and even downcast.

Young, of a delicate and frail constitution, the peril in which he was placed was altogether disproportionate to his means of combatting with them.

He had a boat, arms, tools, and some few provisions.

But he was advancing to an unknown shore, probably peopled by savage beasts and still more savage men.

He had fine weather.

But at any moment a storm might arise, such as he could not cope with.

Even as he thought this, a purple rippling line from the east might have warned him that the struggle was about to commence.

Henry Thornton all this time was advancing towards the land.

He could begin to make out trees upon the approaching shore.

The wind increased every minute, but fortunately there appeared no broken water between him and the island.

His hand was quite tremulous as he clutched the rudder.

It looked very small and very white to manage such a craft.

Every moment the roll of the waves, as they poured on towards the shore, increased.

They began to lift the boat in a most unpleasant manner.

What if there were no bay to run into?

With the increasing wind, to beach the boat was to ensure destruction both to the frail craft and himself.

Cliffs arose to view—an unbroken line —skirted by the usual exuberant reflection of the tropics.

Henry lashed the rudder amidships and went forward.

He was going headlong ashore straight at the cliffs.

Suddenly, when about half a mile from the shore, he turned to his left and saw an opening.

The wind was aft, and the pinnace, being admirably built, was very manageable.

He returned to the helm, and at once steered for the port he had providently discovered.

In twenty minutes more he was sailing up a river, the shores of which were lined with thick, tangled woods.

In half an hour more he had fastened his painter to a tree and leaped ashore, followed by his dog.

Their further adventures for a day or two are scarcely worth recording.

They made short home excursions round the neighbourhood, discovered cocoa nuts and some goats, one of which

Henry Thornton—a very timid and sensitive soul—unwillingly killed.

No savage beasts appearing, and no men of any kind, he ventured further up the river.

At about a mile above he made a remarkable discovery.

The river appeared to burst from a large and magnificent cavern, about thirty feet high, and proportionably wide.

It was perfectly light and airy, and had several chambers, all deep with water.

Here the pinnace was docked, and here for some days Henry Thornton and his dog regularly retreated at night.

Gaining courage, however, every day, the young castaway at length shouldered a gun, and taking his dog as a body-guard, penetrated more deeply into the island.

Thanks to Carlo, who was pursuing a young goat which tore its way up a steep and winding ascent, they discovered the little cave in the rock, which subsequently he turned into a sheltered abode.

Having a good stout axe, some knives, a saw, hammers and nails, the affair was was not after all such a very difficult matter.

The ladder was an afterthought, the young castaway having discovered the occasional presence of savages on the island.

He then determined to have two exits from his abode.

When Ned Summers at length discovered him, under such happy circumstances for himself, Henry had been one year on the island.

"No one would believe," he said, "not my own mother"—he sighed deeply as he spoke—"who saw me a year ago that I and the sickly-looking feeble lad could be one and the same person."

"You look well enough now, though you are delicate for a boy," replied Ned, kindly.

Harry smiled and turned the conversation to other matters, particularly their own safety and future plans.

This Ned Summers, now enthusiastic and hopeful, readily acquiesced in.

CHAPTER XII.

HARRY'S ISLAND HOME.

THE day passed without any events worthy of record.

The two young people kept close within their fortress.

Their provisions were ample for the day.

The time passed rapidly enough, each telling the other his adventures.

They were both deeply interested.

Night came at last long before they were aware of it.

Harry produced a cocoa-nut half full of oil, and a wick, and lit it by means of a tinder-box.

The oil had been procured from a sea monster of some kind he had shot, the wicks from some fungous fibre.

Ned looked on with admiration at the household treasures of his young friend.

It was late when rest was spoken of.

The master of the house then showed Ned a recess where he could lie.

For his own part, opening a kind of cupboard, he pointed to a kind of hammock, in which he was so accustomed to sleep that he could enjoy no other bed.

Ned wished him good-night and threw himself as he was on the pile of dry grass and skins, nor spoke again until morning.

He then found his companion afoot, and the breakfast ready.

To his great surprise, it consisted of some rather tough cakes and a bowl of rich fresh milk.

Harry smiled at the other's bewildered and astonished look.

"You wonder where my dairy is," he said; "you shall see all in good time."

Ned Summers was far too hungry to ask many questions just then, but contented himself with enjoying the good things set before him.

After breakfast, however, he proposed an expedition to discover what the savages were doing.

Harry Thornton hesitated and looked very uncomfortable.

"Ned Summers, do you know," he said.

"that I have a dreadful aversion to shedding human blood? I don't believe I could fire a gun at a man to save my life."

And he looked up at his taller and more manly companion.

"You shall not be called on to do so," cried Ned, heartily. "I dare say your dog will keep them from surprising us."

"Oh, yes, Carlo will do that," replied Harry, evidently much relieved.

They then armed themselves each with a gun, a pistol, and a small axe, while Ned took a good supply of bullets and powder from a store at some distance, a small hole which the cautious and unwarlike Harry had converted into a powder magazine.

As soon as they were quite ready, Carlo led the way down a steep acclivity, almost entirely overgrown with trees.

At the bottom was a small prairie, one of the most lovely of meadows, thickly grown with grass, and on which gambolled some seven or eight goats with their young.

They were quite tame, and showed no fear of either dog or man.

"How is this?" asked Ned, looking in amazement at his wonderful companion.

"Wait and you will see," replied Harry.

Crossing the clearing, which was surrounded on all sides by rocks and trees, they came at last to an opening in the side of one of the cliffs.

It was high at first, the roof being ten feet from the ground.

Soon, however, it lowered until at length it was not high enough to admit of their walking.

The dog advanced boldly and fearlessly, all the while acting the part of guide.

Soon they had to go down on their knees, until at last it was a mere tunnel of about two feet in height.

At the end of this was a rude wattled doorway, which Harry Thornton removing, they issued once more into the open air, at no great distance from the sea.

Thornton then explained how he had followed the dog up this subterranean passage, and thus discovered the retreat, which, otherwise, he would never have ventured to explore.

As their chief object was to discover

what the savages had done, they turned in the direction where, according to Harry, they usually landed, and, after some time, reached a spot on the edge of the wood which commanded a view of the sea.

Not a canoe was anywhere visible on the waste of waters.

Ned then alluded to the river where he had discovered the fleet of boats, and to the place where he concealed the one he had succeeded in capturing.

"Clear now," said Harry, readily. "I know it. When there are no savages on the island, I often fish there."

They had seated themselves for a moment at the foot of a large tree.

It was very hot, and the shade was most desirable.

The dog had left them on some exploring expedition, and they were careful to speak in a low tone of voice.

Suddenly a series of shrieks burst upon their ears, and, rising, they concealed themselves behind a dense thicket of some prickly bushes.

Loud cries, resembling fiendish laughter, followed, and then a man, nearly naked, with frantic gestures, came flying along.

Behind were some ten Indians, the foremost of whom had long swishes in their hands, which they administered without mercy whenever they had the opportunity.

Ned clutched his gun.

"What would you do?" said Harry Thornton, tremulously.

"Save a fellow creature—a white man and English officer, from these inhuman wretches."

Harry made no reply, but covered his face with his hands.

Ned took aim at the foremost Indian, whose hand was raised to strike, and fired.

Quick as thought he snatched Harry's double barrelled gun from him, and again let fly at the amazed and astounded savages.

Three fell, and when Carlo, astonished at the noise, came dashing to join them, no one remained on the battle-field save the victims.

The wretched Petworth had made his escape, while the savages had fled in utter consternation.

Reloading his gun and that of his

companion, Ned walked across to where the Indians lay.

Harry stoutly refused to accompany him, even shuddering at the very thought, nor would Carlo leave his master.

The men were quite dead. The heavy shot with which Ned had loaded the guns had told with decision.

He turned away rather sick and pale, for the sight was a horrid one, and returned slowly towards the tree where he had left Harry.

But Harry and the dog were no longer there.

He called after them in a low and cautious tone, but received no answer.

He became seriously alarmed.

Had the savages returned and captured his only friend, and already beloved companion?

The supposition was too horrible to be believed.

Crouching on the ground, and with his gun ready for action, he listened attentively.

Then a cautious step was heard in the distance to the left.

Another cautious step then was heard to the right.

What could it mean?

He laid himself down flat in order both to listen and see.

Then he saw Henry Thornton, with his dog, emerge from a thicket, and hurriedly prepare to cross an open space towards the tree where Ned was secreted.

Henry looked anxious and alarmed, glancing back every moment.

The dog walked erect, and with ears evidently listening.

What was following them?

The next instant his question was answered.

Samuel Petworth, nearly naked, with a huge stick in his hand, came tearing forth from the bushes in the direction of the youth.

Henry faced him with a white and terrified look, which indicated the completest degree of alarm and trepidation.

"Hand over that gun, you youngster," said the young ruffian, in his most insolent and aggravating tones.

Harry stood with his loaded gun in his hand, apparently quite helpless.

It was quite clear he would not fire to defend himself from the ruffian who was now close upon him.

Indeed, he appeared ready to sink into the earth with emotion.

The dog, however, suddenly confronted the insolent intruder, and prepared to defend his master.

The wretched fugitive from the savages lifted his heavy stick menacingly over the noble animal.

"Hold!" cried Ned, coming up and levelling his gun at the treacherous youth; "one step further and you are a dead man."

"Two to one is manly," said Samuel Petworth, dropping his stick to the ground and speaking with a sullen sneer.

"Murderer in intention if not in act," replied Ned, "away with you, out of my sight, or I may be tempted to kill you even now."

"I shall starve," he said, in a whimpering tone. "I have no arms, not a weapon with which to kill a bird."

"Give him a gun," whispered Harry Thornton, gently.

"To be murdered? No—go; live or die as it may please Heaven," said Ned, sternly. "There are fruits and herbs, and shell-fish enough to prevent you from starvation. Keep away from us as you value your safety."

"We might spare him a little food sometimes," urged gentle Harry.

"If you like to give him some occasionally you can; but do not betray your home to him," replied Ned, in a low tone.

"Certainly not," cried Harry, with suddenly awakened fear.

"Make yourself a hut hereabout," continued Ned, "and when we have anything to spare it will be brought you. But, together or alone, beware how you annoy or follow us; this is your part of the island. Invade ours, or offer injury to my companion, and I will shoot you like a dog."

With these words, Ned Summers turned away with loathing from his treacherous ex-companion.

"Go," muttered Samuel, "go, and see if I don't be revenged on you and your milksop friend."

Harry Thornton, meanwhile, strode alongside his brave and daring companion with a very downcast look.

3

Something was evidently ready to be said, but he gulped down a sigh and said it not.

"You must never come to this part of the island without me," suddenly observed Ned, who had been thinking.

"Why?"

"That fellow is not to be trusted; he will do us a mischief if he can."

"I will be sure to avoid him," said Harry, with a shudder.

It was now nearly evening, and yet they did not decide on returning to their home.

They had need of food to replenish their larder before they again sought safety within their comfortable and cosy retreat.

CHAPTER XIII.

THE CHALOUPE—A STORM IN A WOOD.

THAT night the two young friends camped out, sleeping in a large, live oak tree, and in the morning discovering no signs of the Indians, or even of Samuel, they took the opportunity to collect cocoa-nuts and other fruits, as well as certain savoury roots, and about an hour before mid-day rested on the banks of a stream, one well-known to both, and caught a considerable quantity of fish.

This they secreted, hoping to take it home that night for supper.

They then held a council.

The presence of an enemy on the island, and that enemy a white man, appeared deeply to prey upon the spirits of the younger of the two dwellers in that out-of-the-way corner of the world. Henry Thornton, whose sensitive, not to say timid, character, was already known to Ned Summers, was deeply concerned about the matter.

"We must dismantle the boat," he said, thoughtfully, "or he may run away with it."

"Certainly," replied Ned. "Is it far?"

"No. The sooner we do it the better," continued Henry, leading the way to a small cluster of trees, covered with a dense growth of creeping plants.

Evidently knowing the way thoroughly, he entered the wood, passed round a large tree, and then led the way under the leafy arches of the forest to the banks of the river so often mentioned.

Ned followed closely in his track.

The banks of the river were easily reached, and skirted by the two youths.

Ned Summers was astonished indeed when he came to the great water cave.

He then followed Thornton to a spot where a pathway led them into the hollow.

There lay the boat.

It was of considerable size, and quite capable, if well stocked and victualled, of enabling them to make a considerable sea voyage. This, indeed, was its great value.

But that was not to be thought of for the present.

Thoroughly appreciating the views of Henry Thornton, Ned Summers proceeded at once to dismantle the craft.

They selected a high shelf in the rocky cave, nearly obscured by deep shadow.

Thornton clambered up, and stood upon a small ledge of stone, while Ned handed him up the various contents of the pinnace.

They then carefully examined the boat, and removed a plug in the bottom, used when the craft lay high and dry, to allow rain and other water to run off.

The plug itself was carefully concealed.

Having thus provided against the loss of their larger vessel, the two youths then left the banks of the river, and, satisfied that the savages had departed, determined to further explore the island.

Carlo was to accompany them.

Henry Thornton proposed that they should, as much as possible, avoid the neighbourhood in which they had last seen their dangerous white enemy, who was capable of still being on the watch.

The youth shuddered at the very mention of his name.

"You have never been to a boys' school," observed Ned, with a laugh.

"Never. Why?"

"Or you would not be afraid of such an arrant bully and coward as Samuel Petworth," continued Ned.

"I never fought in my life, and do not want to," said Harry, looking quite timidly in the other's face. "Don't think I'm not brave because I do not like fighting. If you were in danger, you would soon see."

And the boy quite blushed with enthusiasm as he spoke.

Ned laughed, and told him he was a glorious fellow. Then they started in search of further adventures.

Ned had no particular objection to roast and boiled goat flesh; but he at the same time was quite ready to vary his diet.

Henry proposed that they should explore a part of the island he had never yet visited, which he believed might perhaps furnish them with some game and fruit.

Ned was quite willing to make the experiment, so the two at once left the neighbourhood of the river, and took the direction of a distant forest.

They already knew that an island with such a climate must be very fertile; and Ned, therefore, was in no way surprised at the discoveries he constantly made of its vegetable wealth.

Henry, who had not read so much in the style of travels as Ned, related his surprising discoveries with naive admiration and astonishment.

He considered the discovery of potatoes growing wild to be something wonderful.

Ned laughed again.

Henry, all the time he was talking, was making for a grove of lemon trees in full bloom, where he proposed to halt during the extreme heat of the day, which was now far advanced.

Ned was quite willing, and so cast himself down in the shade.

A hearty meal of meat and fruit having been consumed, they took a siesta, leaving Carlo on guard.

When they awoke, the extreme tropical heat of the day had passed, and both felt refreshed and ready for their expedition.

For some time they made their way round a winding kind of path.

Which, however, suddenly ended just as some heavy drops of rain warned them of the approach of a serious shower.

The wood was not many yards distant.

It appeared to be composed of singularly large trees.

Running as fast as they could, they were soon under the umbrageous foliage, which was huge and wide spread.

Scarcely were they beneath the leafy arch of forest, when not only did the rain come down with the force of a torrent, but vivid flashes of lurid lightning illumined the scene, and terrific claps of thunder were heard.

Henry Thornton shivered.

"We must get away from here," said Ned Summers, in a firm and determined voice.

"Why?"

"If the storm comes much nearer, we may be killed by the lightning," replied our hero.

Henry was cowering on the ground, gazing with awe at the terrible scene.

No one in this climate can form any idea of the intensity of a tropical storm.

To add to the din and confusion, the wind swept down with the force of a hurricane, swaying the trees to and fro like reeds.

The noise was perfectly hideous.

"Come away," urged Ned, after surveying the heavens once more.

"Where can we go?" faintly ejaculated Henry.

"Anywhere, away from the trees."

Henry allowed the other to lead him away some few yards, when he fell and could not rise.

The boy had fainted; at all events, he was incapable of movement.

"Leave me," he whispered, after a few moments, "leave me to perish."

"Never; rouse yourself," replied Ned.

"I cannot."

Ned saw that he spoke the truth, and resigned himself to his fate.

Fortunately, though the wind and rain continued as much as ever, the thunder and lightning shortly afterwards ceased.

Ned at once assisted his companion to regain the shelter of a vast tree, where they were in some degree protected from the wind and rain.

For hours the fierce tempest rage seeming never to expend its fury.

At length it ceased, but night had come round again, and neither of them could proceed any farther.

A tree, the branches of which nearly swept the ground, was selected, and into this they clambered, cold, wet and weary.

The dog found a snug bed inside the hollow trunk.

Thanks to the dense foliage above they found a warm, dry and snug retreat —and here they purposed passing the night.

Both were utterly worn out with excitement, which is often more telling on the human frame than fatigue.

Just, however, as they were falling off into a doze, after a brief conversation, the dog gave a low growl.

Then he was silent.

Both peered out into the darkness.

At first they saw nothing.

The wind moaned faintly through the trees, but no other sign or sound could be made out.

They listened keenly.

Presently a low, cautious, warning bark from the trusty dog again roused their attention.

This time they saw what looked like a Jack-o'-lantern moving to and fro.

The light was near the ground.

Then they made out a line of warriors, preceded by one who was keenly examining the ground.

It was a party of Indians, seeking for their trail in the gloomy night.

CHAPTER XIV.

HUNTED AGAIN—FIGHT FOR LIFE.

HENRY THORNTON was now thoroughly alarmed. During the year he had been on the island he had known of the presence of Indians, but they had failed to discover any sign of him.

Now it appeared as if they would never rest until they routed the two unfortunates out of their island home.

Ned was more hopeful. He saw at once the Indians were at fault.

Their marvellous instinct and knowledge of woodcraft had guided them in the right direction.

The storm, however, had proved a friend to the boys.

It had at length obliterated all trace of their footsteps.

The dog, too, was perfectly silent, now that he had attracted their attention.

The Indians presently halted.

They were near a clump of trees, and seemed to be holding council.

Soon it became evident that they were about to camp for the night.

Some began to clear the ground with their hatchets, others to make a pile of wood.

There was plenty of wood sufficiently dry for their purpose.

A fire was soon made, and the whole party, about a dozen, squatted round it.

They were not twenty yards distant from the anxious fugitives.

It was quite easy to distinguish their hideous war paint.

Samuel was not amongst them.

"What is to be done?" whispered Harry Thornton, in a faint tone.

"Can you walk?"

"I must."

"Remain quiet until they slumber, and then we must be far away before morning," was Ned Summers' calm reply.

Thornton sighed.

He had hoped a few minutes before to pass such a comfortable night.

Now they must again front the perils and unknown dangers of the isles.

For some time the savages conversed in their deeply guttural tones, and then one by one they laid themselves down.

At last all slept but one.

To keep himself awake the sentinel walked up and down, round the fire, and in the direction of their own tree.

Suddenly the dog, who had been asleep, gave that peculiar moan which will sometimes betray that these animals are dreaming.

The Indian started, and looked round, and stood still as a marble statue.

He clutched his tomahawk.

"ONE STEP FURTHER AND YOU ARE A DEAD MAN,"

Probably he expected to be attacked by some wild beast.

Still he did not wake the other sleepers.

He took a lance from a pile that leaned against a tree, and waited.

But the noise ceased as suddenly as he had heard it.

Ned now nudged Harry.

"It is time."

"I am ready."

They were not six feet from the ground.

Ned swung himself down.

Fortunately he landed beneath the massive foliage without noise.

Henry handed down his gun, and being stouter in stature than Ned, did not refuse his assistance when he held up his arms.

They now stood side by side, not ten yards from the sentry.

His back was, however, fortunately to them.

Treading as if dear life depended upon every step taken, they got round the tree.

Noiseless and wary the dog followed.

They were now out of sight of the camp, and Ned proposed seeking a temporary shelter deeper in the forest.

Henry nodded his head.

They did not hurry.

One false step would have been fatal to all their hopes of escape.

Advancing as much as possible in a straight line, they were soon some hundred yards away from the dangerous group of warriors.

Both were weary with emotion.

They suffered, too, with thirst.

Under these circumstances, when the dog offered to take the lead, they implicitly followed.

He did not offer to run, but walked leisurely forward with his nose in the air.

Presently his course was downward, over a green, soft sward, still damp from the storm.

Then the pleasant sound of water fell upon their ears.

Hastening forward, they found themselves on the borders of a pool, into which fell a small cascade, with about fifteen feet of fall.

No doubt its volume was greater in consequence of the heavy rain.

Both filled their gourds and drank.

The dog floundered in and bathed with joyous gambols.

They then crossed the stream, which ran out from the pool, and began a steep and rugged ascent.

Henry Thornton stumbled at almost every step.

Ned knew that to proceed much farther would only be to utterly upset him.

He therefore looked about for a halting-place, and soon found a sheltered nook, where a number of stones were piled one upon another.

Here, utterly exhausted, they cast themselves upon the ground and slept until morning.

Ned was on foot at once.

Fortunately they had a small supply of meat left, and, with water, made a hasty meal.

"Ah! my poor goats," sighed Harry, as he drank water and thought of milk.

Ned laughed.

"How do you feel this morning?"

"Better; but sadly in want of a day's rest. Let us get back to the fort."

"Willingly; but first let us throw these wretches off the scent. They are devils incarnate, and will follow us for weeks, unless thoroughly baffled."

"How is it to be done?"

"All about here is rock and stone; follow me, and whenever you see a blade of grass avoid it; in this way we shall leave no trail."

The dog, at a sign from his master, gambolled on in front.

The poor fellow was literally as hungry as a hunter.

Presently, after sniffing the ground with eagerness, he took to his heels, and darted off in the direction of a small wood.

His masters followed.

Suddenly they were startled by wild cries and shrieks, accompanied by fierce and savage growls.

Henry stood still.

"The savages!"

"No; 'tis Carlo and some wild animals —come," said his comrade.

Ned ran on in advance, and the noise becoming louder and louder, he soon found himself on the field of battle.

Field of battle it was.

Carlo, savagely hungry, had sniffed a party of monkeys, and darting suddenly into their midst while engaged in eating some roots, had seized hold of a plump little cub, which he proceeded to devour, without taking counsel with its unfortunate parent.

For an instant the amazed and startled monkeys flew in all directions, utterly terror-stricken and aghast at the strange sight.

Next minute maternal feelings took the place of fear, and the mother flew at Carlo with white, gleaming, and chattering teeth.

The dog, which had already killed and partly eaten the young one, was forced to drop his prey.

A furious combat followed.

Carlo was more than a match for one, but the whole party fell upon him.

Fortunately the two youths came up in the nick of time.

The monkeys showed fight for a moment, but when Ned flew at them with his axe, and began to cut and slash in all directions, they speedily took to flight.

Henry looked on bewildered, and apparently sickened at the sight.

"Bad Carlo," he said.

But Carlo, without taking any notice, went on eating.

Henry Thornton turned away in disgust. The young monkey had something strangely human about it.

Ned laughed.

"You ought to be a girl, Harry," he said, "you are so squeamish."

Henry quite blushed.

"What nonsense you do talk, Ned," said Harry, with considerable confusion.

He fancied that Ned despised him for his timidity; he was very much mistaken.

Onward still, under the trees, some of which were of enormous elevation and breadth, they now made their way, fearful the savages might follow.

Soon, however, after a consultation, they descended to the lowlands, towards what appeared to be a river.

Henry Thornton thought they were not far from home.

An unforeseen obstacle, however, forced them again to turn towards the forest.

A deep and dangerous morass lay exactly in their way.

Here Carlo rejoined them, walking proudly and pleased, as if he had done a meritorious action.

At all events, he had made a good meal.

Harry refused to take any notice of him; but Ned caressed him and patted his ears.

In this way they skirted the morass, and at last found a dry ridge.

Along this they once more advanced.

The morass was on both sides.

Impossible to turn to the right or the left.

At this critical moment the Indians came in view.

With a fearful yell—the horrid war-cry of their tribe—they dashed after the fugitives!

Both turned, and then, by the same impulse, bounded along the causeway.

One thing alone saved them.

The dog ran on in front, instinctively selecting the safest path.

"Keep cool," said Ned; "if we cannot run, we must fight."

Henry shuddered, shook his curly head, but made no reply.

They were nearing a river.

"Can you swim?" asked Ned.

"No."

"That's a pity. Well, we must make the best of it," replied his friend.

At this moment they stood on the brink of the water, and Ned cast his eyes around.

The stream was deep and sluggish.

The dog was already floundering in the water, ready to go over.

Numbers of trunks lined the bank, cast down by the late storm.

Several were afloat, only kept to the bank by a few roots.

These were severed in a moment, and Henry, with the two guns, the powder-horns and axes, at once clambered on the middle.

Ned Summers pushed it off, and then, swimming as hard as he could, urged the raft for the opposite shore.

It was an arduous and fatiguing task.

Henry could not help him.

Presently, however, the raft grounded.

They were in shoal water.

With a howl of triumph, the Indians burst through the fringe of trees on the opposite bank.

Snatching his weapon from the tree, Ned leaped ashore.

Henry followed.

As they crouched on the bank, a cloud of arrows fell around them.

Fortunately, the aim was decidedly bad.

Summers sternly levelled his gun and fired.

The foremost warrior fell flat on his face in the water.

He then snatched up Thornton's weapon and again fired.

The Indians were thrown into confusion, and surrounded their wounded friend.

The boys took advantage of the hubbub and noise to plunge into the wood, where they left a clear and open trail.

This, however, was not to be avoided.

At length, exhausted and out of breath, they halted, and the guns were again loaded.

Their ammunition was in abundance.

Henry again looked keenly around.

The country seemed familiar to him, and yet he was not quite sure.

He looked at the dog.

Carlo answered by a wag of his tail.

Both followed him anxiously, but he only led them to what appeared to be a branch of the same stream they had already crossed.

"I know where we are," said Ned.

And as he spoke he floundered into the water, waded some distance down, and then halted.

"Where are you going?" asked Henry, anxiously watching his proceedings.

"Water leaves no trail," he answered, advancing towards a kind of cliff on the opposite side of the pond.

From this he drew the identical canoe he had captured from the Indians some days before, and bade Henry enter.

Nothing loth, his companion obeyed.

The boat was quite capable of holding half a dozen people, so no objection was made to Carlo getting in and lying down in the middle for ballast.

Ned followed, and urging the boat through the shoal water with great difficulty, presently found himself in deep water.

But not in the same channel he had followed before. That he avoided.

Still it appeared to tend in the requisite direction, and Ned knew the danger of turning back.

Behind were the furious savages, thirsting more and more for their blood.

The death of their comrades would make them remorseless.

As he expected, they were soon in the river where the fleet of canoes had lain.

Its beauty struck Harry with amazement and admiration.

"What a lovely spot! Pity cruel man should make it a scene of rapine and slaughter," he cried.

Ned laughed, for though quite as unwilling to do battle with the savages as Harry, he was not quite so sentimental.

"The question is now what to do?" said he, steadying the boat by means of his paddle.

"Regain our fort; that we can hold against any number," replied Harry.

"The way?"

"I fancy if we descend the river some distance, I shall recognise some landmark," was his companion's ready reply.

They were gliding down the stream without much exertion.

All Ned Summers had to do was to guide the boat, and keep it away from the numerous protruding branches and snags which encumbered the beautiful river.

It wound very much, and while certain reaches were very short, others were of greater length and even width.

Suddenly, just as they were about to turn round a sharp corner, Harry uttered a low cry, and raised his arm, pointing some distance ahead of their position.

Ned looked in the direction indicated, and saw at once a man seated on the bank fishing.

He at once, without speaking, swept the canoe in shore and in the deep shadow of some lofty trees.

These trees hung almost horizontally across the stream.

At the same moment they heard footsteps at no great distance.

The Indians were on their track.

Ned made a sign to Harry, who at once lay down beside the dog, and, by caresses and motions, endeavoured to keep him quiet.

The footsteps and voices grew nearer and nearer every instant.

But the bank was high and extremely well wooded.

While they remained still there was no danger.

At the same moment another sound alarmed them—paddles upon the water.

"Move not for your life," whispered Ned. "Now is the hour of peril."

As he said this he drew the canoe higher up, until it could go no farther, being jammed between the boughs on the shore.

A little hole between two boughs, however, enabled him to look out.

His gaze was intent.

The loaded guns lay close to his hand.

If he was to die, he would die doing battle bravely for his life and that of his friend; he would not be butchered in cold blood by remorseless savages.

Then he heard a low chant or wail, at no great distance.

It was melancholy and weird.

Ned could not make it out.

Presently, however, a large canoe came in sight, and the whole matter was explained.

In the centre was a kind of platform.

On this platform lay two dead bodies.

Ned, himself, shivered at the horrid sight.

They were his victims.

The boat was rowed by eight men, who, as they dipped their paddles in the water, uttered the mournful howls which had so irresistibly attracted their joint attention.

Suddenly they stopped.

A peculiar cry from the shore, close at hand, startled them.

The boat drew in towards the screen behind which was the smaller canoe.

Ned Summers felt his heart bound, as it were, to his mouth.

Harry lay still, with his soft white hand on the dog's mouth.

The men on the bank then spoke over their heads, and appeared to be asking questions.

The answer was not apparently satisfactory, as the others gave a grunt.

The boat then proceeded on its way, the men still giving forth their horrid funeral chant.

Harry looked up, with an inquiring glance, at his friend.

Ned only put his finger on his lips by way of reply to his implied question.

He could hear the men crashing through the bushes, close at hand.

Presently this sound ceased, and Ned was able to explain to Harry what he had seen

A conference was now held, and the resolve come to to camp; in fact, to remain in their place of concealment all day, to emerge only late at nightfall.

The Indians would be sure to halt somewhere below, on the banks of the river, to bury their dead.

Wearily and slowly the long hours passed in silence.

Carlo went on shore, clambering up the steep bank with wonderful agility.

He was evidently tired of inaction, and, probably, also hungry.

He remained absent for hours, and when he did return was heavy, and inclined to sleep.

He had evidently indulged in some ample and glorious repast.

On an island abounding with small game, with hares, goats, and such like, a dog could have no difficulty in living.

It was a pity, said Ned, he would not hunt as well for them.

Harry replied that on more than one occasion Carlo had shared the proceeds of his chase with his master.

On one occasion, when he, Harry Thornton, had been starving for two or three days, nature only sustained by roots and acorns, the dog started in pursuit of some animal.

It was small, active, and in appearance something like a lizard.

The dog caught it just as it was about to run up a tree, and killed it on the spot.

The huge animal appeared thoroughly to enjoy his prize, and presently Harry ventured to take a morsel himself.

A fire was easily made and the meal roughly roasted on the hot embers.

It was delicious, and appeared to give Harry a new lease of life.

Ned, from the description, was able to inform Harry that he had fed on iguana, a very favourite meal with the natives.

In conversation such as this the day passed away.

Night came at last, however, and the two prepared for action.

They both entered the boat again, having left it awhile to repose on the shore.

The night was dark, without a moon, and with the stars obscured by fleecy vapour.

They glided out into the stream.

All was still as death.

Harry, at the express desire of his comrade, lay down in the boat.

Ned took the management of the escape wholly on himself.

By his side were the two guns loaded, while in his hand was the paddle.

He held his breath, scarcely using the small oar, and glancing rapidly from the right to the left.

Suddenly he used his paddle to make the canoe stationary.

He then sent it spinning in shore where the shadows were darkest.

He had caught sight of a large fire on the opposite banks of the river.

He glided along slowly now, scarcely venturing to breathe, and soon came in sight of a horrible spectacle.

A huge fire was built on a hillock; beside this was a scaffold on which were the bodies of the unfortunate slain.

Round the whole were some thirty Indians holding hands, and moving round to the solemn measure of some savage instruments.

Their faces were painted in the garb of woe, which is perhaps the most hideous disguise these children of Nature ever assume.

Ned nudged his companion, who, taking the hint, sat up, looking bewildered and alarmed.

He had been dozing.

The sight was not a pleasant one, though there was no immediate cause for alarm.

The canoe glided slowly onward all the while, Ned merely steering.

Suddenly and unexpectedly the trees ceased, and the two boys were visible against the low horizon.

With a loud howl the savages darted for their canoes to pursue the two unfortunates, leaving the dead for awhile.

CHAPTER XV.

A STERN CHASE.

WHEN Ned Summers saw that he was discovered, he at once adopted a plan that would enable him to gain on his pursuers.

He darted into the middle of the stream where the current was strongest, and, using his oars with great energy, began a race, the victory in which certainly was not likely to fall to the weaker party.

But, while urging forward his boat with all the power and science he possessed, his mind was fixed on some scheme by which to circumvent the others by the force of pure cunning and stratagem.

Glancing back—in a canoe the rower looks in the opposite direction to what he does in a boat—he saw that two war canoes were in the act of being launched, crowded with men.

The Indians made not the least attempt at secrecy.

With awful and savage yells they flew to their work, impelled not only by their naturally savage instincts, but by the demon of revenge.

Henry Thornton said not a word, but was as obedient to the orders of Ned as if he had been his legal apprentice.

The canoe sped rapidly with the current, and for some time Ned simply tried his strength with the enemy.

For a quarter of an hour this continued.

But the Indians were evidently gaining on them rapidly.

This was quite clear.

Ned's brow darkened.

"You must try your hand at this game," he at last said to Harry, pointing at the same time to a spare paddle.

Harry simply nodded, and at once did his best.

The canoe sped along considerably faster.

"Carlo, my boy," suddenly said Ned, "you must go overboard; you can take care of yourself, old fellow."

Carlo did not seem to approve of the suggestion; but when his two young masters insisted, after looking them rather pitifully in the face, he went overboard, and swam as directly as possible for the shore.

"Now, Harry, keep her amid stream while I try and check these ravenous wolves," said Ned. "Paddle steadily, that is all."

Harry nodded.

Ned then took both the guns and placed them on the bows of the boat.

Kneeling, he took steady aim.

Not at the Indians.

They were too numerous for him to cope with, but he might destroy the boat.

As the boat lifted in the air, he fired directly at the water line.

A fierce and angry yell proclaimed a double event.

He had struck the boat and wounded the foremost rower.

The confusion which ensued caused the periagua to swerve round.

For a moment the leak was completely unnoticed.

Ned now fired the double-barrelled, loaded with swan shot and one bullet.

This also struck the boat below the water line.

The savages at once saw that their boat must sink.

The second volley appeared to open the well-sewn seams.

A fearful shout announced the discovery of this calamity.

Next minute they were floundering in the water, and the fugitives were speeding down the river as rapidly as the current and two paddles could urge them forward.

The river now widened rapidly, and they could distinguish the sea in the distance.

"What shall we do—venture out to sea and endeavour to escape that way, or what?" cried Ned, heartily.

"Surely not in this little boat?" replied Harry.

"Why not?"

"The sea at the mouth of the river is very heavy," replied Harry. "There is what is called a bar——"

"Hist! look at yonder point. What is it?"

"Carlo."

This decided their movements, and the boat was urged in shore in the direction of the faithful dog.

Fortunately they easily found a small creek overgrown by luxuriant foliage.

Into this the boat was drawn, and the boys once more took to terra firma.

Both were tired, while Harry Thornton appeared almost to have lost heart.

However, it was no time for repining; and, taking exact note of the spot where they had concealed their boat, they started for some inner and more secluded retreat.

"I cannot go far," said Thornton, who never could undertake long journeys.

At this moment another storm burst over their devoted heads.

The rain fell in torrents, while the trees swayed to and fro as if about to crush them.

Carlo suddenly gave a low bark, and disappeared in a small hole at the foot of a mound.

Ned, stooping down on his hands and knees, prepared to follow.

"Suppose it is the den of some animal?" said Harry, hesitating.

"Nonsense! Carlo would not have gone in so fearlessly. I can hear him gambolling about," replied Ned. "Come along, there's a good fellow."

Harry sighed in rather a doleful manner, which only made Ned laugh as usual, and then followed.

It was pitch dark.

The opening went downwards for a short distance and then became level.

They could now stand upright.

"We are safe here," said Ned, heartily; "but as there may be holes and fissures, it will be better to lie here until morning; we want torches to enable us to explore this hollow."

"As you will," replied doleful Harry.

The boys were too weary and exhausted for further talking, so, finding the ground soft and dry, they stretched themselves out, and were soon in a sound sleep, with Carlo close to them.

When they awoke some faint gleams of light seemed to flitter through the roof of the cavern.

Both started.

They had sought shelter in a cavern-cemetery of some Indian tribe.

It was a vast dome-shaped cave.

On all sides were scaffoldings, on which rested the bones of human beings.

Beside each was a bow, some arrows, and a heavy wooden sword.

This seemed to indicate the spot as the grave of warriors and chiefs.

Harry stood open-mouthed — rather frightened than otherwise.

"Let us go away," said he, "the air smells like a church vault."

"Are you afraid of the dead?"

"No; but a charnel-house like this has its horrors," replied the younger boy.

"It served us a good purpose last night," observed Ned, "and may again. But we must now be moving; I am as hungry as a hunter, and could eat one of these Indians if he were only alive."

So saying he led the way.

Carlo, however, no sooner became aware of their intention than he took precedence.

The open air was soon reached, when both the boys certainly breathed more freely.

The fierce tempest of the night before had passed away, but the ground was still damp.

Birds, however, sang on the trees, and squirrels gambolled in the branches.

A small drove of diminutive deer started off, alarmed at the sight of the dog.

"At them," said Harry.

Away sped the dog after the frightened herd, while the boys followed more leisurely.

They were afraid to fire, as the Indians, though unseen, might have been close at hand.

Their only hope was in the dog.

He left a wide trail, and they easily followed it for above an hour.

Not a sound reached their ears.

The deer had led the dog a terrible way.

Both moved warily, expecting every moment to fall into an ambush.

But field, forest and hill-side were all deserted, and though faint and exhausted, they continued on their way for some time unmolested.

Suddenly Ned halted, and pointed to a thin column of bluish smoke, which arose about a hundred yards in front of them.

It was in a dell, round which grew an apparently impenetrable prickly hedge.

"What is it?" whispered Harry.

"A camp."

"Let us come away."

"No, on the contrary—let us advance. We can only retreat again if my suspicions are not confirmed," replied Ned Summers.

"What suspicions?" asked Harry.

"That our dinner is roasting over yonder fire," he replied, merrily.

Harry, who could not make him out, merely shrugged his shoulders and followed.

Ned made his way round the dense hedge until he found an opening.

Here he suddenly halted.

"Look," he said, pointing to a plot of grass at their feet.

"Well?"

"Carlo has been this way," he continued. "Here he killed a deer—this is blood. Look at these marks; that is his paw—that the hoof of the deer."

"What then?"

"It's cooking ready for us—come along, my boy. I'm sure it's all right."

And Ned entered the bush.

Harry followed.

Both walked slowly.

Suddenly Ned put his finger to his lips, and pointed.

There was the fire, and over it, supported by a triangle of sticks, was roasting a rather large joint of venison.

A man, whose back was turned to them, a savage-looking individual, was turning the tempting meat.

Strangest of all, seated complacently surveying the operation, and as if quite as much interested in the process as the man, was their own dog, Carlo.

Harry Thornton could scarcely believe his own eyes.

Ned Summers, significantly pointing to his gun, and whispering to Harry to follow, suddenly darted forward.

"Surrender, ruffian!" he roared, "or you are a dead man!"

The man at the fire turned round, and disclosed, as he expected, the sinister visage of Samuel Petworth.

CHAPTER XVI.

ON THE TRAIL.

THE surprise of Harry and the cruel young midshipman of the cruiser was mutual.

Samuel glared sulkily at them both.

"Surrender what?" he asked.

"The plunder you have stolen from our dog," replied Ned, with a grin.

"I am starving," he fiercely replied, looking at his heavy stick.

"So are we; and so is the dog."

"Not he; the beast would give me no share until he was satisfied," was the surly answer; "even then he would not leave me."

"Good dog," said Ned, laughing. "Now you, Samuel, just move off. You shall have your share as cook, but shall not sit in our company. Go, or it may be worse for you."

Samuel moved away, cursing between his teeth, but too hungry and helpless to resist.

The meat was done to a turn, and taking out his knife, Ned cut a huge slice off and handed it to Samuel.

Then he and his young friend sat down and enjoyed a meal which they were greatly in need of.

When the meat was devoured by the assistance of Samuel and Carlo, both of whom were insatiable, a search was made for some refreshing fruit, and this was a matter of no difficulty, Harry being well acquainted with all the trees of this wonderful island.

Much renovated, Ned rose to go.

Harry proposed a siesta; but in such company Ned firmly declined.

"Come away," he urged, and whistling to Carlo, turned his back on Samuel Petworth.

"You're not going to leave me, unarmed as I am, to die of starvation," whined Samuel, advancing towards them.

"No such treacherous scoundrel comes with us," said Ned, sternly. "You know my decision. When your house is built we will keep our word."

"But in the meantime," observed Harry, gently, "the poor fellow must not starve."

Samuel looked at the speaker keenly, and a cynical smile, that made Harry avert his head in alarm, passed over the countenance of the traitor.

"Come away," urged Harry, as if utterly forgetful of his former observation.

"Samuel Petworth," said Ned, "be warned by me. If you attempt to follow us, to spy over our habitation, I'll shoot you like a dog. You have attempted to murder me once and would again."

"I solemnly promise, on my honour," began the young villain, assuming a humble and contrite manner, at variance altogether with the glance of his eye.

"A murderer has no honour, no word; but listen. As long as you keep away from us, and do not molest us in any way, you shall have, at fixed and stated intervals, a certain supply of provisions. Make yourself a hut, a home, as I have told you, and with our occasional assistance you will find means to live."

Without another word the two left him.

"You two," he said, as soon as he was alone, "you two mean to lord it over me, do you? Well, mark me, Ned Summers, your time is not for long, and then, I have no doubt, I and Master Harry Thornton may, perhaps, contrive to knock up a very comfortable alliance—ha, ha, ha, ha!"

Waiting until they were some little distance off, he followed their trail with the keenness and avidity of a red Indian, taking care, however, to keep out of sight.

Ned and Harry were about a hundred yards ahead of him; but though they turned every now and then and looked behind, they saw nothing of the solitary tracker.

In this way they advanced about half-a-mile, this time making the best of their way towards the habitation of young Harry.

He appeared to think himself safe only when once more ensconced in his island home.

Suddenly Carlo gave a low growl, and turning, they saw Samuel flying over the ground in the direction of their hiding-place.

He was running as for dear life, followed by half-a-dozen Indians in their war-paint.

Both clutched their guns, still, however, keeping behind some low bushes, and hoping that the chase might pass by without their being discovered.

But Samuel, after a few minutes, headed directly for where they lay concealed.

"Lost, lost!" whispered Harry, dropping his gun, just as Samuel bounded over the frail barrier. "Fire!" he cried, in a wild but commanding voice, as he stooped to pick up the fallen gun.

"Back!" shouted Ned, levelling his piece. "Harry, run for your life! we are near the grave-cavern; the savages will not enter there."

And, picking up his gun, he took to his heels.

A shriek and a loud laugh made him turn in a few minutes, to see Harry struggling in the arms of the young ruffian.

Harry shrieked wildly for help.

Samuel held him firmly with one hand, while with the other he waved to the Indians to approach.

Ned's rage was boundless.

Why had he not killed the wretch, and why should he have thus basely betrayed them to the Indians?

If he had only known the truth!

It was too late, however, now to repair the damage.

To all appearance his companion—the boy he had learned to love—was lost to him for ever, and he seemed no longer to care even for his own life.

Still, it was utterly useless for him to be taken also.

The only chance was to remain free.

With this conviction, he darted into a thicket with the two guns, and then fortunately finding himself on the top of a steep incline, slided, sitting, to the bottom.

The Indians were too delighted with their capture, however, to take any notice of Ned, towards whom, in a few minutes, Carlo came, howling and moaning.

As soon as Ned thought himself safe, he began to reflect.

Short as had been their acquaintance, he now discovered that Harry Thornton had found a soft place in his heart.

He loved the gentle, tender-souled boy as he would have loved a younger brother.

And as much as he loved him did he hate the false, treacherous Samuel.

What was to be done?

Probably the Indians might make short work with them both, in which case he would be utterly desolate and lone.

At all events it was worth a trial to save Harry from their clutches.

How to begin?

Well—his heart was as true as his hand was firm, and the worst that could happen was sharing the fate of his friend.

After some repose and thought, Ned, finding that he was unpursued, rose from his place of concealment, examined the priming of his two guns, and restraining the ardour of Carlo, took his way along the foot of the slope down which he had fallen so unexpectedly, in the direction where Harry Thornton had been captured.

He had a very vague idea of what he should do, but, like many others, he trusted very much indeed to the chapter of accidents.

The sun was going down in the west, ere he, in a roundabout way, reached the spot, where the vile treachery of Samuel Petworth had given poor Harry up to the machinations of their enemies.

Not a sign of white man or redskin was now to be seen.

Ned peered around, while Carlo sniffed about anxiously.

At length the dog gave a low whine; he had found the trail.

He looked up imploringly at Ned Summers, and wagged his bushy tail.

"On, on, my faithful creature," said our hero; "come what may, we will not desert him."

And he at once followed in the track of the unfortunate boy and his savage captors.

Over morass, through dense thickets, through woods, across a stream, marched Ned, weary, footsore, and sorrowful, but never daunted, until the midnight hour was nearly approached.

Then Carlo, whose paws were bleeding from thorns and briars, lay down, as if exhausted, on the sward.

"Tired—poor fellow!" said Ned; "so am I—but, still, I wish we could go further on. Sleep and I will be unacquainted to-night."

The dog, as he crouched at his feet, whined in a low, warning tone.

Then Ned rose and looked about.

They were close to a camp of Indians, which proved, on examination, to lie in a hollow near their feet.

There were some faint embers in the centre, and around this the whole party lay.

A dozen sleepers at least, and two watchers, erect and armed.

Where was the treacherous Samuel Petworth?

Where the unfortunate Harry?

Ned could scarcely advance near enough to make this discovery.

At all events, he determined to try.

He surveyed the spot exactly.

The camp was bordered on one side by a thicket, while on the other side was a spring.

Between the two was the fire.

Around, with their feet to the centre, lay the whole party.

Beside the spring was one tall tree, against which leaned the sentries.

They were smoking.

Their eyes were closed; but occasionally, as if to keep themselves awake, they spoke, in dreary and guttural monosyllables.

Ned drew nearer and nearer, compelling Carlo to keep slightly behind.

In this way he at length reached the verge of the thicket.

The sleepers were not more than five feet from him, and the nearest sleeper was Samuel Petworth, the traitor.

Where was Harry?

Ned looked slowly around.

All the sleepers, except Samuel, appeared to be stalwart warriors.

Harry was nowhere to be seen.

Ned's heart was very sore at this discovery.

What had become of his unfortunate companion, his friend, his comrade?

Surely they could not have murdered the poor boy in cold blood!

Just as this idea crossed his mind, Carlo, who had been quietly sniffing about, suddenly flew at Samuel, and caught him by the throat.

Ned had only time to draw back into the thicket, when the whole camp was in a state of wild confusion.

Samuel, with loud and furious curses, caught the dog round the neck, and tried to throttle him.

The dog, however, finding himself about to be attacked on all sides, let go and leaped into the thicket.

Ned had contrived to crawl to some considerable distance, but Carlo readily found him!

Pursuit there was none.

No one ventured for one moment to think that a mere boy would come near a camp of armed men.

Ned, however, thought it wise to conceal himself in the dreariest hole he could find.

He was resolved to follow them unto the death until he discovered the fate of Harry.

Next morning he easily made out the movements of the Indians.

He did not, however, make any attempt to move.

They were preparing, he soon saw, to take their departure.

With difficulty restraining the dog, he lay still until he heard them pass at no great distance, their shuffling and limping gait betraying them at a very great distance.

Still Ned Summers never moved until he was satisfied the whole party of savages were out of sight.

Then he rose and cautiously returned to the camp they had just left.

It was completely deserted.

Carlo, however, found a sufficient supply of bones to satisfy him.

Ned stood leaning on one gun with the other slung at his back.

He was watching for the slightest sign of his beloved Harry.

None showed themselves.

"Lead on," said he, in an angry tone to the dog, which was wallowing in the spring close at hand.

Carlo needed no second word.

Lowering his head to the ground, and getting possession of the scent, he started forward in an animated manner.

Ned followed.

Instead of being downcast, he walked forward erect and proud, determined to succeed or die.

"THE WHOLE PARTY OF MONKEYS ATTACKED THE DOG."

For hours, however, nothing was seen of those who were ahead.

Ned was compelled to satisfy his hunger with berries, roots, and sweet acorns.

Water was not wanting.

In this way, aided by his dog, he kept not far behind the marching party.

He more than once actually heard their loud-toned voices.

Now Ned knew that they were not more than eight or ten in number, with, he expected, two prisoners.

They were armed simply with clubs, and bows and arrows, while he had three deadly barrels loaded.

Why should he not surprise them, kill three or four by means of his fire-arms, and then, while the panic lasted, attack them, and rescue Harry, who must be their prisoner?

If he failed, why, then he could only lose his life.

Second consideration, however, convinced him that to attack them in the open day was simply madness; all he could do was follow them up, which he did, until they made a halt during the noontide heat.

About three hours after mid-day the Indians broke up their camp and continued on their way.

Guided by the burning embers, Ned entered the clearing where they had made their fire.

Carlo, as usual, began to gambol about in search of bones and offal.

Ned looked round in a melancholy mood.

Suddenly his eye caught, fluttering on a branch, a small piece of black velvet.

He flew towards it.

He was right.

He had often noticed it round the neck of his companion.

It was fastened on a horizontal branch.

Ned eagerly clutched it, and found that it brought with it some choice morsels of food—venison and Indian corn cake.

His heart beat wildly with joy.

Not only Harry was safe, but Harry was satisfied that he was following.

Welcome, indeed, was the refreshment, but more welcome still the pleasing intelligence that Harry was most certainly alive.

He sat quietly over his meal for some time, shared it, of course, with Carlo, and then went on his way rejoicing.

He knew that they could not go much further in that direction.

The sea was at no great distance.

Were they about to carry his friend into captivity?

If so, where?

Well, he could only follow and wait.

The further journey was, however, doomed to be very short.

Less than an hour after he quitted the mid-day camp he was in sight of the ocean.

There it lay before him, calm, blue and beautiful.

Scarcely a ripple moved the translucent waters.

Ned's heart beat wildly.

The canoes were drawn up on the shore.

About a hundred yards from them was a perfect village; some twenty wigwams surrounded by a formidable stockade.

From the height at which he stood he could make out no sign of prisoners or Indians.

Carlo, however, continued on his way, and, by a rugged and winding path, led him direct towards the wigwams.

Again the sun began to set.

Suddenly Carlo stood still, with tail and ears erect, as he heard the *bark of dogs.*

It may be true that the canine race, when wholly abandoned to themselves, lose the faculty of barking—from the absence of the human voice, which certain philosophers declare is necessary for them to hear; but it is quite certain that Indian dogs are the most noisy, yelping curs in creation.

Carlo, who had heard nothing of the kind for nearly a twelvemonth, could scarcely command himself.

Ned, however, caught him by the collar, and checked his otherwise headlong course.

The dog evidently intended making a totally unaided raid on the village.

This would have ruined everything, betraying his presence and his hopes.

The dog once checked, like the well-bred and obedient dog he was, yielded.

The two descended the slope together.

Night fell, as is always the case in tropics, suddenly.

It was quite dark when the two reached the confines of the village.

The camp-fires were already lighted, and Ned determined to act at once.

Carlo was left tied to the foot of a tree, about fifty yards from the camp.

Ned advanced slowly, almost desperately—alone, to carry out his plans.

There was no moon.

He was able to get to the stockade before he even ran any chance of being noticed.

Fortunately, he had selected the shadow of a row of trees by means of which to reach the primitive wall of the camp, which was simply a wattled stockade, eight feet high, with a ditch on the outside.

To a sailor this presented no great difficulty.

In another moment, a tree growing conveniently at hand, Ned was over the stockade and in the interior of the camp.

A wigwam was close to him.

He crawled along the ground until he reached it, and then lifted boldly the skin of the tent.

His amazement may be conceived, when he discovered, with his arms tied to two tent-poles, Harry Thornton, in the dress of an Indian squaw, very pretty and becoming, even in that garb, but still disguised.

"Harry!" he whispered.

"Heaven have mercy on me! That voice!" gasped the unfortunate prisoner.

"'Tis Ned—keep up, Harry—I am near!" continued Ned, in a low, hearty voice.

"Save me now, or let me die!" faintly ejaculated Harry.

CHAPTER XVII.

THE ESCAPE.

NED was perfectly bewildered to find Harry in the costume of a squaw, confined, too, in a separate prison from Samuel.

As, however, the important business was to escape, he forbore to ask any questions.

Harry was secured by the waist to the pole of the tent, but not otherwise bound.

His companion, a woman in reality, seemed to keep constant watch upon him.

A tomahawk lay close to her hand.

Ned was well aware that she would not hesitate to use it, if necessary.

What was then to be done?

Any loud noise would be fatal!

Still, no time was to be lost!

Lifting up enough of the tent to allow his head to pass through, he slowly, with something of the snake-like progress adopted by his enemies, began his venturesome attempt.

A breath, a stumble, the faintest, slightest noise, and he was lost.

Harry sat with his eyes closed.

Painted, adorned with gewgaws, and made up admirably, he looked a very handsome squaw, thought Ned.

But why this inexplicable disguise?

This, however, was not the time to waste his thoughts on such a subject.

He was soon beside the woman, who, though watching the unfortunate boy, had still her eyes nearly closed.

Suddenly Harry moved forward, and the woman woke up thoroughly.

This was the moment caught at by Ned.

He knelt, and clasped his hands round her neck. A slight gurgle followed.

"Help me, Harry!" whispered Ned; "thrust something in her mouth!"

The woman struggled more violently; but, finding that Ned squeezed all the tighter, she suddenly ceased.

Harry, who seemed amazed and astounded, looked round the tent, and then made out some articles of Indian costume, which, without regard to their nature, he thrust into the mouth of the woman.

With admirable celerity, Ned tied them behind.

He then contrived to tie her hands and wrists.

"Come!" he said, in a low tone; "walk slowly—do not stumble or speak, or we are lost!"

Harry made no reply; but, snatching up a bundle that was close to his hand, he prepared to follow.

The night was still and calm.

Fortunately, it was dark.

No moon, no stars, nothing but dark, heavy clouds.

The door of the tent was open.

Ned peered out.

Far away on the edge of the village, at the entrance, was a small fire.

One man stood close to it.

This was the sentry they had to fear.

Harry, as they walked, shook as with the ague; and Ned was every moment afraid he would stumble.

"Calm yourself, Harry," he said, "or we are lost!"

Harry nodded his head, and crept close to him.

Ned at once put a tent between him and the sentry, and then looked round.

They were close to a small wood, and he at once made for this.

But his arms and ammunition lay on the opposite side, and must be secured.

"Will you remain here," asked Ned, "while I fetch my guns?"

"Yes."

"Do not move a step," replied Ned, "or in the darkness I shall not be able to find you."

"I will not move," said Harry, gently.

"I will not be long," responded the brave youth, and began his journey.

He had to turn the whole camp.

Treading lightly, never pressing his foot on the ground until sure that he was not pressing on a dry stick, Ned advanced on his way.

He kept the camp in sight, but he screened himself from all danger of being seen from it.

At length, after twenty minutes of patience and crawling, he was close to the tree.

He took the guns and stood erect.

The sentry was not twelve feet from him, and one false step would have been ruin.

Suddenly he stood in the act of listening, his glaring eyes directed full upon Ned.

Our hero stood motionless.

He was beneath the dark shade of a yew-like tree.

Slowly he backed, keeping a strict watch on the other, who, as if uncertain, made a step or two in advance.

Ned still retreated, until at last he touched some bushes, through which he slowly backed.

Here he was lost to sight.

The sentry, apparently satisfied, returned to his place, and Ned silently returned in search of Harry, who awaited him on the skirt of the wood.

He had not moved, but he had concealed his strange disguise by putting his own clothes over it.

Ned laughed lowly as he gazed at the now rather comical figure before him.

"You looked far better as a girl," he whispered.

"Don't say that again," replied Harry, sadly. "I know I am not brave like you; but do not call me girl."

"Well, I won't," continued Ned, good-naturedly.

They now, clutching their guns, entered beneath the leafy roof of the wood.

As soon as they had gone about a hundred yards, they held council.

To remain anywhere near the savages was impossible.

Where to go?

Harry was quite lost.

The only thing was to try and make a straight line from the camp.

Ned looked up.

Not a star.

Suddenly a slight noise was heard close at hand, as of something bounding in the bushes.

Both halted, and hastily levelled their guns.

"Stop—don't fire," cried Harry; "'tis only Carlo."

And so it was.

The faithful dog had succeeded in getting loose, and after a careful search had, indeed, found them.

They were saved.

The sagacious animal looked up in his master's face, who waved his hand to him to advance.

Carlo trotted on slowly in front, as if he himself were not very far from being fatigued.

Presently he halted on the borders of a stream, and began to trot across, not to swim.

Both followed, and in this way, soon reached the bottom of a rocky eminence, up which the dog led the way.

When the summit was reached, they found themselves on a ledge, sheltered from all wind, and very much like a natural cavern.

Here they resolved to rest until dawn, when they would retreat to their cavern, and there await the departure of the savages.

The dog nestled at their feet, and both the young people being tired, imitated his example.

CHAPTER XVIII.

PURSUED.

WHEN Ned arose, he found that Harry had been before him, having descended to the river, and obliterated the paint with which the savages had daubed him.

He had, too, removed the woman's dress, and stood erect in his own garb.

They had nothing to eat; but, under the circumstances, they cared not.

The matter to be looked to was escape.

They found themselves, now it was light, on a kind of table-land, which Harry appeared to recognise.

"Why, we have worked round in a very marvellous way," he cried. "We are not three miles from my cavern."

Ned was delighted to hear it.

At this instant a well-known sound caught his ears.

It was human voices.

Ned fell to the ground, pulling Harry with him.

There they were, a dozen Indians, armed with spears, bows and arrows.

They marched in the usual single file, and came straight to the river.

"Follow," said Ned; "there is nothing but to run openly."

Harry at once obeyed, and, after drawing back out of sight, took once more to his heels.

Before them was a small rocky plain, and over this they could hope to pass without leaving any trail.

Ned encouraged Harry to make a dash, as the only chance of saving their lives.

Carlo bounded before them.

They had reached the very edge of the rocky plain, when a loud yell proclaimed that the enemy had sighted them.

They were straining every nerve to come up.

Before the unhappy fugitives were some thick bushes, into which they plunged.

Plunged to fall down, down.

Harry gave a loud shriek, and then all was still.

When the savages came up, not a sign of the fugitives was to be seen.

Then arose a loud clamour, the savages running along the edge of the brushwood, but not venturing to enter it.

They held back like men who knew the danger they were likely to incur.

Presently, however, one party went one way and one another, peering carefully at the ground.

At length they seemed satisfied, and going round the brushwood, moved in a direction which made it likely they would soon meet again.

Meanwhile, what had become of Ned and Harry?

The bushes grew over a deep but dangerous fissure, utterly concealing it from view.

Into this the boys had plunged, like Curtius into the yawning abyss.

Fortunately they were light weights, and their clothes caught in the briars.

They were, it appeared, suspended in the air.

"Are you safe, Harry?" said Ned, suddenly.

"Yes; but where are we?"

"I cannot say," replied Ned, "but I fancy in a pretty fix."

"It is as dark as pitch."

"Where is Carlo?" was the answer.

The dog replied by jumping up and caressing their feet.

"All right, the fall cannot be great," said Ned, as he let go.

He touched ground without any hurt, and then aided Harry to descend.

They were, to all appearance, in a dark hollow without any means of exit.

Dark as Erebus.

Ned looked up; the canopy was itself, to all appearance, impenetrable.

He determined to strike a light.

They always had a supply of tinder, steel and flint.

They soon had a small torch alight.

The fissure was about thirty feet long, and without apparent issue.

But Carlo soon attracted their attention by a growl.

Advancing to where he stood, they soon found in what place they were.

In the lair of a wild beast.

Fresh picked bones lay at their feet.

With a shudder of horror they looked around, while Harry bade Carlo search.

He did so, and soon brought them to a narrow opening.

The animal that could come through could not be very large.

At this moment the voices of the savages fell on their ears.

Having no knowledge of the place, they motioned to Carlo to precede them.

He had to stoop and crawl.

They had to wriggle like snakes on their stomachs.

First Ned threw down his torch.

In an instant the bushes and trees were in a blaze.

Luckily smoke goes upward, or they must have been suffocated.

As it was, the draught through the hole they had to crawl through nearly took away their breath.

It came like a sirocco.

The dog, ignorant of what it was caused by, howled terribly.

At length, however, the tunnel increased in size, and became almost light.

Again they saw bones scattered about —bones which, from their size, seemed to vary between hares and goats.

Of these, however, Carlo took no account.

They were old and dry.

"I think it would be wise to remain here," said Ned.

"Why?"

"The savages will think us burnt, and give up all pursuit."

"But the wild beast?"

"At worst it can only be a large wild cat," urged Ned, "and surely we can shoot that."

Harry shuddered, but made no further objection.

He was too tired and faint.

Presently the dog, which had gone to the mouth of the cave, uttered a low growl.

Ned darted out.

There was a huge wild cat, with his back up at sight of the dog, standing with a tolerably-sized kid in his mouth.

Carlo, nothing daunted, darted at the animal, which turned tail, dropping the kid.

Ned, with a merry laugh, picked it up, and took it into the cavern.

It was quite dead, having been bitten at the neck.

"Won't we have a feast!" said Ned, who at once proceeded in the most philosophical manner to pick up small pieces of bones and wood.

This done, he unhesitatingly made a fire, and, cutting up the unexpected prize, proceeded at once to broil some by means of his ramrod.

Harry looked on, scarcely conscious of what was passing.

When, however, Ned handed him a nice, well-done piece of kid, he took it with a smile.

It was very necessary under the circumstances.

Having both made a hearty meal, they felt the necessity of water, and hence resolved to pursue their journey.

The cave-mouth looked north, so that they were on the right track.

After listening attentively for every sound, and finding none, they left the cave; and, without taking any notice of Carlo, who always contrived to find them out, went slowly over the plain in search of the river.

It was soon found, and after drinking they descended its course until they found a ford, and, before an hour, were once more within the enclosure, where the goats greeted them with a merry bleating that was quite satisfactory.

Carlo had preceded them.

CHAPTER XIX.

LOOKING AROUND.

FOR several days they remained quiet in their secure and pleasant retreat, working at several light jobs, living on milk, and dried roots, and goats' flesh, being very careful to make small fires without smoke.

Much time was spent in conversation, the principal topic being that of escape.

What else, indeed, could they care much to speak of?

Ned believed in the possibility of doing so.

The chaloupe, well stocked with provisions, and provided with water, would take them on the track of ships.

There was a time, about two months in the year, when the weather was always fine, and when they might safely navigate those seas.

"You will try, then?" asked Harry.

"Most certainly. It wants four months to the time. All our spare hours can be spent in getting together the requisite provisions," was Ned's cheerful reply.

Five days passed thus, and every day Ned began more and more to like his gentle, kind friend, just one of those boys he would have been proud to shelter and defend at school.

Then Ned determined to see once more if the Indians had left the island.

Harry hesitated at first, but Ned urged that this sedentary life was not good, that they required a provision of roots, of dried fruits, and of goat's flesh, with a supply of cocoa-nuts, which, during the coming wet season, was almost essential to their health.

Harry sighed ere he consented.

"Why not take the goods the gods provided, and wait in peace?"

Ned insisted, and Harry, as usual, gave way to the more bold and resolute character.

They started at early dawn on the sixth day, choosing the sea coast, that is to say, a ridge of rocks in sight of the sea coast, for their walk.

By this means they hoped, without exposing themselves, to catch a glimpse of the canoes belonging to the savages.

The first day their journey was extremely arduous and sharp.

At night they encamped in a small clump of trees, making no fire, trusting to the dog to warn them against wild animals.

When they awoke in the morning, their surprise may be imagined.

Some eight or ten canoes were in sight.

But they were approaching the shore instead of leaving it.

The canoes were full of warriors, who, in a few moments, leaped out on to the strand.

They were manned by over forty men.

About ten prisoners also accompanied them, their arms fastened behind their backs.

Ned frowned darkly.

"What is it?" asked Harry.

"We are about to witness a horrible sight," said Ned. "Come away."

"What horrible sight?"

"Do you see yonder naked savages?"

"Yes."

"The warriors are about to kill and eat them."

"Not without a struggle though," cried Harry.

"How?"

"Look."

Ned turned, and saw at no great distance, creeping from tree to tree and bush to bush, between twenty and thirty armed warriors.

They were their own persecutors!

Anyone could see by difference of dress and colour, that they belonged to a different tribe from those who had just landed.

Ned at once guessed that they were about to attempt to rescue the prisoners, probably members of their own tribe.

In the meantime, the fresh-landed warriors were preparing—some a fire, while others danced about with swords and javelins.

Between the expected combatants and the white boys was a dried-up water-course.

"Let us get nearer," said Ned. "Perhaps we may do some good."

Harry, who apparently did not like to stop behind, followed.

Creeping out from behind the clump, they stooped low.

When they got about a hundred yards from the clump, matters stood as follows.

The warriors who had just landed were to their right, the prisoners in the middle, the other savages to the left cautiously approaching.

They were evidently preparing for a charge.

Suddenly the prisoners, who were fastened with withes, saw the approaching foe.

With one accord they began to run in that direction.

With a fearful yell the armed warriors started in chase.

They were better armed than the foe, and much more numerous.

They passed within thirty yards of where Ned and Harry stood.

By an impulse, which he deeply regretted the minute after, Ned aimed at the foremost warrior and fired.

He fell prone to the earth.

The rest stood still for a moment, and then, advancing, picked him up.

He was quite dead.

They stood still around him, bewildered and astonished.

This gave time to the prisoners to reach their friends and be set free.

With a joyous bound they embraced, and, though several were young women, rushed to the charge.

This act roused the others to defend themselves.

A terrible hand-to-hand fight ensued, from which Harry shrank with horror.

Ned, not sorry himself to get away, having loaded his gun, retreated along the water-way.

When they reached the old clump of trees, the fight was over.

The later arrivals were defeated and made prisoners.

The effect of Ned's shot had been something fearful.

He himself deeply regretted having interfered, as one party was certainly no more to him than another.

The thing was done, however, and could not be undone.

With a sore and dejected heart, he turned away.

The sight of so much bloodshed was sickening.

Besides, it was clear their island was well known to the inhabitants of the mainland, who made it occasionally a battle ground, at other times a place for hunting and feasting.

What peace could they hope to enjoy?

Their life would be intolerable.

Even if gunpowder held out, they could not use it, and game would never be procured.

Besides, hunting was a pleasure in which Ned delighted.

He would rather venture to the main land than live in this continual dread.

They determined to ascend a hill at no great distance, and watch the savages.

The fight, we have said, was over, but when they looked again they found, to their great surprise, that the two enemies had fraternised.

Why?

Only one idea suggested itself.

Against them.

Then a fearful hunt would take place over the whole island.

What was to be done?

Return to the fort, fight, or dodge round the island?

Harry was for the fort, urging that for weeks they could live comfortably.

But Ned was never made for confinement.

He preferred even the attempt at immediate flight in the chaloupe

"Do just as you will, Ned," said Harry Thornton, gently. "I will only obey your orders in future."

Ned smiled, and they continued ascending the hill, which a little before sunset they succeeded in doing, and found at once that, as they expected, they were on an island.

Not a desert island.

That is a misnomer—on a deserted island, except by occasional visitors.

Suddenly Ned gave a wild start.

"What now?"

"A ship in the offing."

"Where?"

Ned pointed it out, coming in slowly towards the land, at a distance of three miles.

This explained the conduct of the

savages; they, too, had seen the ship, and had made up their differences in order to capture a prize so valuable.

What should they do?

Strive to save the ship, of course.

From the fact of there being an uninhabited island, it was to be supposed that this vessel was coming for water.

Both the young hearts bounded with joy, and, fatigued as they were, they began descending the hill in the direction of the vessel.

It must be night before they could reach it.

Should they be before the savages?

Ned determined to make a desperate effort to aid, doubtless, his countrymen.

Harry was quite as delighted at the opportunity.

The vessel in sight was a brigantine—that is, half schooner, half brig, having two masts, a mainmast and a foremast.

On the former there was a sail running fore and aft, and on the latter there was a foretopsail, and a fore-top-gallant sail, all of course square sails, and fastened to the yards.

Ned, in his own mind, had no doubt she was English, and equally had no doubt that man-of-war, merchantman, or privateer, she would gladly take them on board.

As, however, it was war time, and many French cruisers were about, it was necessary to be careful, as the island home would be better than imprisonment on board a Gallican privateer.

"What say you, Harry?" asked Ned.

"But for the savages I am in no hurry to leave the island," naively replied Harry.

Ned was rather surprised at this, but made no remark, as they were nearing the sea.

CHAPTER XX.

THE BRIGANTINE.

THE two boys ensconced themselves behind a large clump of trees at no great distance from the strand.

The vessel was heading directly for the land, as if about to enter a bay formed by two long, projecting points.

They were going very slowly, with scarcely any sail set, evidently sounding as they advanced.

This was a wise precaution, as the water shoaled rapidly, and suddenly all sails were taken in, and the anchor let fall.

Still no flag.

Boats, however, were rapidly put out, and amongst others the long boat, fitted, as Ned had fully expected, with barrels.

Water was, then, the object of their visit.

Other two boats accompanied this one, and into these descended numerous sailors.

They were not half a mile from the shore, and the boys easily made out that they were heavily armed.

They watched them keenly.

As they neared the shore, Ned anxiously scanned their countenances.

His hope was that they would prove to be English, and therefore friends.

In this case their escape would be a certainty.

His feelings then may be imagined when they proved to be a hideous collection of negroes, mulattoes, Spaniards, and men of a whiter caste, but certainly pirates by the very cut of their jib, as Ned observed.

Harry drew back from the contemplation of their hideous and ferocious countenances with unfeigned horror.

"Ned!" he said, clutching the other's arm, with him an unusual mark of excitement.

"Well, Harry."

"Let us away. The sight of those men inspires me with disgust," he continued.

"I will be careful. But be sure they will not come this way. They are making for yonder spring that trickles from the rock," replied Ned.

He was right, and very soon the whole party were on shore, the barrels rolled upon the beach, and the chief part of the men hard at work.

There were two exceptions, in the shape of white men, apparently officers.

One, who wore a nondescript uniform, and whose belt bristled with pistols, while a hanger and musket added to the martial character of his appearance, moved on one side with a younger companion.

The first was a burly ruffian of about thirty, with huge, ruddy whiskers and heavy moustache.

The second was a youth, not more than sixteen, pensive and delicate, decidedly English; at all events, so they fancied.

He was armed with a kind of dirk, carried a small gun, and one pistol.

They were about fifty feet from where the boys crouched in an almost impenetrable retreat.

They sauntered slowly along, apparently not very pleased with one another's company.

"They are coming this way," said Harry.

"They will not come here; what could attract them? They will pass within hearing, however, and, do you know, Harry, that pale, pensive youth interests me?" replied Ned.

Silence now ensued, as the strangers were close at hand.

"Cheer up, boy, and don't be spooney; a short life and a merry one is my motto," said the elder sailor, with a grating laugh.

"An honourable life is my motto," replied the boy sadly.

"None of your sanctified nonsense for me!" savagely cried the officer. "Why, what's more honourable than our trade? We ain't got no king or country, it is true, but then our ship is king and country both."

The boy sighed.

"Don't we have plenty of money? Don't we enjoy ourselves, go where we will? Haven't I seen more of the world than most men? Fred Blount, I'm ashamed of you!"

"I shall never be a pirate, Lieutenant Robinson. You have never been unkind to me; you saved my life when my father was killed before my eyes; to protect me against the brutality of the captain, you made me an officer and put me in your watch. Do me one more favour—leave me behind—maroon me, as you call it."

"No. Take care I don't repent my former kindness," said the sailor, sternly; "never while I live shall you——"

He did not live to complete the sentence.

A volley of arrows pierced head, chest, and heart, and laid him low on the green and pleasant sward.

Then the whole band of united savages burst from cover, and came bounding in their direction.

The youth stood irresolute, looking towards the crew of the pirate.

Life is sweet, and he was preparing to run for it, when a voice as from heaven arrested his footsteps—

"This way—quick! Pick up the gun."

He looked around amazed.

Mechanically he obeyed, however, picked up gun and game-bag, and entered the clump, where two unmistakable English boys faced him.

"No time for talk," said Ned; "we must fight for dear life."

The situation was as follows.

The Indians were not forty feet off, coming down like an avalanche.

To the right were the sailors, a hundred and fifty feet off.

No time was to be lost.

Harry, roused probably to desperation, levelled his gun with the others.

Three sheets of flame—three reports, followed by the discharge of the pirates' heavy gun, startled equally savages and corsairs.

The former stood still, uncertain how to act.

"This way," said Ned. "Leave them to settle the business between them."

The others did not hesitate, but securing their arms, followed, nor did they halt until they were half a mile distant.

Volley after volley, cries of triumph, shrieks of suffering and dismay, sufficiently indicated what was passing behind them.

Presently, when in a valley which led by a circuitous route to their central cave, Ned halted.

He whispered a word to Harry.

Harry nodded his head, and the three seated themselves on the ground.

"Yonder ship is a pirate," began Ned

"Yes, but——" urged the boy.

"You are no pirate. We heard your conversation with the dead man. You are English, of course?"

"My parents were English, but I have never seen England. My name is Fred Blount. I was born in India, where my mother died. My father being invalided, came home, intending to put me to school. On the road home, our ship was taken by pirates, and every soul on board slain except myself."

"Poor fellow! How long ago?"

"Three years; since when I have never been on shore until now. My life has been one long agony. The presence of my father's murderer, the captain, strikes awe to my very soul."

"You, of course, have no desire to return to join this ship."

"Death rather!"

"Well, we, having no such calamities to deplore, have been very unfortunate. My dear friend and brother here has been wrecked over a year. I have been deserted a week or two only. We have contrived to find home, food and shelter. Now, if you like to join our association, and will swear to be a true brother, we will ensure your escape from the pirates."

"Make me your servant—slave—what you will—but do not give me up to the wretches who murdered my father," cried Fred.

"Never!" cried Ned.

"Never!" cried Harry.

"On the contrary," continued Ned, "we admit you as a companion and a brother, so follow on."

Fred Blount was profuse in his thanks, and with a bright and hopeful expression of countenance, took his way in company with his new-found friends.

They were fortunately at no great distance from the cave, the narrow entrance of which amazed and delighted Fred.

His wonder and delight were, however, something remarkable when he saw Carlo rush in among a flock of goats, and begin gambolling with them as old friends.

He appeared to fancy himself on some enchanted isle.

The others smiled, and led the way to the hut on the hill.

Fred was beside himself with delight.

He seated himself on the ground fairly subdued by deep emotion.

"You seem to have descended from heaven to save me," he said, unable to repress his tears.

The others only smiled, and then Harry, taking a bowl, went out, and soon returned with a goodly supply of milk, which to the unfortunate youth appeared nectar, after ship tea and coffee, bad rum, and tainted water.

They then explained their position to him, and then resolved into council.

As their numbers were increasing, it became necessary to enlarge the hut.

Harry stuck to his locker, as they called it, from habit or some more powerful motive.

It became necessary, therefore, to carry the cave further in on the other side.

This they began at once, and, it being wise to keep close for a day or two, continued at the work for nearly a week.

CHAPTER XXI.

A FIERCE FIGHT.

AT the end of this time they had not only perfected their residence, but become very great friends.

Fred, from education and nurture, had been originally as delicate as Harry, but his residence on board had roused his energies, and given him strength.

Still he was not so manly as Ned, to whom the others looked up as leader in all things.

In everything, however, they acted together, and, the week being expired, resolved once more to sally forth in search of adventures, as on a voyage of discovery.

This time they made up their mind to use the chaloupe, and took with them as much food as they could carry.

It was destined to be a voyage of startling adventure.

"HARRY GAVE A LOUD SHRIEK AS HE FELL."

In this way they gained the river, launched their miniature vessel on the stream, took in water both for drink and ballast, and glided down the river, three happy, joyous Boys of England.

It is not in the nature of British lads to be cast down, and though Harry was graver and more thoughtful than the others, no one would have imagined, to see them, that they were poor ship-wrecked waifs from the ocean.

The voyage down the river was delightful in the extreme.

The ever-varying views, the glorious foliage, the multitude of birds with bright plumage, made an ever-shifting picture.

At length the channel widened, and they came in sight of the open sea.

It was a splendid day.

The water was smooth, with a light breeze.

They could run no danger, and resolved, as far as the wind would allow them, to make a tour of the island.

It had so many bays and inlets that they could run in at any time and take shelter.

This resolved on, they pursued their journey.

The left bank of the river was formed by the promontory, which projected on one side of the bay where the brigantine had anchored.

The wind being fair that way, the chaloupe's head was turned in that direction, and, with a joyous bound, darted out to sea.

A quarter of an hour elapsed ere they rounded the point.

A wild cry from Fred startled them.

"Look! look!"

There lay the brigantine at anchor!

They could hardly believe their eyes.

What could it mean?

The boat's head was rapidly turned, but, as the wind blew, they could not return the way they came, but ran out to sea.

Not a sign from the vessel.

It appeared deserted.

What could be the meaning?

Ned used his spy-glass.

Not a soul was on deck.

There it lay riding slowly at anchor, e some phantom ship.

Where were the crew?

On shore; in huts.

But why had they thus temporarily deserted their vessel?

Fred could not make it out.

Were they determined not to leave without him?

The very thought made him sad.

Suddenly Ned gave a hearty laugh as he once more directed his glass on the shore.

The sailors, in strange and fantastic garbs, were either dancing with dusky brown beauties, or seated by their sides.

"They're on the spree," he said; "only fancy if we were to capture the ship and sail away."

Both Harry and Fred shuddered.

All this time the chaloupe, under full sail, was flying out to sea.

The village was being lost to view.

As soon as this was certain, they changed their course, making for the land.

One object of their voyage was answered; they knew that the pirates had not left the island.

But how about the black women?

Had they fraternised with the Indians, and selected this island as a place of refuge when too hotly pursued by hostile cruisers.

This was a question which they had no means of answering.

At all events the presence of the pirates was to them a source of continual dread, while, even if they presently took their departure, there was always the fear of a speedy return.

Well, there was nothing for it but patience and circumspection.

They must be exceedingly cautious and wary, collect food, and live as much as possible within their safe retreat.

The life would be a little monotonous, but anything was better than a residence on board a pirate ship.

All this while they were running along the shore before a stiff breeze.

They kept as near the island as was safe, and lucky for them was it that they did so.

Ned's keen eyes were soon occupied glancing round the horizon. A low black line was clearly visible in the distance.

Ned sprang up.

"Whew!" he cried; "here's a pretty how-d'ye-do! The savages are coming in a perfect army. Douse the sail!"

As he spoke, he loosened the halyard, and the chaloupe, being at no distance from the shore, ran at once into a small land-locked bay, where the boat was at once dismasted, and concealed under some of the luxuriant foliage.

"What is to be done now?" asked Harry, timidly.

"Let the fellows fight it out," said Ned.

"The white men will be surprised and murdered," replied Fred.

"Serve the villains right."

"No. They are not all bad," urged Blount; "there are several worthy enough lads among them. I vote we warn them if we can, without doing any injury to ourselves."

"Just as you like," said Ned, always good-natured. "How is it to be done?"

Well, Blount didn't exactly know; but, as they had the start of the savages, they determined to make their way in the direction of the pirate village, and seek their opportunity.

They were well armed; the pirates evidently in the midst of a drunken orgie, and they had little to fear.

Harry made them smile as he advanced, he looking more like a martyr going to the stake than a brave Crusoe marching to the wars.

As the crow flies they were not more than three miles from the spot selected by the pirates as a residence.

In this direction they determined to make, and, having reconnoitred, trust to the chapter of accidents.

It was very hot, and though they kept beneath the dark shadows of the trees, they were long ere they reached the confines of the camp.

The drunken yells, the shrieking, the laughter which greeted their ears were anything but encouraging.

Still, they contrived to approach by means of the small rock above the spring which had attracted them on shore, and overlook the camp.

It was as they expected.

Not an Indian warrior was to be seen.

Whatever the fate of the men, the girls of the tribe had all been captured.

Fred shuddered.

"Do you know," he whispered to Ned, while Harry sat sombrely aloof, gazing down at the scene of wild disorder with feelings of utter disgust, "what will be the fate of these women?"

"No."

"When they are tired of them they will be sold into slavery. I have been two voyages to Cuba, after what these fellows call blackberrying."

"There is one remedy for that; let the Indians surprise and put them all to death."

"Murder—still murder!" said Fred

"No; let us warn them somehow. Who can that be with a log of wood to his leg?"

Ned looked.

Engaged in some menial occupation in connection with cooking, near a large open-air fire, over which a huge pot was boiling, while several kids and other animals were roasting, stood a wretched, abject-looking being in rags, alternately turning the spits, feeding the fire, and stirring the contents of the pot.

His ankle was fastened by a chain to a large block of wood, and every time he wished to move he had to lift this log.

His groans were awful.

Every now and then he would sit down and cry, upon which one of the pirates would come out and give him half-a-dozen strokes with a rattan on the back.

Upon this he rose and hastened to resume his work.

"Don't you know him?" whispered Harry.

"No," replied Ned.

"Samuel."

"Good Heaven! to what is the wretch reduced!" cried Ned, in dismay. "Well, at all events, he shall have the merit of saving the pirates."

"How so?"

"You will see. Hide yourself carefully, and be ready to start at a moment's notice."

Ned, as he spoke, selected some gloomy-looking trees on the edge of a slope seaward.

The other two obeyed without a murmur.

"Samuel!" he then exclaimed in a deeply sepulchral voice.

The boy looked up.

He could see nothing

"Samuel," continued Ned.

"Who speaks?"

"One whom you have injured and wronged, but who wishes to do you a good turn. Warn the pirates that the Indians are upon them at least a thousand strong. One hundred war canoes are in the offing."

The young midshipman turned slave, knew scarcely what to do.

"Will you save me, Ned Summers?" he said, humbly.

"That I cannot do at present. All depends on circumstances; in the meantime warn the pirates."

Samuel tried to obtain further information, but Ned at once declined to answer.

At this moment a pirate came out of a tent and looked at the cook.

"Sir," said Samuel, humbly touching his hat.

"Well?"

"Savages!"

"What do you mean, idiot?"

"The savages are coming—hundreds —thousands!" urged the unfortunate wretch.

"Where—when?"

"Two hundred war canoes."

"You fool! how can you know?" said the pirate, savagely.

Fortunately the man was nearly sober.

"How can you know, I ask?"

"My comrade, Ned, sir, just now."

"Either the boy is mad," said the pirate, to himself, "or there is some truth in the matter. At all events there is method in this madman. Look out, ahoy!"

A man replied from the branches of a tall cocoa-nut tree.

"Ahoy!"

"Look out at sea."

"Aye, aye."

"Can you see anything?"

"Yes."

"What and where away?"

"A fleet of savages just going round the point."

The man at once dashed into the village and alarmed his companions.

Several were sober.

They rallied round the officer and at once listened to his words.

"On board, my men! the Philistines are upon us!"

The man collected a few together, launched a boat, and made at once for the brigantine.

The captain was himself very ill; but

roused by the intelligence, at once came forward and gave his orders.

Just in time.

Scarcely had they set foot on the deck, when a mighty fleet of savages rounded the point of the island, while another party dashed into the village from the shore.

Their yells of disappointment were terrible to hear, and the three boys, well aware of what their fate would be, if captured by the infuriated savages, resolved to keep close and await the course of events.

They had secured a post not likely to be assailed by either party, and to all appearance out of reach of all missiles.

The war canoes, trusting to their numbers, never hesitated, but made a furious dash at the anchored ship, letting fly a volley of arrows, and then preparing for the contest with spear and club.

The pirates were not idle.

No sooner were the boats in a cluster, close at hand, than a gun was depressed, and a rattling volley poured into their midst. The scene that follows beggars description!

For a moment they seemed stunned at this sudden and extraordinary reception; but then, as if roused to a pitch of fury, they dashed at the ship, and began clambering furiously up its sides.

At the same moment a number of those on shore pushed off on logs, in small canoes, some even swimming with one hand, while they clutched a deadly weapon in the other.

The first party, over a hundred in number, had gained the deck, and Ned, who had the telescope in his hand, saw that in a hand-to-hand encounter, the savages might perhaps, get the best of it.

"They have driven the crew to the quarter-deck!" he cried, in an excited tone, "and are preparing for a desperate charge!"

"What is this the pirates are doing?

"I see, hand-grenades, rockets," he added, keeping his eye upon them all the time.

"Ah! the savages give way only for a moment.

"On, on, they press, wielding spar, club, and tomahawk; then a gun, a swivel, is uncovered, and down go the Indians."

5.

As he spoke the whole ferocious band, terrified and decimated by the chain and canister with which the swivel or Long Tom was loaded, leaped into the sea, swimming, some on shore, others to their boats.

The pirates took no notice for some few minutes, but as soon as the confused horde reached the shore, they fired a whole broadside.

Ned had not noticed that this was directed full at them.

When, therefore, an iron messenger of death came ploughing up the earth and stones close to where they were secreted, his astonishment was greater even than his alarm.

Harry looked very white, but never moved, while Fred grimly removed some dirt that had fallen on his clothes.

"Close shave," he said, with a rollicking laugh.

"Too close to be pleasant," replied Ned, "and I advise a shift of quarters; but,

no, the brig is drifting with the tide. We shall be out of range in a moment."

He was right, and when again the pirates poured their relentless broadside upon the Indians, the balls crashed into the woods, nearer the village.

The ship was then silent for awhile.

At the end of a few minutes, however, the boats were again manned, and the pirates, armed with guns, pistols and swords, prepared to land the swivel gun, firing all the time over their heads.

But when the pirates reached the huts, they were empty.

The bandits, unable to revenge themselves on the natives, set fire to their huts, and going on board, sailed away, rather the worse in every way for their visit to the island.

To the boys, their departure was the source of unmitigated delight, and they fervently hoped they might never see them again. In this, however, they were mistaken, as the sequel will prove.

CHAPTER XXII.

THE UNINVITED GUEST.

THE departure of the pirates, and the disappearance of the savages, left the three young friends some respite from dangers which they could neither repel nor control, and enabled them also further to prepare both for the winter season and the voyage, which they so eagerly contemplated as a possible means of escape from their now wearisome captivity.

Their first determination was to continue their journey, as their boat was not safe in its present place of concealment, should either the desperadoes or the Indians come back to the place.

They determined, however, to camp one night on shore in peace, the more that they had secured a fine fat kid, an ample supply of yams and sweet potatoes, and some very juicy, ripe grapes.

As a rule, in the circumstances in which they were placed, eating and drinking were only thought of as a necessary law of nature; but it would have been very unnatural if once now and then the young

people had not wished to enjoy a real feast.

They selected a hollow in the ground, shaded by trees, to make a fire, round which, when the gala repast was concluded, they intended to repose for the night.

As soon as the ample supply of wood had burned to hot embers, the young cooks commenced their operations, and soon a savoury odour of broiled kid and roast yams began to pervade the atmosphere, exciting in all a degree of appetite which may be more easily comprehended than described.

Persons constantly in the open air, and taking continual exercise, feel a very different sort of hunger from what is known in town.

Scarcely, therefore, were the meat and vegetables pronounced cooked, than all clasped their knives.

"Hush!" suddenly exclaimed Ned Summers. "The odour has penetrated afar off. We shall have uninvited guests

To your arms," he whispered, "and each behind a tree."

The two others silently obeyed, while he lay at full length on the ground and listened.

As he did so, his bold heart beat wildly with horror.

Some heavy animal was slowly making his way through the bushes in their direction.

Either it was some large member of the feline tribe seeking in a rampant way to approach their camp, or, terror of terrors, it was some huge snake, against which they could make no resistance.

Flight was quite as useless and vain as defence.

And yet, with a boy whose motto was always "Never say die," something must be done.

Their guns were heavily charged, and perhaps a simultaneous volley might check the progress of the monster.

"Boys," said Ned Summers, in a calm and resolute tone of voice, "some mysterious animal is about to attack us. It will be in sight in a few minutes. Fire steadily at its head, and then load again."

"All right," said Fred.

"I will do as you tell me," replied Harry, in a tremulous tone.

"I'll give the word," continued Ned, "as, lying down as I am, I shall see it first."

A low moan was now heard—something horrible and heartrending.

"Ready," said Ned. "I can see where it is moving the bushes."

"Don't fire!" responded a human voice, in a lamentable tone.

"Sam Petworth!" cried Ned, with a dark frown; "by Heaven! the miserable wretch has scented our food. Come in, if you be the person I think."

"Can't walk."

Ned now summoned Fred to his side, and advanced to the summit of the hill, where they found Samuel Petworth, actually crawling along the earth, with his log of wood still trailing at his right heel.

He looked so abject, so miserable, so utterly a being to be pitied, that the two good-hearted boys silently raised him up and led him towards the fire.

They acted like the old man in the fable, who warmed the frozen viper.

The issue will show whether Samuel Petworth was any better than the snake.

He thanked them in his low, hollow tones, and walked, groaning and sighing, to the fire, beside which they placed him.

They then examined his chain, and found that it was fastened by a kind of anklet.

Still no means offered of taking it off.

It appeared to have no joint, while to slip it over his swollen foot was impossible.

Henry, without being able to disguise his disgust and repulsion, presently advanced with a gourd of water and a large wisp of grass, with which he washed the sore and wounded limb.

He then bent low, and carefully examined the anklet.

As he expected, it somewhat resembled the ring on which keys are placed.

With a deft and dexterous turn, Harry soon slipped the chain off the leg.

The anklet remained.

The wretched youth heartily thanked the young castaway, and then cast wistful and ravenous eyes at the food, which was just done to a turn.

Ned cut him a huge slice, gave him some yams, some water, diluted with rum, and then, leaving him alone on the other side of the fire, the three proceeded to eat their interrupted meal.

I had almost written "enjoy," but, in presence of that scarecrow, the word would no longer have any meaning.

They scarcely spoke, and when they did so it was in low and cautious whispers.

Sam ate in sullen silence. He devoured his food with the rapidity of starvation.

Then he asked for more.

It was given to him without a murmur.

Then arrangements were made to pass the night.

None of the three felt safe in the presence of Sam. It was true they were armed, and he was not; but, should they sleep, he might, if not murder them, rob them of guns and ammunition, and thus reduce them to utter desperation.

Ned Summers reflected as to what was to be done. One solution alone offered itself. One must watch all night.

The other two would then be able to sleep in safety.

Three hours, or thereabouts, was given to each, and when the matter was discussed Harry Thornton proposed to be first watch.

He could not sleep, he said; the unexpected arrival of Sam Petworth had driven all ideas of slumber from his head.

The two others readily agreed to give way.

Each then took his gun, and passing the leathern sling over the left arm, prepared for slumber.

Sam was sent to a respectful distance, under the shelter of a thicket.

Sore, exhausted and tired, they had little to fear from him.

They never reflected on the miraculous curative powers of food and rest, and the invigorating glass of spirits.

Harry began his watch in a mood of unusual gravity.

Of all those deserted on the island, far away from home and friends, this gentle being felt it most.

On many occasions he had found difficulty to hide the fallen tear.

You know some are more tender-hearted than others, and unbidden tears will flow sometimes from the eyes of the bravest.

When Harry saw that his two companions slept, he slowly rose, still clutching his gun. His eyes were streaming.

Blame him not, brave boys, for the explanation will be given in due time.

Retiring a little way from the camp-fire, he kneeled at the foot of a tree and prayed fervently.

This lasted ten minutes.

When he strolled back to the fire, all traces of tears had disappeared, and he was much calmer, and more resolute.

Had he seen two eyes fixed upon him from the opposite side of the fire, gleaming with a savage and sinister expression—an expression strangely mocking—the poor boy might have been less calm and resolved.

As it was, he determined to do his duty to his companions.

They had collected a goodly supply of fuel, and the fire was burning low.

For an instant he laid down his gun to pick up an armful of wood.

A sound startled him. He turned round, and nearly fainted at what he saw!

CHAPTER XXIII.

DESOLATION AND REGRET.

WHEN Ned Summers woke with a start, some hours later, it was to find the fire almost out, so far gone that he with difficulty revived it.

"Harry!" he cried, "where are you? Gone to sleep, poor fellow," he added.

He was busily engaged in reviving the fire as he thus spoke.

Soon a slight blaze was coaxed, after which the dry wood easily made a bright flame.

Ned looked around.

Fred slept beneath the camp tree.

Harry was nowhere to be seen.

With a wild bound the brave boy rushed to where Sam had last been seen.

"The miscreant!" he cried; "I see it all. He has been shamming. Up! up, Fred!"

"What's the matter?" cried the sleepy boy, rubbing his eyes.

"That unhanged gallows-bird, Sam, has stolen away our poor Harry."

"What!" said Fred, a crimson glow overspreading his countenance.

"Poor, gentle Harry; this wretch will make a slave of the boy. Of course he has taken his arms from him; but, by Heaven, I will take no rest until we find them; day is not far distant. What say you, Fred?"

"That I will willingly lay down my life for Harry Thornton," said Fred, quietly. He was not loquacious, but when he spoke, he spoke well.

"And so would I," observed Ned, thoughtfully; "there is something so soft, gentle, and *girlish* about the boy."

"There is," said Fred, dreamily. "I cannot understand him."

"Where is the dog?" suddenly exclaimed Ned. "Surely he cannot have stolen him too."

"No; there he lies on his side, breathing, it is true, but insensible."

Ned examined his body, and found a gaping wound on his head, inflicted, most certainly in his sleep, by a heavy log of wood, which lay beside him.

They dashed cold water on him, they bathed his foaming mouth, and a long sigh indicated that he was coming to.

A gourd of water was then placed by his side.

Carlo was rarely fed by his masters.

He preferred wild game caught by himself to cooked food.

He had been on the prowl when Sam Petworth had come to the camp.

Finding him in the camp, he fancied that all was right.

"It wants but an hour of daylight," said Ned; "by that time the dog will be better. Eat and drink, Fred, for when once this chase begins, no one knows where it may end."

Fred obeyed, and Ned Summers shortly after followed his example.

Neither of them, however, had any appetite.

Their brows were darkened, their lips compressed, their faces blanched.

If Harry had seen them, he would have discovered how much he was loved.

Then they waited, cleaning and examining their guns in preparation for action.

Suddenly a faint grey light, the herald of dawn, fell upon the tree tops.

Ned started to his feet.

"Carlo! Carlo!" he cried.

The dog half raised his head, looked at them, and staggered to his feet.

The bowl of water was cleared in an instant.

He then shook his head roughly and moaned.

"Find, find," said Ned, pointing to the ground.

The dog growled savagely.

He tottered, however, and fell.

"We must wait," observed Ned, gravely; "without the dog we can do nothing. They cannot have gone far."

"Too far, perhaps," said Fred, drily. "That Sam is a demon."

"Who shall return whence he came," cried Ned, pointing significantly below.

At the same time he caressed Carlo, gave him some titbits, and brought him another gourd of water.

The noble animal seemed revived, and, wagging his tail, signified that he was ready.

He at once took his way in the direction by which the coldblooded villain had crept upon him.

He had, then, returned the way he came.

The dog moved slowly.

He was evidently still dizzy from the fearful and cowardly blow which had stunned him in his sleep.

He, however, gained courage at every step, and presently, the trail leading to a small stream, he wallowed with delight in the water.

Then, bounding across the rivulet, he soon found the track.

It was clear.

The pair of footsteps, one of rude shoes, the other bare feet, were clearly visible.

Which way was he going?

To the sea-shore, to the tents of the revellers, they thought.

Both clutched their guns convulsively, keeping their eyes fixed in advance.

The boy Sam was capable of any base act of treachery.

At every moment the dog appeared to revive, and to advance more readily on the track.

He looked back every now and then, showing his great white teeth and red gums.

It looked bad for anyone who should stand between him and his master.

But Sam was now armed, and clearly to be dreaded.

At length the dog halted a minute.

He had come to the edge of a hard, stony plain.

He was at fault.

"Remain here a moment," said Ned, "while I cross over to yonder trees."

Fred nodded.

The dog remained behind as told, with the younger boy as they wished.

The arid strip was about a hundred feet long and fifty broad.

"Now, Fred," cried Ned, when he reached the other side, "walk the dog right round."

Fred obeyed, and the dog trotted on before him.

Suddenly Ned gave a wild and horrible shriek.

"This way—help!—murder!" he said.

Fred and the dog rushed madly across the clearing, to find Ned standing over a small spot, where a fierce struggle had evidently taken place.

A number of spots of blood were on the ground.

The dog's hair stood up like bristles, his eyes glared, his tail wagged furiously.

"Murder—vile murder has been done!" cried Ned, in furious exasperation. "Oh! that I had the villain by the throat!"

"Where is the body?" said Fred Blount, more calmly.

"The blood—the blood!"

"There has been a struggle, a fight perhaps for the mastery of the gun," continued Fred, gravely. "But we shall soon see."

"Come on!" said Ned, fiercely.

Again the dog went on; this time again in the direction of the sea.

They could see the huts.

How those two noble boys' hearts panted and beat as they reflected how soon now the dread mystery would be solved.

They were within a hundred yards of the low huts.

With a wild, savage, furious howl, the dog caught up a fresh trail of blood, and sprang into the brushwood out of sight

Both followed as fast as they could.

A loud, savage barking impelled them to renewed exertions.

In five minutes more they were in front of a large hut, the door of which was fastened, and at which the dog was barking wildly.

With one blow of the butt end of his gun, Ned dashed in the door, and recoiled in gratified amazement.

"Hold back the dog," cried a well-known and welcome voice.

CHAPTER XXIV.

RETRIBUTION—SURPRISE.

ON a pallet left by the pirates, and on which the pirate chief had slept during his short sojourn on shore, pale, ghastly, and to all appearance dying, was Samuel Petworth.

By his side, bandaging up a severe wound in his arm or shoulder, was Harry.

The younger boy was paler than the elder, as if the terrible task he had undertaken was either too much for him, or too painful to his sensitive feelings.

As silent and grave, after tying the furious dog to a young tree, Ned and his companion gazed upon them, Samuel looked up with a sullen and savage scowl—a scowl of defeated malignity.

"What is the meaning of this?" said Ned, sternly.

Sam only growled.

"I will tell you all," said Harry, gently, "but not now, nor here."

"Water—water!" gasped Sam.

Fred, at a sign from Ned, went away to the small stream and fetched a gourd full.

Sam drank it savagely, and his wound being dressed, declared his desire to be alone.

The young savage, though apparently wounded unto death, was sullen and unforgiving.

They went out and closed the door behind them.

Harry Thornton tottered to a green spot under a tree.

"Tell us what has happened?" said Ned, gently.

"My brave friends and companions, did you miss me very much?" asked Harry, with a sickly smile.

"Didn't we?" cried Fred. "Ned here was nearly mad—that's all."

Harry looked at him with a beaming smile, which made Fred wince. He was jealous, though he would not own it.

"I should have killed the base traitor and ruffian, if I had not found him so helpless," exclaimed Ned, hotly.

"He is punished," said Harry, gently, and told his story briefly.

He was about to replenish the fire, when a noise startled him, and, looking round, he saw Sam in the act of braining the dog.

The shock was so great that Harry was, for a moment, speechless.

Sam, meanwhile, snatched up the gun, and, levelling it at the sleepers, spoke—

"One word, and I blow their brains out!"

Harry yielded with a shudder.

Sam told him to walk on in advance, and not to turn to the right or left without his permission.

The trembling boy obeyed.

Visions of awful horror were before his eyes; and rather than have gone off in willing slavery with this vile young ruffian, he would have died.

But he threatened Ned and Fred.

Under this pressure he yielded.

An hour before dawn, exhausted and worn out himself, Sam sank at the foot of a tree.

Only for a moment.

He took breath, and then tied Harry hand and foot.

After which he slept an hour.

Then, as the daylight came, he was again on foot.

There was nothing to eat or drink except some cocoa-nuts on the tree.

Sam ordered Harry, with a sinister smile, to climb and get some.

Harry refused.

Sam made some exasperated remark or other, which appeared to raise the ire even of quiet Harry Thornton.

He dashed at the gun.

A struggle ensued, and in this struggle the gun went off, and Sam fell bleeding to the ground.

"Then why did you not leave him, and come back to us?" cried Ned.

"Leave a dying fellow-creature!" exclaimed the boy, gently. "Not I."

He went on to say that Sam implored him to staunch the wound as well as possible, and then to assist him to the pirate village, where he could find a bed and probably some food.

Harry, finding him really so weak, and having secured the gun and loaded it, did all he could for him.

At the end of an hour they reached the hut, and Sam, complaining of burning fever, lay down.

But the pain was still hot and fierce.

Harry fetched some water, found some rags left by the pirates, and, repulsive as the task was to his sensitive nerves, was in the act of binding up his wound when they came upon him.

"And now," said Ned, "what is to be done with the cowardly young ruffian?"

"Nothing," urged Harry, eagerly. "Surely he has been punished enough."

"What say you?" asked Ned, addressing the other hitherto silent, but deeply interested, listener.

"He is in your hands, Ned."

"This is my decision. If he dies, he shall be buried, and there is an end of the scoundrel. If he lives, he shall retire to some remote part of the island, and if he ever comes near us, he shall be shot like a wild beast of the forest."

"He will starve."

"Let him. No such luck. As he is a perfect savage, let him live like one. Such is my decision, unless you like to shoot him right off."

To this neither of them acquiescing, the first decision was held to be the leading one.

A hut was then selected, in which to repose during the heat of the day.

The pirates, in their hurry, had left behind them many useful things in the one or two houses which escaped the conflagration, such as salt pork, peas, and one or two bags of excellent biscuit.

On the latter all made a meal, and then, giving the poor dog a supply also, they lay down, too glad to seek repose and shelter.

When the heat of the day was passed, Harry, ever thoughtful, took a pannikin of water and oatmeal, with which to moisten the patient's lips.

At the end of an hour he returned with a very grave and solemn countenance.

"Is the wretch dead?" cried both.

"No; but he is in a burning fever," said Harry. "I must nurse him."

"You?"

"Yes! Must we not return good for evil?" replied Harry Thornton.

"Well, you are a saint," said Ned, laughing; "but you shall have your way. Cure him first, and then, if he don't behave himself, we'll shoot him afterwards."

Harry smiled, collected a few necessaries, and, after promising to return soon, rose to go.

"I will take turns with you, if he really wants watching," said Fred.

"No," replied Harry, nervously; "I

will see to whatever he requires. As soon as he falls into a sound sleep, you will find me near you."

They shrugged their shoulders, but, being in the habit of giving way to Harry in all matters of feeling, they yielded and allowed the sensitive boy to go to his self-imposed and horrible task.

Years passed before they ever knew the extent of the suffering their young friend endured.

The ravings of the wounded man were awful, to Harry inexpressibly so ; but he never grumbled, never found fault.

Four days this lasted, during which Ned and Fred hunted, fished and cooked, besides collecting provisions for their grand water expedition.

Carlo was quite recovered.

Nothing but a scar remained to tell that he had been wounded.

Harry at length pronounced Sam Petworth convalescent, that is, the wound was healing and the fever gone ; the patient was only weak and frail.

"He is now my patient, then," said Ned, sternly, and he walked off to the hut, as prearranged with Fred, carrying a supply of water, cooked meat, and biscuits.

These they placed by his bedside.

"Samuel Petworth," said Ned Summers, "you have a dozen times deserved death, and this time nothing has saved you but the wishes of Harry Thornton. He declares you out of danger. Now I neither know nor care what is your case. Here is food and water for a week. Make the most of it."

"You leave me to die?"

"No ; but recollect that until further orders you do not leave this village. Eggs, fish, and fruit abound, with fresh water."

Sam scowled, but made no reply.

"Should you be found on any other part of the island, unless by my leave, you shall be shot like a dog. Above all, touch Harry Thornton again only with your finger and you die."

"Your precious Harry !" sneered Sam, with a strange, hateful glance.

"My friend and protégé, whom I will die to defend," replied Ned.

"Doubtless," continued Sam, with ferocious energy. "Well, never mind, you are the strongest, and I must yield."

"You had better."

And with these words Ned Summers went out, followed by his comrade, who had not said a single word, but who merely thrust his hands into his trousers pockets, hitched them up, and whistled.

"He'll give us trouble yet," he presently observed. "Pity the skunk ain't dead."

"Let him beware," replied Ned ; "to shoot a fellow creature, except in desperate self-defence, is against all my principles and feelings. But we three cannot sacrifice ourselves for one bad and wicked man."

"Certainly not."

That evening they once more camped in the Indian village, and next morning, after giving Sam an additional supply of water, started.

They had made a sledge for the beef, pork, peas and bread, which to were invaluable, as well as a small of powder.

As they disappeared, Harry and t' dog walking first, Ned and Fred dragging the heavily laden sledge, Sam Petworth peered forth from his hut, shook his fist, and cursed them heartily.

"I'll be even with them yet! Harry Thornton," he added, with bitter and concentrated hatred, "I will reach your heart yet! Ned is your pet—the one you look up to, is he? Well, your punishment shall yet come to you through him!"

Leaving Sam to his well-merited fate, the three boys took their way in the direction of the chaloupe, which they intended to victual as completely as possible, and leave carefully guarded against the rain, until the time came for their great and adventurous voyage.

A boat expedition is not a matter to be much considered by experienced old sailors, but to three boys a journey into unknown regions was a matter of serious import.

But our heroes had gone through too many dangers to be daunted by future perils.

"HE DID NOT LIVE TO COMPLETE THE SENTENCE."

CHAPTER XXV.

PREPARING FOR THE VOYAGE.

AT last the time came round when the great attempt was to be made by the three boys to escape from the island.

The chaloupe had not only been well provisioned, but a kind of cuddy had been erected, with a deck over it.

In this was stored the provisions, the ammunition, and here also was the only sleeping-place of the three castaways.

After long consideration and discussion, it had been decided by our youthful crew to divide the day into three watches.

Two were always to be on deck and one below for exactly eight hours.

In the first place, the cabin was very small, with barely sleeping accommodation for one; in the next, one alone on deck might be apt to fall asleep, and thus be the means of causing some serious accident.

The course to be followed was due west, as that was the direction from which the savages had come, and there probably was the great continent which they hoped to reach.

Though inhabited by savage Indians, in all probability there would also be inhabited towns belonging to some European race, and no matter what their nationality, they would not be cruel or unkind to the unfortunate boys.

Except in past ages, and chiefly then among Spaniards, shipwrecked English seamen were sure to find a welcome.

It was, therefore, with keenly hopeful hearts that the last preparations were made for what might be the most important event in their lives.

Not but they all regretted leaving an island which had very many attractions.

Still, they were not made to fall back into savagedom, while each had a separate motive for returning home.

It was dawn of day when, after a hearty meal, they went down to the shore, and prepared to push off.

Harry Thornton had pleaded for Sam, but the others had sternly refused to have anything to do with him.

He had sinned, and he must be punished.

The only thing Ned would do was to give information to some man-of-war, who would probably go and take him off, putting him on the ship's books as a reward for their trouble.

Lots had been drawn for watches, and it fell to Fred to go below, which, as he was a remarkably good sleeper, he by no means objected to.

The wind was pleasant, but strong, and the chaloupe at once glided through the water, with a rapidity that promised much for the success of their journey.

Under the lee of the island, the water was, of course, for some time smooth.

Carlo sat gravely in the bows, as if he had been the appointed look-out, while Ned Summers and Harry Thornton occupied the roof of the cabin, from which they steered and kept their eyes upon the sails.

Both, at the last moment, felt a sort of vague regret on leaving the shores of that lovely isle; but, as we have observed, the hope of home sustained them above all.

Scarcely had they got one hundred yards from the shore, when a loud hail was heard, and Samuel Petworth came bounding to the edge of the water, into which he ran up to his middle, begging and imploring to be taken off.

Harry Thornton hid his face in his hands. Ned was simply stern and resolute, refusing even to answer him.

Slowly and sullenly the baffled young villain returned towards the shore, and the youths believed they had seen the last of him.

"Poor wretch!" said Harry; "what will become of him?"

"Join the pirates as cabin-boy," replied Ned; "and only too good a situation for him."

And so the unpleasant subject was allowed to drop.

All that day the young Crusoes kept on the same tack, the wind never changing; but towards night it came on to blow more heavily, and just after the evening meal, which they ate in common, it was resolved to take in all sail and lay to for the night, as darkness set in with a wind in such a way as to render it impossible to see either land or breakers ahead.

To retard their progress still more, the anchor was thrown overboard, thus impeding their advance.

Harry, who was of least use in a boat —though active and willing, he was not so strong as the others—had the cabin on this occasion, while Ned and his friend occupied the deck.

A watch was absolutely necessary, and they agreed to take it in turns.

Ned Summers soon was alone.

He was not sleepy; he was, in fact, uneasy and restless, as if something unexpected and unpleasant was about to happen.

The night was singularly dark; not a star was to be seen in the heavens, while, if there were any moon, it was totally obscured by dark and gloomy clouds.

Ned listened keenly for any sound as of the wash of waves on adjacent rocks.

He heard nothing but the dismal howling of the wind and the continuous rush of the waves on the bows and sides of the boat as it came head to wind.

Then there fell upon his ears a sound so startling, so unexpected and astounding, that, mechanically, he clasped his hands and thanked Heaven.

It was the distant, unmistakable sound of a ship's bell.

Yes, there was no mistaking it; some vessel was journeying at no very great distance in the fog, which for some time had overspread the deep.

Ned strained his eyes over the wild waste of waters, to catch, if possible, a glimpse of the ship, which he firmly believed was at hand to save them.

He could see nothing, but still the bell tolled in a dreamy kind of way, as if the man who pulled the cord were weary and half asleep.

Unwilling to awake or disturb his wearied companions, Ned stood with his arms round the mast, listening and looking both.

Presently, as he gazed in the direction of the sound, he saw something dark, like a huge rock looming in the distance, and, in the drear fog and mist, looking like some vast phantom ship.

There was the mighty hull, the faint tracery of the tall masts, and the outline of the complicated rigging.

Unable to contain himself any longer, Ned Summers caught up a gun from off the deck, and fired.

When the report was over, and the smoke had cleared away, no ship was anywhere to be seen.

Harry and Fred, however, were wide awake by his side, asking wildly what on earth was the matter.

"A ship! a ship!" cried Ned, wildly, as he pointed in the direction of an increasing bank of black fog.

"My dear Ned, you have certainly been dreaming," said Fred, merrily.

At that moment, however, the sound of the bell was distinctly heard across the waste of waters.

The two hastily-aroused sleepers were at once awed into silence.

A hurried conference was now held as to what was best to be done.

Ned Summers was sure the vessel had no sail on, but was running with bare poles before the wind, so that by the morning it would not have gone a very great distance.

Had the sea not been so heavy, and the wind so high, he would have proposed following in her track.

This, in the darkness, however, was out of the question, and so there was nothing for it but to wait.

CHAPTER XXVI.

THE DERELICT AND WHAT BECAME OF IT.

NEVER was dawn of morn watched for more anxiously.

The three boys cowered on the deck; despite the stiff norther, their eyes strained in the direction where the ship had disappeared.

For some time the bell was still heard; gradually, however, its sound became fainter and fainter, until it was lost altogether.

As the dawn approached, and the sun's beneficent rays made themselves felt, the clouds were rent in twain, the dense sea-fog was dispersed, and the wind even began to lull.

Ned Summers swept the horizon, and suddenly announced, amid breathless excitement, that he could once more see the ship.

All hands at once out with the reefs, and every effort was made to get sail on the gallant boat, which ten minutes later was bending to a stiff but steady breeze, and heading for the vessel, which Ned declared to be a large three-master.

But suddenly his eyes dilated, just as the faint, afar-off tinkle of the bell was heard,* and the vessel rose steadily to view.

It was without sail, and not a living soul was to be seen.

Ned scanned the rigging, the poop deck, the forecastle.

Not a living being.

"What can it mean?" thought Ned, frowning darkly, as a terrible series of ideas rushed upon his excited and heated brain.

He had a strong suspicion.

This was some handiwork of the pirates, he firmly believed.

Still he was determined to unravel the mystery.

The huge and apparently deserted vessel was not a mile distant.

It waddled through the water, swaying now a little to larboard, now to starboard, and yet never wholly swerving from its course.

No human hand was at that helm, he now well knew.

An awesome silence fell upon the three boys, who never once took their eyes off the ship.

Presently they were within a hundred yards of the strange vessel.

Ned began decreasing sail.

"Harry, you be boat-keeper," said Ned, with a significant look at Fred;

"we will go on board and see what's what."

"There is some danger?" urged Harry.

"No; only, perhaps, some horror. Nothing *living* is on board that ship," replied Ned.

Harry Thornton shuddered, and made no further remark.

In two minutes more they were grating alongside the vessel, and Ned made fast the painter.

He then ran up the ladder which hung from the starboard gangway.

As his foot touched the deck, he uttered a fearful cry of horror, which was reiterated by Fred.

On every side were signs of a murderous conflict, the deck having at least a dozen corpses lying about.

The helm was lashed amidships.

The state of the bodies indicated that the conflict had been recent, and probably interrupted by the fierce gale.

"Follow," said Ned, in a low tone.

And he led the way into the cabin.

Here lay other bodies, two of whom, from their costume, evidently were pirates.

Ned looked around.

The lockers were untouched, some valuables lay about, and it was clear that, as he expected, the pirates had been forced, by a sudden squall, to leave the ship.

"Let us away!" gasped Fred.

"One moment! The ship is a derelict, and may contain things useful to us," cried Ned—"powder and shot, above all."

As he spoke, he picked up a large flask which lay on the ground.

He then entered the steward's pantry, and secured several bottles of wine and spirits.

For about twenty minutes the boys were busily engaged removing useful stores.

They were handed down to Harry, without a word being said about the bodies.

Soon they had secured sufficient plunder, without overloading their craft, and prepared to leave the horrid scene of carnage.

"I should like to bury them as sailors wish to be buried," said Ned.

---

* The progress of sound over water with the wind is something wonderful. The writer, in the Gulf of Mexico, has often heard the voices of men in distant boats on a calm day, long before the boats could be seen with the naked eye. To a certain extent, the same is true on level plains and on the prairies.

cannot do it. Heaven!" cried Fred, pointing to the westward.

Ned leaped on a gun, of which there were six on each side.

A fleet of Indians, some hundred in number, were close on board; that is, about a quarter of a mile distant.

Simple flight was impossible, as their canoes can go in the wind's eye.

"We must scatter and disperse them," said Ned; "let us load the cannons."

Without a moment's delay, he snatched up a rammer, and, drawing back a gun by the slings, he thrust in the instrument used in loading.

The gun *was* loaded.

It proved on examination that the starboard broadside had alone been fired.

The larboard battery was, luckily, on the side of the savages, who came up in one cluster.

So many boats must, of course, make a long line.

"To the helm!" shouted Ned. "Keep her steady—don't let her swerve an inch when I speak. A little more to starboard —so—keep her so."

And with a bit of lighted rope, which he easily ignited in the cook's galley, he ran from one gun to the other.

Six successive reports followed, and a perfect storm, as of iron hail, was poured upon the Indians.

An awful and fearful shout arose from the infuriated savages, who thought the ship deserted, and who expected a fine prize of iron and wood and other useful articles.

"Now for a race!" shouted Ned; "while they are in confusion we may escape."

"Sail, oh!" shouted Fred.

Ned turned, and there, not three miles distant, was the pirate coming down upon the derelict.

The storm having abated, they were coming back to complete their work of plunder and destruction.

Without a word the boys ran down the side and pushed off.

Both the pirate brigantine and the Indian canoes were thus hidden from view, and this circumstance was probably their only chance of escape.

They found Harry very pale and anxious. The sudden report of the guns had astounded him.

He saw at once that something was the matter, and that it would be necessary to be off.

All hands set to work, and he light and buoyant sails were soon set.

The chaloupe made a course so as to keep the ship between them and their enemies.

The boat flew over the water like a thing of life.

Ned steered, as everything depended on even the minutes gained.

A quarter of an hour elapsed—a quarter of an hour of deep anxiety.

Then a wild yell was heard, and the ship seemed alive with demons.

The savages had gained the ship, and were busily at work plundering.

They apparently were not noticed.

Away—away went the chaloupe, until the cries of the savages became indistinct.

Then a loud report was heard.

The pirate was coming up, and was pounding the derelict in order to clear it of its savage captors.

Gun after gun followed, and then all was still.

By this time they were a good distance from the awful ship, and Ned Summers advised to take in all sail, lower their mast, and trust to their oars.

The others readily acquiesced, and the small party of fugitives were soon floating, a speck on the waters, with one only idea now in their heads.

To escape from the wretched men who dealt in wholesale robbery and murder.

The sun was soon so hot as to render labour very hard, and, directing the other two to get under an awning made by the mainsail, Ned determined simply to keep before the wind, as that took them away from the northward and eastward.

The day passed, and night came, a night not so dark as the preceding one, but still dirty.

To sail was dangerous, as they now had no guide.

Not a sign of land, not any known star, by which to set their course.

Again they resolved to lay to.

Scarcely had they done so, when sudden lurid glare illumined the heav

At first it was but slight, then it creased, and suddenly it burst into a of flame.

The pirates had fired the doomed

to hide their iniquity and bury their dead.

Ned gazed at the huge blaze with melancholy interest, and, as he did so, suddenly felt the boat's keel graze some hard substance, and then heel over to port with a jerk which nearly sent them overboard.

They were fast in a small channel, between two rocks.

Leaping to his feet, Ned clambered overboard and bade his comrades do the same.

The boat just floated, and, taking an oar, Ned sounded.

Deep water in front.

There remained only to scramble on shore, and tow the boat out or forward.

After some difficulty, they contrived to get on the rock, and succeeded in drawing the chaloupe into a small bay, surrounded on all sides by lofty trees.

What with excitement and fatigue, the boys, though utterly ignorant of their whereabouts, were only too glad to find this unexpected retreat.

They, however, found that there was a strong current through the bay, and were soon compelled to moor the boat stem and stern.

It was this very current which had sucked them into this snug retreat.

Still its existence proved that there was another outlet.

Ned who was less fatigued than the others, induced them to remain on the boat, while he kept the first watch on shore.

They acquiesced, on condition that they were awakened in turn.

Taking Carlo with him, happy and joyous to be on *terra firma* again, he shouldered his gun and took his way along the bank, keeping the water in view as much as possible.

He soon found the outlet, which was narrower than the one by which they had entered, and where the water ran like a mill-race.

Of course, they would have to go back the way they had come, which could only be done by lightening the chaloupe.

Satisfied with his examination, Ned was about to return, when a low growl from the dog aroused his attention.

There was danger at hand, either from man or beast.

Ned carried pistols and a sword, as well as his gun.

Still, the best policy was secrecy, and yet he wished to know the nature of the danger.

He stooped low and listened.

Nothing.

"Find—find," he whispered to the dog, and the intelligent brute started before, halting suddenly about fifty yards from where he had given the first alarm.

Ned at once comprehended the situation, as well as the fearful danger they had escaped.

The launch belonging to the pirate rose and fell close at hand on the swelling waters.

It was anchored some distance from the shore, to which it was further fastened by a rope.

The crew—as truculent a set of ruffians as ever were collected—sat round a fire.

Their voices were plainly heard.

A burly fellow, of stout build and stalwart height, was addressing them.

"I tell you I seed them with these here two eyes, as plain as I sees you, and they were lost just about here. Now, I ain't a-going to be done by three trumpery boys—it's just what we want for the two messes. So I tell you, mates, they must be found and taken on board, where, arter they have had three dozen apiece, by way of *smart* money, they'll do."

The men laughed hideously, and resumed their pipes and grog.

Ned stood transfixed with horror.

A flogging was terrible to think of for himself, or even Fred; but Harry Thornton would die under the infliction.

Once he levelled his gun, with the intention of shooting the man; but, burning as his anger was, he reflected on the consequences.

With a dark frown, he turned on his heel and rejoined his companions, who slept soundly, ignorant of the stupendous danger that menaced them.

Ned, however, did not awake them at once.

He needed time for reflection.

It was, indeed, quite midnight when he stepped on board the chaloupe and roused his heavily-sleeping friends.

"Boys," he said, as soon as they were able to understand his words, "there is danger at hand. The pirates have tracked us to this lonely spot—now, don't be frightened."

"I am not frightened," replied Fred.

"I am only sad," observed Harry.

"I am going to tell you something dreadful, and which must make even you, gentle Harry, fight for your life. These men intend, if they capture us, to flog us first, and then make cabin boys of us on board their murderous craft."

"Sucking pirates," said Fred.

Harry Thornton only groaned with unspeakable anguish.

"We must not remain here," continued Ned, "but shall have to abandon the chaloupe to its fate. I trust it will be concealed enough by these heavy boughs. At all events, we have no choice."

"We are ready."

"My boys, our motto to-night is—do or die! Each must take two guns, and as much food and ammunition as he can carry."

His orders were obeyed in silence, and ten minutes later, the overhanging boughs of the trees being bent down, like a green roof, over the boat, the three bold young adventurers sallied out into the night, utterly ignorant of where they were, and of what was about to become of them.

Ned, with Carlo by his side, led the way, and soon reached the rapid.

It was not three feet wide, and was easily leaped over.

They now were launched, like many other travellers, upon the unknown.

Ned still walked first, his guns carried one on each shoulder.

The country was here wild and rocky, and ascended rapidly, when suddenly they came again to the region of trees.

Here the ground was level, until they came to the edge of a narrow chasm.

It was, however, easily crossed by climbing the trees which skirted the abyss, and dropping from the extreme end of one of the boughs which hung over it.

On the other side, after passing through a long but narrow slip of cocoa-nut trees, the ground sloped upward very rapidly.

Just where they crossed was a narrow, dark ravine, which ascended to the summit of the hill at an angle of forty-five degrees.

It was the bed of a torrent in winter.

Up this they scrambled for about thirty yards, the dog first, when they came to a small platform.

The hill on each side was too steep to be climbed.

It formed a natural fortress.

"We could hold this against a hundred," said Ned. "At all events, here we will halt for the night."

No sooner said than done, and in ten minutes all slept.

Harry was the first to wake, but made no attempt, on this occasion, to prepare breakfast.

He allowed his comrades to sleep soundly.

They, too, awoke, however, shortly after, and, nibbling a biscuit, with a draught of water, were soon ready for the march.

At this moment numerous voices fell on their ears, and they knew they were pursued.

Ned looked upwards.

The gully was narrow and steep.

"Boys," he said, "we must make a stand here. The gully is so narrow, that one alone can act with vigour. Put the guns in a row, and as fast as I fire do you load."

They only nodded, and got ready powder and bullets.

A quarter of an hour elapsed; the voices continued, and then were heard much nearer.

They were tracking them.

Suddenly the burly boatswain appeared at the bottom of the gully.

"This way, my hearties; I can see marks of their feet—only they've a cust big dorg with them."

"Back, as you value life!" cried Ned.

The boatswain roared.

"Ha, ha! my bully boys, there you are! Come down, and, except a sound flogging, no harm shall be done you."

"The first man who moves up our way dies. Go, leave this island, and do not seek to make us the slaves of wretched thieves and murderers!"

As he spoke a rush was made upwards.

Steadily, with perfect nerve, Ned fired one gun after another—six in number —two being reloaded while he discharged the others.

The pirates bellowed with rage.

When the smoke cleared away, nothing of them, at first, was to be seen.

Then Ned Summers became aware that four fellows were crawling up on their hands and knees.

He had already noticed a number of loose stones sticking out of the earth on each side of the gully, one of which—the largest—was nearly loose.

With his sword he dug close under it, and in a few minutes it was gone spinning down the gully, and carrying with it something like half a ton of other earth and rubbish.

"For your lives!" said Ned, and snatching up two guns, he led the way to the summit of the hill, whence they could look down upon the scene of the late conflict.

And what saw the three boys?

Out of sixteen desperate pirates, men used to defy double their own number, six lay on the ground dead and wounded, while several others limped about with manifold curses and oaths.

It was not only the ignominious defeat that enraged them, but the fact of its being accomplished by three such puny mites of humanity.

A council was held, and then it was resolved to feign a retreat, and then, attacking the youths suddenly in this way, to become their masters.

A sudden disappearance followed this determination.

It lasted ten minutes, and then a dash was made, the men dividing themselves on the side of the slope, and bounding, with desperate strides, for the station occupied by the lads.

They reached the platform this time without any difficulty.

To their amazement and confusion it was quite empty.

CHAPTER XXVII.

A STRANGE VOYAGE.

NED SUMMERS, when the desperate crew retreated, at once judged that the pirates had made up their minds to a stratagem of some kind or other, and resolved to be beforehand with them.

Whispering to his obedient companions to follow in his wake, he led the way, and soon reached the top of the hill, which, however, commanded no prospect, it being a large expanse of table land, skirted by a dense fringe of forest.

Towards this they hurried as to an ark of refuge.

Death was preferable to being taken by pirates, and none thought of fatigue or foot soreness.

Carlo bounded on before.

The dense mass of trees was reached, and a halt declared.

Though it was noonday, under the leafy arches it was in most places dark—dank, and the damp actually rose in steam from the ground.

It was a true tropical forest, with its trunks close together, its branches interlaced, its rich, seething undergrowth, and, Ned thought with a shudder, its snakes.

Not huge, fabulous serpents that swallow elephants and such-like *bonnes bouches*, but good-sized dangerous animals which are to be found in real life.

There are, however, circumstances in which animals are less to be feared than man, and this unfortunately was one of them.

Ned whispered his comrades to follow in single file, sending the dog forward first.

It was useless as yet to attempt disguising the trail, so that he made no attempt to secrete his steps.

All clutched their weapons, eager to put as great a distance as possible between themselves and the foe.

The way they took sloped downward rapidly.

By winding in and out of the trees, and avoiding the denser undergrowth, Ned contrived to progress rapidly, until suddenly they heard the dog floundering in water, and were next minute themselves up to their knees in a rice swamp.

They had found the bottom of the hill with a vengeance.

Ned, however, did not hesitate one moment, but retreating slightly, skirted the edge of the water.

The swamp was open and clear, dotted

6

here and there with small and beautiful islets of timber.

Ned wished they could only get on one of them.

At all events they would be concealed from the pirates' view.

As he walked along he revolved in his mind what was to be done.

At this moment he heard the distant shouts of the sailors, who had hit upon their trail.

Ned halted.

A huge tree lay uprooted, its trunk in the water, which here was deeper than ordinary.

The roots were few, and none attached to anything on shore.

The lower boughs had been crushed by the heavy fall.

Ned rushed into the water, and when up to his chest heaved at the log.

After some little difficulty it grated on the mud.

"Heave all, for your lives!" he said, fixing his gun on the log.

The others rushed in and pushed.

Still the old log glided, with an odd kind of noise, along the mud.

In two minutes more, however, it floated free and buoyant.

"Climb up," whispered Ned, "and whatever you do, keep your guns ready and your powder dry."

The two boys clambered on the mighty trunk, and, as it still floated, soon followed, having first chopped off a good-sized straight bough to serve the purpose of a pole, or boat-hook.

Slowly, almost imperceptibly, through the wild rice, the log advanced, getting every moment into deeper water.

Suddenly its motion increased, but in quite an unexpected way.

The log appeared stationary for a moment, and then the part nearest the shore swung round in the stream.

The head had evidently caught in something.

"Hold firm," said Ned Summers; "she'll perhaps roll over."

In another instant their strange craft was broadside to the shore, and then a current catching the roots, the huge log was dashed out beyond the limits of the wild rice into a deep and open channel.

The jerk released the boughs, which, on the upper side, stood some ten feet out of water, and the singular raft was wholly independent of the earth.

The boys still kept a recumbent position.

They were now floating between the line of rice and some small timbered islands along what appeared a lake, but which might be only the wide reach of a river.

They were effectually concealed, as they advanced, from the pirates, even if they had gained the shore.

Now what was to be done?

Ned Summers, as usual, had an idea, and in furtherance of it, pushed out towards the islets.

One in particular caught his eye.

It was chiefly covered by cocoa-nuts, and would thereby afford them some means of refreshment as well as shelter and repose.

"I think we'd better hide; out in the lake we shall be in reach of gun-shot," said Ned, after a keen examination of the locality.

"Decide for us," replied Harry; "we are ready to obey, eh, Fred?"

Fred Blount merely nodded.

There will always among three men be a chief, and therefore why not among boys?

This once decided on, Ned pushed valiantly, and the log obeying the direction of his pole, they were in a few minutes again grating on the bottom of the river or lake.

They all landed, drew the log as near as possible to the shore, and crouched down.

Not a sign of the pirates was as yet to be seen by the fugitives.

But as it is never wise to halloo before you are out of the wood, they lay close for half-an-hour.

"They must be gone, I think," said Fred.

"Better be cautious," put in Harry.

"A few minutes more," observed Ned, who for some time had been gazing upwards.

"Prime," remarked Fred, following the direction of his eyes.

"What is prime?" asked Ned.

"The cocoa-nuts; pity there's no monkeys to throw them at us?"

"Never mind the monkeys," said Ned, throwing off his heavier clothes; "I'll soon have some!"

The other two looked at him with wondering and admiring eyes.

Having reduced his garments to merely his trousers and shirt, Ned began plaiting a kind of rope from some of the varied creeping plants, and at length had a piece about seven feet long.

This he passed round a stout cocoa-nut tree which grew rather out of the perpendicular.

It trended towards the water of the lake, over which the summit hung.

He tied a firm knot in the cord, and then entered within the circle.

The tree was of goodly size and fair proportions.

Hoisting the rope as high as he could, where it was supported by the rough bark, Ned clasped the tree and ascended as far as possible.

Every time he gained a foot, he thrust the rope up as far as he could reach.

Then, with his knees against the tree, he had but to lean back to rest and breathe.

The two boys watched him with extreme wonder.

Neither of them was as learned as Ned in the lore of travels, which, above all reading, is pleasant and useful to the rising generation.

Soon he was half way up, and the trunk being smaller and more projecting, his course was easy.

Though he still retained his useful assistant cord, he scarcely used it.

In another moment he was snugly ensconced in the boughs, and the boys below made ready for the welcome shower of cocoa-nuts. But not only had Ned disappeared, but he was wholly silent.

Then a low, firm voice was heard directly over their heads.

"Keep close—sharks alongside!"

It was time.

From the height at which he looked down upon them, the pirates appeared close to them.

They stood in a cluster on the edge of the rice swamp, in consultation.

Gesticulations could be seen, and the hum of voices heard distinctly, but no meaning was attached to the words.

But their eyes were cast in every direction.

Evidently they were rabidly furious at being baulked by three boys.

Then, after a further consultation, they turned their heads to the westward and speedily disappeared beneath the leafy canopy of the forest.

Ned Summers watched them out of sight, and when the last lagger had turned his back, began cutting off the cocoa-nuts with his knife and throwing them down within reach of his comrades.

As soon as he had stripped the tree, he contrived to slide down far more rapidly than he came up.

His friends awaited him with the utmost impatience.

Though hungry and faint, they were first eager to hear his report.

As, however, it was only what they had a right to expect, very little remark was made.

A meal was made of the welcome fresh fruit, a meal at which Carlo gazed with undisguised contempt.

He, at all events, had not learned, during his travels, to be a vegetarian.

After some sniffing and hesitation, the great beast suddenly came to a determination, and, plunging into the water, swam ashore in search of more savoury and satisfactory food.

The boys, as the hottest part of the day was advancing, lay down, and, after a languid attempt at conversation, fell into a sound and heavy sleep.

When they awoke, it was dark.

Carlo lay snoring at their feet, evidently the better for a very plentiful meal.

In a few minutes more, the three boys were seated under a large tree, in anxious consultation.

To remain on the island was not possible, while there could scarcely be a shadow of a doubt that the pirates were not far off.

Desperate and vindictive men like these were not likely to be easily put off the scent.

How was this to be found out, and in any case how were they to leave?

CHAPTER XXVIII.

A CHAPTER OF ACCIDENTS—THE FIRE SHIP.

NED SUMMERS was in all things the guiding spirit of the party.

Harry from the first had yielded to him.

Fred made scarcely any resistance.

He sat between his lieutenants on the extreme point of the island.

Before them was a reach of river about a quarter of a mile wide, and nearly three quarters long, after which it appeared to take an abrupt turn between some moderate-sized hills.

Ned Summers, all the time he was speaking, examined the whole scene keenly.

The night was moderately dark, with scarcely any wind; no sound was to be heard but the dull roar of the distant sea beating upon a rocky shore.

The water at their feet glanced swiftly by in the direction of the gap.

The two shores were lined with high bushes, behind which were lofty trees.

"Very quiet," murmured Ned. "I wonder if it be deceptive, and if it conceals an ambuscade."

"Shouldn't wonder," said Fred.

"Hope not," observed Harry.

"Well," continued Ned Summers, "I mean to find out, as well as discover which way the river runs."

He had another motive, but that he kept to himself.

"How is it to be done?" asked Fred, who was in quite a brown study.

"Well, you see," said Ned Summers, in the tone of an admiral laying down the plan of a naval engagement, "my own opinion is those fellows are lurking about to try and catch us."

"We must stop here, then, and live on cocoa-nuts," growled Fred.

"No; I mean to find out the truth. The island has plenty of wood, drift and other materials to make a raft; but first I mean to start a fire ship."

"A fire ship!" cried the two others, amazed and puzzled.

"Yes. The trunk we came over on is a big thing and will attract attention. If the beggars see it floating down with a light on it, they will be up like a nest of thieves."

He then retreated into the centre of the island, where he bade them make a small clear fire, after which he left them awhile.

The two boys obeyed him implicitly.

He himself began with his hatchet to cut away a round space in the centre of the top of the tree, screened on all sides by the standing boughs.

To this, when completed, he transferred some hot coals, and a whole pile of dry cocoa-nut shells, surmounted by oily fresh ones.

Then he thrust the floating tree out into the very middle of the stream.

It went broadside on at first emitting from the "prow" a volume of smoke and sparks. Its progress was majestic and slow in the extreme.

All but the head was shrouded in darkness, and that even emitted very little light.

Suddenly, however, the smouldering fire burst forth into a blaze, just as the motion of the fire raft began to be quicker and more progressive.

Still all was silent on both shores.

Quicker and quicker went the log, now sending up a bright blaze to the heavens

Suddenly, as Ned Summers had expected, a loud cry was heard.

The boys rushed to the reedy bank and listened attentively.

"Boat, a-hoy!"

No answer, of course, was given to this rough and ready appeal.

"Boat a-hoy! Round too, or we fire."

Silence still.

A volley of musketry was the answer, and then some half dozen men dashed off upon a raft, which the pirates had prepared to search the island with.

The burning log went majestically on its way, quicker and quicker.

On, on went the raft, its occupants cursing and swearing most energetically at the supposed fugitives.

"Avast!" suddenly cried one, as they nearly reached the middle of the open space of water.

"IN THE STRUGGLE THE GUN WENT OFF."

"Hold hard !" roared another. "By gum, we're being sucked into some cursed current."

"Thought so," said Ned Summers, with a grave smile.

At this moment, a volley of execrations burst from the terrified pirates, as, avoiding the log as much as possible, they tried to force their way up stream.

But the prospect of going over some tremendous fall was not half the difficulty.

From the opposite bank, yelling, yelping, and shouting, came at least a hundred armed Indians in long canoes, which they had carried by main force over land.

The pirates leaped into the water, turned tail, and fled.

Swimming was the only chance, as the raft was wholly unmanageable.

But swimming against well-manned canoes is no easy work, and it would have fared ill with the sailors had not their companions on shore discovered their situation.

When the head canoes were about five and twenty feet from the swimmers, and just as the Indians gave a joyous war-cry, there was a bright sheet of flame, several reports, and piercing yells from the periaguas.

Still they advanced, though again a deadly volley was poured upon them.

By this time the fugitives had touched ground, and added their broadside to the fire of their companions.

Then, with a loud, ringing cry, they waded to the shore.

But though the infuriated Indians lost a great number of their warriors, they made for the shore, and, after a desperate hand - to - hand engagement, drove the robbers of the sea some distance before them.

A terrible and partially hand-to-hand conflict ensued.

Curses, yells, and whoops were heard, filling the air with horrid sounds.

Then there came the noise of a fierce struggle, followed by dropping shots, which indicated that the pirates were slowly retreating up hill, followed by their fierce and vindictive foes.

"A nice kettle of fish !" said Fred, speaking for the first time since the surprise.

"Now's our time," replied Ned, who

had watched the raft and log disappear to the left—that is, to seaward.

A lot of wood, drift, and other material was collected, and the three boys commenced making a raft of their own.

They had no tools but wood, withes, and long, creeping plants; but the earnest desire to escape from their dangerous position urged them on.

In an hour a raft capable of carrying them all, just level with the water, was constructed, with two sweeps and a scull behind for a rudder.

This Ned Summers took the management of, while the others, carrying their guns on their backs, were placed at the sweeps.

Ned's plan was to cross to the opposite shore, from where they could still make out the conflict to be going on.

He knew it to be a difficult task, but he had been very careful in observing which way the empty rafts had gone.

Edging as much as possible out of the current, which drove them in the direction of the shore they wished to avoid, Ned now lost sight of the spot he wished to gain.

The task was a dangerous and almost hopeless one.

A raft is always a difficult craft to manage; but when in a current, and with two such slightly-built oarsmen as Fred and Harry, the task was almost beyond their joint power.

Ned Summers could do nothing to help them.

Slowly the overloaded craft went on its way down stream.

But the current soon showed its power.

The raft refused to obey its rudder.

Suddenly Ned pricked up his ears.

A low, hollow murmur attracted his attention.

What was it ?

The roar of the sea ?

No.

The whole stream, lake, river, arm of the ocean, whatever it might be, going over a waterfall !

Faintly he had dreaded this—dreamed of it—but at length it had come true.

"Pull away, boys," he said, in a stern, hushed whisper, "or it's all over with us."

"How so ?" asked Harry, looking at him with his soft and gentle eyes.

"All this water is trying to suck us

over a fall," replied Ned, "and only desperate struggles can save us. Pull with a will."

And with his long, rough oar he thrust at the bottom, which every now and then he reached, and succeeded in propelling the raft a little nearer the shore.

But now the frail structure is in the suck or in-draught of the stream, and Ned feels the cold perspiration forming on his brow.

Nothing can check the force of the onward current.

All this time the dog is swimming beside the raft, occasionally resting his paws on the edge.

"Boys," said Ned, solemnly, "you must prepare for the worst. We have been in many perils, but never in one equal to this. We are caught in the rapids of a heavy waterfall, and only a miracle can save us. Sit steady; say your prayers, and Heaven be merciful unto us!"

As he spoke, the raft darted forward, was caught in the eddy, and turned right round, dashing the sweeps out of the hands of the boys.

"Lie down!" roared Ned, in a loud, appalled voice.

The boys sprawled, as best they might, on the raft.

Guidance was now useless.

A low moan from Carlo showed that the noble animal himself scented the danger.

He turned right round and began to swim against the stream.

The watercourse had suddenly become narrower. The water itself spun along in furious and boiling floods.

In the centre was a rapid current, about thirty feet wide, running like a mill race.

On either side the stream, checked by a line of reef, came back in eddies, marked by two lines of foam.

This formed a kind of back-water.

To go down the fall was certain destruction, and Ned knew it well.

His keen eye rapidly selected a spot where to make a trial.

His pole was in his hand, and suddenly thrusting it into the water, it touched the ground.

With an amount of strength which surprised himself, he made the raft move more towards the left.

Next instant it lay motionless between two fierce and furious currents.

One in the middle of the stream where the river made its plunge; one where such of the water as could not continue to take the same road was sent with almost equal violence towards the opposite shore.

The meeting of these two currents, the overplus, which could not force its way over the rocks, caused the eddy or back-water in which they now lay in temporary security.

Ned gently urged the raft to the very edge of the fall, and then only understood the true state of affairs.

Beneath the centre of the cataract was a fearful boiling cauldron, to have fallen into which would have been certain death.

On every side minor falls, spurts, little cascades were to be seen; but this was the principal and only dangerous one.

What was to be done?

To go back was equally dangerous to going forward, and Ned at last proposed that they should abandon the raft, and scramble down the rocks, trusting to find their way to the shore by means of the mass of stepping-stones which his keen eye had already selected.

Setting an example, and keeping his pole to sound with, he made his way from the raft to the kind of strong backbone which crossed the rift.

Here, as he expected, he was scarcely ankle deep in water.

"Follow close," he said, peering before him, feeling with his oar, and in every way acting the part of an experienced guide.

Harry clung so close to him as to touch him, while Fred kept nearly as close to Harry.

In this way they clambered to the foot of the falls, amidst the wildest din they had heard for many a long day.

At one time the mass of water had evidently come steadily over from side to side, but time had gradually worn away the middle.

Everywhere the rocks were curiously honeycombed.

Half an hour of perilous walking, of advancing and retreating, followed.

Some channels had to be leaped, and

with all these the pole became an essential.

Carlo had by this time rejoined them, and was leaping about in high glee.

Evidently the clever animal knew what he was about, and had contrived to find food, as usual.

At last the shore was reached, and the three exhausted and tired boys cast themselves on the ground to regain their breath.

"We must not remain here," said Ned, after a short rest. "When the fight is over, they will be searching for us—Indians and pirates. I'd as soon die, as made prisoner by either."

"So would I," replied Fred.

Harry only sighed.

Brave, resolute, and determined as he was, he had no idea of dying.

There was yet within his breast the earnest hope to see England and his friends again.

Glancing at their feet, Ned noticed some shiny objects in the still water.

These he drew out, and found that they were the bodies of fish just killed by the heavy fall from above.

Selecting the best and the fattest of these, he fastened them with some withes.

Provisions were scarce, and every waif was valuable.

They would have to camp somewhere, and food would be necessary.

Giving them about a quarter of an hour to rest and gain breath, Ned was once more on foot, and leading the way up a stony and difficult bank.

It opened on some wooded plains, of variegated aspect.

It seemed, when they had gone a mile, strangely familiar to both Ned and Harry.

"Harry," whispered the elder boy.

"What is it?"

"Why, do you not know——"

Harry looked about him, shook his head, hesitated, and then laughed.

"Do you see yonder trees?" asked Ned, pointing to a tall grove.

"Impossible!"

"No, Heaven be thanked!" said Ned. "I know it now. Go on, Carlo; find—find!"

With a low bark, cautious, but joyful, Carlo responded.

On, on, the three weary, hungry, and exhausted fugitives went now.

They knew the place.

Behind yonder trees was the entrance to the valley of the goats.

The entrance to their own fort, to the home on the island, where they had met with so many adventures.

Here, at all events, they would have shelter, and would be able to defend themselves against the whole force of the pirates and of the Indians combined.

They seemed to rouse and regain new energy as they advanced.

Ned Summers was quite jovial, while even Harry contrived to get up a slight smile.

"Home, food, dairy, butcher's shop, and bed," said Ned encouragingly.

He knew how to raise their flagging spirits.

All smiled.

The prospect was indeed cheering.

Presently, with a low whine of recognition, the dog ran on, and disappeared through the narrow opening, which led into the valley where they had so long abandoned the goats while in search of adventures by sea and land.

In a few minutes more he was followed by the others, and the Boy Crusoes were once more at home.

The first thing, as the goats came up, was to stoop, and by means of their old gourds, to obtain a supply of milk.

The animals appeared themselves glad to see their masters; like nearly all the brute creation, once used to the society of humanity, they were lost without them.

CHAPTER XXIX.

HOME COMFORTS—OUT ON THE HUNT—A TERRIBLE LOSS.

THOUGH Harry Thornton was certainly in raptures at returning to the home which he had, unaided and alone, founded in the wilderness, the two other boys were almost equally delighted.

Their journey had been so painful and perilous, as well fruitless, that the prospect of repose and quiet was pleasant even to the aspiring spirit of Ned Summers.

But after a few days, so inconsistent is human nature—boys as well as men—he was fuming to be out and about again.

There was plenty of meat, milk, and even a sort of bread, with a moderate supply of fruit, but Ned was one of those who never can be still—never be satisfied with good food provided, but always hankering for that which was difficult of attainment.

"I feel as rusty as my old gun," he said, one morning, after scarcely eating any breakfast, kicking his heels on the edge of the platform in front of the house. "Something must be done."

"Tired of home already!" replied Harry, with a pout and a shudder.

"No. One must, however, have some exercise. Care killed the cat, you know, and idleness would soon kill me," continued Ned.

"What do you propose to do?" asked Harry, with a sigh of regret.

"Have a day's hunting, to be sure," replied Ned Summers.

"But the pirates—the savages?"

"They have had enough of it long ago," said Ned, tartly; "besides, we had just as well be dead, as close prisoners up here."

No further opposition was made by either Harry or Fred, and soon after breakfast, armed to the teeth, and accompanied by Carlo, the three once more sallied forth upon the plains and mountains of the island.

They were now in the height of their summer season; the foliage was in all its glory, the different tropical fruits of that favoured region were ripe, and the wild island in the far distant seas was more like a paradise than anything else.

Man, however, is never wholly satisfied, and the three castaways would have given the whole territory, and all it contained, for the most sandy scrap of English seashore in sight of a town.

As soon as they were once out of the cavern entrance to their fort and residence, all three held their guns ready, sending Carlo on in front to scout and reconnoitre.

The dog readily obeyed, without showing any of that suspicion which so often led him to run with his nose to the ground, and to examine carefully every thicket.

This roused the animal spirits of all.

With no danger at hand, with nature casting her favours around with so lavish a hand, everything seemed beautiful.

Their way, as usual, was towards the sea.

Now that the pirate craft had in all probability taken its departure, they might hope for other ships to come in sight.

But unless very active measures were taken, it was not likely that anyone would land upon a spot which in all probability bore a very bad name.

Ned proposed that every day they came that way an hour should be spent in cutting down wood, and adding it until it formed a huge pile, ready to be set fire to in the event of a sail being descried.

The others readily agreed, and an hour was spent in cutting down trees, in lopping branches, and then in dragging them to a bare space of sand and rock that faced the wide and open sea.

This done, the three boys made a hearty meal of fresh oysters, gathered on the shore at low water, goat's flesh, and milk, after which they continued their journey.

Ned led the way, in the direction of the chaloupe, about which he was anxious, as, in his heart, despite disappointments and rebuffs, he was determined, at the worst, to make that the means of final escape, if all the rest failed.

The other boys were far less anxious about the fate of the boat, their recent journey having been quite sufficient for them.

After leaving the sea-coast, they struck across a small, scantily-wooded plain, where the dog put up a number of fine fat birds, which Ned was too good a provider to neglect.

They, in fact, made all parties look forward with anxiety.

Presently, however, Carlo stood still, as if he had discovered something new.

He sniffed on the ground, and then, running forwards towards a small thicket, raised a fine fat deer, which bounded off in the direction of the nearest wood.

Ned Summers took steady aim and fired at the unexpected prize.

The deer bounded in the air, evidently

wounded, stood still, with outstretched legs, one moment, and then again sought safety in flight.

Ned, who was the most inveterate of sportsmen, at once threw his gun into the hollow of his arm, and bounded after the stricken animal, leaving the others to follow as best they might.

Carlo naturally accompanied the foremost sportsman, and soon sniffing the blood from the wounds, made easy running.

The wood in which the deer had sought refuge was soon crossed, and then the young sportsman found himself going up a steep and difficult ascent.

The deer was not two hundred yards ahead of him, evidently distressed and exhausted from loss of blood.

Carlo, now not to be restrained by the call of his master, made one dash forward, and, after a very feeble resistance, pinned the animal to the ground.

Ned lost no time in getting up and driving the animal away.

His long, sharp knife then finished the poor creature's struggles, and before his comrades joined him, Ned had nearly skinned his prize—if not with the neatness of a butcher, at all events with as much expedition.

The carcase was cut up, the inferior pieces cast to Carlo, and the rest divided between the three, to carry with them for supper that night, and for salting and smoking.

This done, they proceeded on their way, night coming on before they resolved upon a final halt.

A very dense bottom, surrounded on all sides by heavily-branched trees, was selected as a camping place.

A fire was made, supper cooked and eaten, and then the deer's meat—except the legs, kept for salting—was cut up in long strips and placed on a platform of sticks to be smoked.

This operation performed, and each of them clutching his gun, they cast themselves on the sward and went off into a sound sleep, from which none awoke for hours.

It was in the grey of morning.

Carlo, drawn off by some animal, was at a distance.

The boys slumbered heavily.

Nothing to warn them.

Round about their camp strange sounds would have been heard, had th been less wrapped in dreams.

The steps of men coming up.—

Light steps.

Then dark, painted faces, plumed heads, tattooed and nearly naked bodies came from under the trees.

Twenty warriors, armed with tomahawk, spear, and bow and arrow.

Grimly, slowly, and without a word spoken, they formed in a circle round the unconscious boys.

Then there came from their savage throats a war-whoop so hideous and horrible as to induce the three unfortunate lads to leap to their feet, deafened almost by the horrid clamour.

One glance at once revealed the extent of their misfortune—the fact that they were hopelessly at the mercy of the savage Indians.

As if delighted at their dismay and discomfiture, the triumphant redskins continued dancing round them in a circle, with a low, monotonous kind of chaunt.

Suddenly they ceased, and several, rushing forward, seized the prisoners, and, in the most summary way in the world, bound them each to a separate tree.

Then, without taking the slightest notice of their captives, they seated themselves on the ground and began eagerly to devour the viands so unexpectedly provided for them.

In a quarter of on hour not a scrap was left ; the prisoners meanwhile enjoying no other part of the meal but the odour.

As soon as the meal was concluded a kind of council, or big talk, was held, which ended in the savages separating into three parties of six, who then selected each party a prisoner.

The first party, having somehow or other obtained first choice, selected Harry, and, pushing him on before them, disappeared in the forest.

The second, some little time later, chose Fred, who, with a tearful glance at Ned, was compelled to accompany his captors, leaving Ned desolate and alone, in the hands of the most villanous and truculent-looking of the party.

Bad as was the position, and hopeless the future, Ned would have felt very much less wretched had not the three been parted.

It appeared like a total disruption of their happy connection, a finale to their pleasant life.

But repining was useless.

The grim warriors to whose portion Ned had fallen appeared in no hurry to follow the others, and the youth was sadly at a loss even to understand the cause of the division of parties, unaware that, like nations of an older growth, redskins are particularly jealous of their trophies of victory.

For about an hour they sat smoking their red sand-stone pipes, and luxuriating in the repletion which had so unexpectedly fallen upon them.

Then all rose, looked at their keen hatchets, examined their bows and arrows, and then conferred in their guttural, incomprehensible language.

One of the savages finally examined the withes which bound our hero, and, with a frown, discovered that he had worked them loose.

With a savage scowl, he shook his tomahawk right in the other's face, after which, releasing him, he proceeded to tie him more securely.

A straight pole was laid on the ground, and to this he was fastened by the waist.

Then two other poles were fastened across, to one of which his ankles were attached, and then his outstretched arms to the other.

Having several times tried the efficacy of this mode of securing his enemy, the savage rose.

He was alone.

The others had long since disappeared beneath the leafy arches of the forest.

Next minute Ned Summers was alone in the camp of the savage redskins.

CHAPTER XXX.

CARLO TO THE RESCUE.

THE position was not only humiliating, but was excruciatingly uncomfortable and painful.

The remorseless savage had tied the strips of leather from the unlucky deer so tight round Ned's ankles and wrists as to actually cut into the flesh.

When once alone, however, Ned Summers made a desperate attempt to break his ligatures.

In vain.

Exertion only caused them to cut more deeply into the flesh.

He ceased his exertions therefore.

Moaning with pain, Ned was in a humour that boded ill to the savages, could he have been for that instant with arms in his hands.

Repining, strong language, and threats were, however, simply useless.

Patience was all he had to depend on.

Hark!

What sound is that?

Someone, with extreme care and precaution, is crawling through the bushes.

Who can it be?

An enemy or a friend?

The latter supposition is scarcely possible, as the only two friends of whom he knows anything in that island are in as bad, or worse, plight than himself.

He strives to turn in the direction of the sound; but his swollen wrists and ankles at once compel him to lie still.

Still the steps advance.

There is something slow and trailing, like a wounded animal, in the sound.

It is close at hand.

He looks up.

Sallow, nearly naked, his rags scarcely holding together, a stout stick his only weapon, stood the author of all his misfortunes—the wretched midshipman, Samuel Petworth.

Gaunt, half starved, the light of semi-insanity in his eye, the youth grinned a ghastly smile as he looked down upon his old fellow-midshipman.

"So—caught in a trap!" said Sam, in a strangely hollow tone.

"Cut me loose!"

"What for?" sniggered Samuel Petworth.

"Are you a Christian?—do you own to having white blood in your veins," cried Ned Summers, "and will you leave me a prey to the brutal redskins?"

"Where is Harry?" asked Sam, looking about him with a keen and cunning glance.

"A prisoner, like myself," exclaimed Ned. "But make haste—the wretches may return."

"You won't hurt me?" whined Samuel Petworth, after a moment's thought.

"Hurt you! No—only be too grateful. Take my knife, and cut away quick."

The other drew Ned's long knife, which the savages, in the gloom—it being in a leather sheath—had not noticed, and passed it slowly across his thumb.

"Sharp," said Sam.

"Yes, sharp enough," replied Ned. "Cut away, and talk nonsense after."

"No hurry," drily remarked Sam.

"What do you mean?"

"This," cried Sam, with a fierce and savage gleam in his little, grey, ferret eyes, "either this knife ends your existence——"

Mechanically, as he spoke, Samuel loosened one wrist—the right—by a sharp cut, which brought blood.

"Or you swear to me, as soon as they are rescued, to divide the other two boys between us. You shall have Fred Blount for your fag," he grinned; "I will have Harry Thornton."

"I have no right to dispose of my friends. Besides, why should I yield up one so delicate to a savage like yourself? A pretty slave he would be!"

"You are mistaken," said Sam, drily. "I love the—the boy, and will have him."

"All this is idle talk," cried Ned. "The savages are probably returning; we can discuss this matter at a future time."

"No time like the present. *Swear or die!*"

And the long knife gleamed in the air, held on high by the half-insane youth.

All this time Ned's right hand had been lying limp and useless beside him.

The raw green hide had cut deeply and inflicted a wound.

The blood had been checked in its circulation, and the whole arm felt more dead than alive.

But Ned Summers was not a boy to be taken unawares.

He had once or twice stretched his muscles, and felt that sense and energy were returning.

The wretched outcast lifted his knife.

"Once — twice — *murder!*" roared Samuel, as he let fall the knife, to defend himself from the furious attack of Carlo, who, after a long morning's hunt, had condescended to return to the camp.

While Samuel shrieked, writhed and struggled, Ned picked up the murderous weapon, and unfastened the other cord.

Then, and only then, he called off Carlo.

The dog had pinned Samuel by the back of his neck, holding him fast without any very great damage, though, as he was naked from the waist upwards, not without some severe scratches and bites.

Foaming at the mouth, panting with rage, Sam would have flown at Ned, but the sight of the knife and the presence of the dog restrained him.

"Ned Summers," he hissed between his set teeth, "this must end. The world is not big enough to hold us two. Throw down your knife, send off your dog, and fight me like a man."

"Why you should hate me, I know not," replied Ned, sadly. "But go your way, lest I be tempted to tie you whence I have just escaped."

Sam looked at him with furious rage at being baulked of his fell desire, and then, with a wild cry, he whirled his staff over his head, and disappeared in the deepest recesses of the forest.

Ned, still stiff and awkward, shook himself, kicked out his legs, and soon brought life and energy back to his frame.

As he did so, his toes came in contact with something that made his heart bound.

Stooping amid the dry leaves which had made them a bed, he found that all three guns lay together untouched.

Snatching them up, he strapped one on his back, and casting the others one over each shoulder, made a sign to Carlo, and entered the forest in the direction in which he had lost sight of his friends and companions.

Carlo appeared fully to understand what was expected of him, as he at once assumed a jog-trot step and led the way in which his master wished to go.

Ned moved very slowly, as he was fully aware of the character of the people he had to deal with; they were equally cruel and cunning.

In front were those who had stolen away

.is friends and companions; behind those who had left him, to all appearance, so securely tied.

He was alive—armed, it is true; but what was one boy, even provided with firearms, against a horde of bold and desperate savages?

Nothing would have been easier than to retire to the secret castle on the hill, and there abide the final retirement of the savages.

Ned, however, was not one to abandon friends in distress; and if even he perilled his life, was quite determined to follow in the footsteps of Harry and Fred.

Slowly, deliberately, the brave dog kept some distance in advance.

He soon found that Ned was not able to move very fast, though, as he warmed to the task, he did feel both more energy and life.

Up hills, over small plains, along dark valleys and gloomy dells, winding in and out, until, instead of an island, their retreat seemed an endless continent, Ned and his faithful companion towards sunset reached a wood, which spread in every direction over a rolling and slightly diversified plain.

No sign of the fugitives.

It was evening, and almost dark, so that Ned resolved to camp.

That Carlo might not go astray, he tied him by a loose thong to his wrist.

With his sturdy dog and his three guns, he lay down at the foot of a wide spread tree, and soon slept the sleep of the fearless and the just.

An hour elapsed.

The forest was still and silent as the grave, and then Carlo put his nose close to the other's ear, and gave a low, whining moan.

Summers understood him well.

Ned raised his head and peered slowly around.

At first his head appeared dizzy, and he could scarcely make out where he was.

He then listened attentively.

Nothing.

Still the dog moaned, and fixed his eyes in a westerly direction.

Yes, there they were, six bloody savages, 'n their war-paint, with their head-dresses relieved against the sky, on the summit of a small ridge.

They were passing along in Indian file,

like the ghostly forms of the former inhabitants of those far-distant isles.

Ned clutched his gun nervously.

They were not fifty yards distant, and coming directly his way.

In another moment they would be beneath the shelter of the forest.

They were following the trail, and by means of the clear, cold moonlight, had easily traced the dog and man over the hills and plain.

Under the canopy of leaves the task became somewhat more difficult.

Unfortunately for Ned, these redskins were not of those savages who, until intimate with Europeans, were ignorant of fire.

To light up a clear pine torch, and hold it down to the trail, was the work of a minute.

All was lost.

In another moment they would be upon him.

Flight was of little avail, as the cunning knaves would still follow him.

Well, Ned was not going again to submit to the fearful thraldom from which he had just escaped.

They came on, one behind the other, the first holding a torch, the others clutching their heavy tomahawks.

Ned Summers had his three guns close to his hand.

He lifted up the largest and heaviest, loaded with heavy duck shot, took steady aim, and fired.

A fearful howl, a horrid screech was heard, and then, when the smoke cleared away, two Indians lay sprawling on the ground.

The rest had, as was their usual practice, rushed to cover.

Ned Summers had himself retreated behind the tree, and, treading lightly, made the best of his way from the night camp he had selected.

A dismal howling and screeching followed him; but Ned, regardless of the enemy, and thinking only of his own safety, hurried away as fast as his feet could carry him.

Carlo trotted on as unconcernedly as possible.

That worthy seemed on perfectly good terms with himself, and selected paths which were certainly easier than those around.

At length they came to the verge of the wood.

Something shone translucent in the bright moonlight at no great distance.

It was the mighty ocean, in all its greatness and glory.

Amid the rocks, and by fording here and there a small branch of the sea, he might, Ned thought, hide his trail.

After a moment's reflection, he skirted the edge of the wood, intending to dash down a small gully to the left.

He counted without his dog, who wagged his tail, looked up at him, and signified his intention of going quite another way, even back into the wood which they had just left.

Believing the animal, like most of his race, to have a motive for what he did, Ned, who had loaded his gun as he walked along, followed.

The dog went forward about a hundred yards, and then stopped.

Ned looked around, and presently saw a faint light, something like the twinkling of a star.

His heart leaped into his mouth.

Had he fallen upon the camp where his comrades were guarded by the Indians?

He saw to the priming of his three guns.

One he held in his hand.

The other two he cast on his shoulders, and, bidding the dog hold back a little, crept on.

He strove to emulate the cunning and patience of the Indians themselves.

The fire burned low in a hollow, to which the wood sloped.

Ned trod slowly and carefully, never putting his foot to the ground until sure that he did not tread on anything likely to betray him.

In this way he soon reached the camp.

It was a small, clear, sparkling fire round which sat four men, moodily smoking their pipes.

Leaning against two large tree trunks were two other ghastly-looking redskins.

A moment's reflection told that they were corpses.

Between them lay the body of a man tightly bound, and towards this the Indians continually pointed, with savage mien, with glaring eyeballs and ferocious scowls.

It was the half-naked body of Samuel Petworth, whom the Indians had caught crouching round their camp, with some vague idea of food and warmth, and whom they were about to punish for the misdeeds of others.

Presently the pipes were laid down, and in their places the savage and implacable Indians clutched their tomahawks.

The spectacle was going to begin.

Sam looked at them in stupid wonderment, as if he scarcely knew what was about to happen, nor cared much. His brain was certainly affected to a certain degree.

Whatever in one sense of the word may be the nobility of the Indian, there can be no doubt of his savage delight in cruelty.

Cruelty of the most refined character.

Samuel Petworth gaped at them with a mien almost as wild and savage as themselves.

The pipes consumed and finished, they surrounded the dead bodies of their friends, and danced a singular measure to a still more singular tune.

Then they brought a pile of wood to where the wretched white man stood, naked and despairing.

It was quite clear that they intended to torture and then burn him.

Now Ned was, of course, deeply antagonistic to Samuel Petworth.

And yet it went against his noble and generous heart to leave him to the devices of the savages.

All this while where was Harry—where Fred?

Had they been with him, his attack on the savages would have been a certainty.

His eyes were never taken off them.

Sam looked at the proceedings with a lack-lustre eye.

Abject terror had seemingly bereft him of his senses.

The savages danced with joy.

Their happiness consisted in quelling the courage of their victims.

Had he only shown a decent amount of courage, they would have respected and perhaps spared him.

For the coward they had no mercy.

The pile was made, some splinters of wood were ready, with which to tear his flesh, and the torch was lit.

The savages approached him in a body.

Ned hesitated no longer, but let fly the double-barrelled gun he had obtained from the pirate lieutenant.

An awful yell followed, and then the savages fled.

Ere they were out of sight, Ned gave them another shot.

Then, without delay, he ran up, loosened Sam's withes, and freed him.

"Now run for your life."

Sam grinned in his face.

The man was a howling idiot.

Ned could not wait to be recaptured, so turned away, hoping that the instinct of preservation would induce him to follow.

Scarcely had he done so when Carlo began to howl.

Ned immediately took the hint, and selecting an open space, where the trees were thin and sparse, took to his heels.

He was speedily aware, by the crushing in the bushes above, that he was pursued.

Taking advantage of the darkness, he rushed into a thicket and came to a pause.

Instead of running, he moved with the most extreme caution.

Carlo moved majestically forward.

Still the noise of pursuit could be heard in the distance.

It became, however, more and more indistinct.

At length it ceased.

Ned, who could not be still, continued on his way until he reached the shores of the mighty ocean, close to the great beacon pile they had erected.

Ned seated himself on the naked rock, and was affected almost to tears.

Suddenly he rose, and dashing his hand over his eyes, moved hastily up and down.

"I must be a man, or else how can *they* be saved?"

A wild cry arose from his throat next instant—

"Heavens!"

What is this looming in the distance against the sky?

A tall and stately ship.

She is afar off, moving in a stately way slowly past the island.

She is under easy sail, and there is little wind.

Frantically, more like a madman than a rational being, he now rushes to the beacon, strikes his flint and steel, creeps into the deep hollow they have left in the centre of the huge pile, both to create a draught and keep the smaller fuel dry.

It is like tinder.

A spark, a flicker, a flame.

Hurrah! the beacon is fired.

Slowly at first, then more quickly, the flames burst forth, caught the adjacent wood, lapped the larger beams, and then spread rapidly.

Hurrah again! the indraught is felt, and the flames come forth with a roar.

The beacon is on fire.

Ned now stood back behind a rock, and waited with a wildly-beating heart.

The flames gained ground every moment; the damp wood resisted at first, but finally the whole was wrapped in one huge, fiery embrace.

Forty feet perpendicular in the air.

The day and the hour had come.

CHAPTER XXXI.

NED REPORTS HIMSELF.

FOR some minutes, it seemed an age, the ship went on her way.

Then suddenly the helm was shifted, and the top-sails thrown back to the wind.

She was laying to

How the brave boy's heart beat with joy and hope, not for himself, but for Harry and Fred.

Then he saw a boat—boats—put out,

and into these he saw large bodies of men descending.

Was it the pirate? No!

Such a noble vessel must, indeed, be rather superior to that which had infested the island.

It is—yes, it is a man of war!

They come, four armed boats, in the direction of the island.

"ON EVERY SIDE WERE SIGNS OF A CONFLICT."

7

They suspect a snare, a lure, something to lead them to destruction.

They advance slowly in the direction of the beacon.

Ah! what sound is that?

A large number of savages are coming down, attracted by the fire.

The boats are still a hundred yards off.

Ned does not hesitate.

Off with his superfluous clothes, down with his weapons, and into the sea he plunges, followed by Carlo.

The sea is smooth, and swimming easy.

The savages, with wild yells, line the shore, forty or fifty in number.

The boats halt for a parley.

Ned swims out vigorously, and, when half way from the shore, raises a loud and despairing cry—

"Help! help! help!"

The boat dashed in, and in five minutes Ned was hauled in the boat.

"Who and what are you?" said a well-known voice.

"Ned Summers *come on board*," was the startling answer.

Just as if he had gone on shore for an hour's duty.

A loud hurrah from the men was the response.

It was his own ship.

"And Petworth——"

"Ashore, free; but there are two dear friends prisoners."

"On! on!" cried the brave lieutenant; "drive the beggars into the bushes."

The boats advanced, and when within forty feet, just as the Indians poured in a volley of spears and arrows, fired a volley, not only of musketry, but of cannons, one from the bow of each launch.

When the boats struck the beach, not an Indian was to be seen.

It wanted now two hours of dawn, and the commander of the expedition at once ordered the men to rest, after placing sentries to guard against surprise.

Then the officers crowded round Ned to hear his wonderful story.

They listened in amazement, and before he had concluded, every listener had determined to risk anything to save the two companions of Ned's strange adventures.

Ned himself was wild with impatience.

He was with difficulty made to eat some beef and biscuit and to drink some grog.

He, however, felt much better afterwards.

At dawn they were all ready, and discovered that their volley had done great destruction.

Seven were dead.

Carlo sniffed the ground with fierce impatience.

He scented the blood.

After a hasty conference, it was determined to follow the dog.

The sailors, apart from those who were left to guard the boats, numbered forty-eight men.

They carried cutlasses, guns and pistols.

All were ready and willing to help in the release of the two boys.

The lieutenant, the very same who had given permission to Ned Summers and Samuel Petworth to roam at pleasure, led the van, with our hero by his side.

Both panted for victory, while Ned himself felt no satisfaction in the idea of escape without *dear* Harry and *poor* Fred.

Much as he liked them both, Harry was the preferred.

The dog led them on steadily over rocks, to the edge of swamps, across a dense strip of forest, until at length he once more turned towards the sea.

All turned.

It was quite possible the savages would attempt to escape by sea.

They might take Harry and Fred with them as prisoners, or they might kill and——

Ned shuddered at the very thought, knowing these wretches to be cannibals.

The lieutenant thought some minutes.

They were on the summit of an acclivity, and just about to descend.

"One moment," he said.

From a wooden case behind him, which he unslung, he brought forth a large signal rocket.

Ned stared.

"This will warn the ship to keep a good look-out. They will see it."

It was soon fixed to a stout stick, a light obtained, and ignited.

Far into the air it rose over a hundred feet.

The dog began to yelp in a low tone.

He was evidently impatient, and the sailors were none the less so.

Onward was the word and the act—on —on, until at last the dog looked up knowingly in their faces.

They still advanced, and soon saw that they were approaching the goal of their wishes.

A large Indian village was in sight, down upon which they rushed with a loud shout—but to find it empty.

The Indians had seen the beacon and the ship, and had fled with their prisoners, but where?

This was the difficulty.

Ned was nearly frantic with disappointment, and proposed a general search of the island.

Not a moment was to be lost.

The island was searched thoroughly, but not a single Indian was found.

About an hour before sunset, however, they came upon a horrible and revolting sight.

Samuel Petworth, gibbering like an idiot on the sea shore, and uttering frantic cries.

"He is mine, my prisoner!" he shrieked, as he danced about, and pointed towards a low line of land to the southward and eastward.

"The savages have fled to the other island," cried Ned; "let us follow."

"We must communicate with the captain," replied the lieutenant; "I dare not stay a moment longer without consulting him."

"They will be murdered."

"Rely upon it there will be no delay. In fact, I will simply write a few lines and await orders on shore."

"All right, sir."

The lieutenant simply wrote to say that some English youths were prisoners with the savages, and had been removed to the larger island.

"May I take the boats and try and rescue them?"

With this the gig was sent on board.

"I will stop a week rather than leave English lads in the hands of the rascals," was the reply. "Lead the way; I will follow."

"Now, then, my lad, we have a roving commission. But where is that wretched Sam?"

None had taken notice of him, while he himself, having discovered a deserted canoe, was making with wild energy for the distant island.

"Rely upon it you are right, Ned."

CHAPTER XXXII.

THE STRANGE ISLAND.

AS the savages were of course alarmed at the presence of the frigate, it was necessary to use the extremest caution.

The larger island was about twenty miles or less distant from the one where the Rival Crusoes had so long made their home.

Nothing would therefore be easier than to reach it during the dark, conceal their boats, and commence their search of the island by daybreak.

These islands, though marked on the charts, were rarely visited by Europeans.

The natives were particularly savage, and, as they produced neither gold dust nor ivory, afforded little temptation for commercial capacity.

Their coasts, therefore, were very little known.

All, therefore, that could be done was to exercise great caution, and navigate a kind of blind navigation in No Man's Land.

As they passed over the tossing waves, Ned gave fuller details of his adventures.

With his dog at his feet, he gave all the particulars he could remember.

"You've had a fine time of it, Ned," said the lieutenant, when he finished. "Shouldn't have thought Sam Petworth would turn out such a duffer."

"He was sullen when in the mess, and hated me from the hour I stepped on board," replied Ned.

"There are some natures like that. I suppose, however, we've seen the last of my joker," observed the lieutenant, carelessly.

"I know not. I fancy Sam will turn up like a bad halfpenny again," sighed Ned.

He was right.

After about two hours of slow and cautious pulling, they made out the dark outline of the shore.

"Silence, my men. A word may betray us to the savages," said the lieutenant. "Jones."

"Yes, sir."

"That dingy of yours will float wherever it is damp—push on and see if you can make out a safe landing," said the luff.

"Aye, aye, sir," was the ready answer.

While the other armed boats followed slowly in single file, the dingy advanced like a pilot fish more than anything else.

Presently it was lost to view, and the other boats were at once ordered to lay on their oars.

In a few minutes the dingy returned.

"What news, Jones?"

"We are at the mouth of a narrow bay or river, with vast trees on all sides —plenty of anchorage."

"Lead the way."

Jones required no twice telling, but took them all into what, on further examination, proved to be a land-locked bay, where the boats would be easily concealed from any but those coming seaward.

They were drawn up almost under the overhanging foliage, and then all crept beneath the trees.

The captain, ever thoughtful of his men, had sent his own chaloupe after them with rations of meat, bread, and rum.

Jack, with that and tobacco, can always make himself tolerably comfortable.

But there was one injunction strictly laid upon all, to keep close together, and to speak in whispers.

Ned, having supped with the lieutenant, retired under a dense bush with his only near and dear friend, the faithful dog.

It was Harry Thornton's dog, and hence he loved it more than he ever could any other animal.

His thoughts were sad and depressed. Under the circumstances in which they were placed, could he ever hope to see his dear friend again?

But though for a long time he uselessly wooed slumber, at length the tyrant god overcame his resistance, and he slept soundly.

He had even to be awakened.

The men were at breakfast, and this essential preliminary having been adjusted, the lieutenant entered upon the duties of the day.

Fifty-two men were ashore. In duty to the ship's boats, so important a part of her equipment, it was impossible to leave less than a dozen well-armed men in charge.

The lieutenant had paid great attention to that part of Ned's story which had reference to the pirates.

They might be prowling about, and at any moment make their appearance.

A rumour had gone forth that a pirate station—a slave baracoon, very much the same thing—was concealed among this group of islands.

"Prize money and promotion, my lad," said the lieutenant, as they finished their breakfast, "if we could get hold of this rascally pirate."

"I would rather have Harry," replied Ned.

"You are as spoony as a first love," laughed the lieutenant.

It was now arranged that the officers and men detailed for the expedition should follow the shore in search of any signs leading to a village.

"Keep close, Jones, and send up a rocket if there is any danger. Both I and the captain will know what that means."

"Aye, aye, sir. But I shall be able to hold my own against all the enemies likely to attack me," said the old quartermaster, rather loftily.

"Against niggers and blackbirds, yes— but there's a few white men about worse than the savages, so keep your weather eye open," replied the lieutenant, gravely.

"I'll look sharp after that sort of cattle. I'm glad you spoke. The pinnace has its long Tom in the hold. I'll just haul it on deck and have it ready," continued Jones.

"That's the ticket, my lad," said the lieutenant, heartily, and with increased confidence, commenced the march.

The wood in which they had sought shelter was composed of very lofty trees, with underbrush.

The lieutenant, Ned, and the dog marched first, the others coming in single file.

The dog appeared rather proud of the notice which was taken of him, and strutted as loftily as any actor his brief hour of importance on the stage.

"That beast deserves a silver collar if ever dog did," observed the lieutenant.

"If we escape, and my friend is released, I will take care he has one," replied Ned.

For an hour there was no change in the character of the country, but the wood gradually thinned, and soon a river came in sight.

Ned suddenly tapped the lieutenant on the shoulder, and pointed to where a man was seated with his back to them, fishing.

He was a black, wore a huge Panama hat, and was so absorbed in what he was about that he appeared to hear nothing of those who approached.

The lieutenant lifted his hand by way of warning, and the whole troop halted.

The officer, Lieutenant Titcomb by name, selected one powerful sailor, and advanced slowly, followed by Ned and the powerful dog.

They were close upon the man, had touched him on the shoulder, ere he started up.

He was a full-grown negro, very powerful, exceedingly ugly, and yet good-humoured.

"What you want, sah?" he said.

"Tattoo Block, by jingo!" cried the sailor.

"Dat my appelleration," continued the darkey. "Where you knew me, sah?"

"On board the 'Bacchus,' Indiaman."

"Right you am, sah; now me head cook and bottle washer to dirty pirate."

"The deuce you are!" said Lieutenant Titcomb; "step this way, my fine fellow. I should like a little conversation with you."

Tattoo Block stepped on one side, and in a few words explained that some years before he had been captured by the pirates, who, finding him to be an excellent cook, had kept him in that capacity.

"But where are the pirates?" asked the lieutenant.

"Don't know—'em cut away daylight dis morning," cried Tattoo Block.

"But what about the savages," asked Ned, rather sharply, "who stole two boys?"

"Dem run away too," said the negro.

"Had they two English boys with them?" said the lieutenant, smiling at Ned's eagerness.

"Yes, and one mad chap get here in the night," continued Tattoo Block.

"Sam Petworth!"

"My lad, be calm," said the lieutenant, loudly, "and allow your superior officer to speak. I make every allowance for your anxiety, but things must be done shipshape and Bristol fashion."

"I beg your pardon, sir."

"Have the pirates gone after the blacks?"

"Not knowing, massa, can't say. But dis chile bery much tink so."

"Have you no clue—nothing to guide you?"

"Well, dis infant tink ship go to Baracoon Island."

"By Jove, can you guide us there?"

"Cut my tongue out, massa."

"My lad, you have the word of an English officer that you shall be well rewarded and protected against the scoundrels," said Titcomb.

"Must go by wattah (water), sir," put in the negro.

"Which way, my boy?"

"Up dis creek; troo tree or four island—dis nigger find de way."

"Be off, Thomson," said the lieutenant to a young top-man; "you are a good runner, I know—bring up the boats as quick as possible."

The top-man drew in his belt, touched his hat, and started on his journey.

"How is it you are alone?" asked the lieutenant.

"Dem in such a debil of a hurry run away, dey no tink ob me," groaned the black; "besides, dem coons know I neber swim away."

Satisfied with this explanation, the lieutenant ordered his men to seek repose while he heard as many details as possible relative to the pirates.

Some things he heard made him very grave.

The boats arrived in two hours, and the smallest was at once sent to the ship with a carefully folded letter, addressed to the captain.

It was marked "Private and Important."

Then the expedition started.

The river, they found, was in reality a narrow channel between two islands known only to the natives and the pirates.

Is was wide enough for the pirate ship to pass through, towed by its boats and its yardarms fore and aft.

"I understand now," cried Lieutenant Titcomb to Ned, "why that rascally slaver and pirate Red Dick always escapes us."

"How so, sir?" said Ned.

"I was on a cruiser for three years after him, and he always escaped about here."

"The cunning rascal!"

"I'd give something to come face to face with that scoundrel. I'd give twenty guineas," cried Lieutenant Titcomb.

"Dem's mine," said the negro, coolly; "me just bring you face to face. Dat one name ob the debil; Captain Brand him Red Dick."

"My lad, you make me happy. That scoundrel has done deeds which are revolting to humanity. Apart from the prize money which we shall gain if he be captured, humanity demands the destruction of himself and gang."

The passage was intricate, and no one but a person who had been there before could have guided them.

Every now and then they appeared about to rush up a blind channel, ending, it appeared, the river.

Suddenly Tattoo Block cried a halt.

"Now, sah, you hide all dem boats. De pirate he tam cunning, but you see some fun."

"How so?"

"We close to de Crow's Nest, where am de sentry. If him see us, him fires rocket—one, two, tree, dah! and den him beggah absquatulate."

"A sentry! But what are you going to do."

"You gib me gun, pistol, sword, yer see. Come behind me, but no let him see lilly bit ob white skin, or him cut him lucky, like de frog jumper."

The lieutenant, though for a moment slightly suspicious, finally gave the negro his weapons, and then the dog being se-

cured, followed the negro, in company with Ned and Bob Slack, who had recognised Tattoo Block.

The coloured cook stepped ashore, and making signs for silence, walked with slow and cautious step under the trees, until they came to a small lake, in the centre of which was an island.

In the middle of the island stood four trunks of cocoa-nut trees, on the summit of which was a platform.

Under this platform, leaning his back against one of the pillars, was a tall, thin, Yankee-looking individual smoking.

"Got yer napping, have I?" muttered the negro, slouching along with his hand behind his back.

"Waal, old iron pot, what's up?" asked the other, puffing away vigorously.

"Only, old pepper-pot, as I've caught you napping, and if you move one inch I shoot you dead," said the negro, levelling his piece, and wading up to his waist across a narrow channel which separated that shore from the island.

"Why, you owdacious skunk, what d'yer mean?" said the other, whose weapons and other fixings were on the platform above.

"Dis yar, you ugly son ob a sea cook, dat you dis chile's prisoner," said the black, chuckling; "now you, sah, bring up de boat. Tattoo Block him enough for one——"

But at this moment the Yankee drew a knife, and, while the negro was speaking, aimed a terrible blow at his head.

"Dat's de game; yah! yah! one for him nob," said Tattoo Block, swinging the gun round, and bringing the stock down upon the pirate's head with a blow that would certainly have felled an ox.

The ruffian was dead.

"Him spy no more," said the negro, drily.

In a few minutes more the boats came sweeping round the bend, the dangerous pass of the Crow's Nest being surmounted.

By nightfall they were at the end of the most dangerous part of the channel, and about to enter upon a more open sea, with islands scattered about.

"How far is the baracoon island?" asked the lieutenant of the negro.

"Good ten miles, massa. Men tired?"

"'Pon my word, darkey, I thank you f—

the hint. Supper and splice the main brace, my lads," said the lieutenant, cheerily; "I should like to surprise the rascals in their beds."

"Den, massa, it must be in de morning, dat de trap," cried the negro.

The men at once proceeded to eat their supper, drink a stiff glass of rum to keep out the malaria, and then, after a pipe, snatched as much slumber as they could.

The lieutenant posted sentries, ordered them to rouse him at four, and turned in on shore under a spare sail to keep out the dew.

Ned lay beside him, with his noble dog very near at hand.

Sleep overcame him on this occasion very soon, and he remained in a heavy slumber until he was startled by something touching his face.

He lifted up his head, and found that the dog was whining in his ear.

He sat up, and the dog wagged his tail in the still starlight.

Ned knew that something was up.

He snatched up his gun and sword, and, without giving a thought to his companions, went out from the tent after the faithful animal.

A cry, a cry of distress, was heard in the distance, a cry he seemed to know.

The dog gave a low, moaning howl, and rushed on the track.

Ned bounded after him, more like a madman than anything else.

Some fearful catastrophe was imminent.

Ten minutes more, he was in sight of the sea and of two figures; one that of a tall, gaunt man, the other of a shorter personage.

The latter was being lifted into a boat as he came in view.

"Stay, villain, wretch, murderer!" roared Ned, taking a bound like a young tiger.

"Save me! help!" said the unmistakable voice of Thornton.

"Ha! ha! ha!" was the wild, weird cry of the infuriated madman.

And casting the boy into the bottom of the boat, he gave a shove with the oar against the bank, and sent the canoe flying out over the dark and stormy waves.

He stood up, waved his oar on high, and uttered an exultant shout.

Ned, exasperated to the last degree, fired.

A hollow laugh was the only response, and then the mad midshipman seated himself and rowed away into the night.

"Lost! lost!" cried the youth.

"Ned," said Fred Blount, running up, "where is she?"

"Heaven! What has happened?"

In a few words Ned explained. But his narrative was of a character which will have to be condensed in our own words.

CHAPTER XXXII.

THE INDIANS.

THE reader is already aware of the almost total destruction of the band which had taken Ned a prisoner.

The sufferings of Harry and Fred with their captors were very much of a similar character, though, for reasons which may or may not be obvious to the perspicuous reader, they were rather more gentle to Harry than to the hardy young sailor.

Be this as it may, they finally, after many and cruel hardships, were reunited in a deep valley that, through a narrow gully, opened up a view of the sea.

Here all the savages collected together,

remaining strictly concealed, and making no fires.

There was evidently danger in the wind.

To the wretched captives this was no consolation, as there could be little doubt the only enemies at hand to be feared by the savages were the pirates, as deadly foes to themselves as to the blacks.

In fact, if they were to be slaves for ever, it would scarcely be a matter of choice.

"As far as I am concerned," said Harry, when, with strict guard kept over them, they were allowed to converse, "I would rather be the drudge of a black than of those wicked, blaspheming men."

"Poor Harry!" replied Fred, kindly, "you were never intended for this sort of thing."

"Truly, the tender care and nurture of my parents did not prepare me for this," sighed Harry, and then, with a deep sigh, he added, "now that Ned is gone, I don't care to live."

"You count me for nothing," said Fred, sadly.

Harry actually blushed crimson.

"Oh, yes, Fred, I like you so much—but then, you see, I—well, I mean I knew Ned first," was the rather involved reply.

"I quite understand," answered Fred, "but no matter which you prefer," he added, taking the other's hand in his, "remember, I am now, and if we live, for ever, your brother."

Harry shook slightly, and then looked Fred in the face curiously.

Fred gave a strange, peculiar smile, and Harry looked down upon the ground.

"Harry, my life is yours! Do with me as you will. Shall we endeavour to escape?" asked Fred.

"You are generous, good, and brave; let me look upon you ever as an elder brother," replied Harry, "and be guided by you in all things."

Hark! what wailing cry is that?

A prolonged howl arose at the entrance to the camp, and two men, wounded and footsore, entered.

The sole survivors of the band that had carried off Ned Summers.

"He has escaped!" cried Harry, joyfully.

"Heaven! by what chance?" said Fred.

The wounded braves were now in the camp, and, surrounded by all their fellows, relating their adventures.

The savages heard in silence.

When they had finished, a fearful shout of execration burst from their throats.

Then, with a wild cry, a number of the exasperated wretches flew at the prisoners.

A speedy exit from this world, torn to shreds, would have been their fate, but for a dash made by the elder warriors, who stood before them, a serried rank of projecting spears.

Frantic words were exchanged, and

then those who had been so eager for revenge gave way.

They even laughed with ferocious glee, the laugh of demons over lost souls.

Then some patted them on the back.

"Ah! ah!" said one young ruffian, who had been saved by a cruiser from a slaver, and served three years with the English, "make fine roastee—then eatee him up."

"Cannibals!" cried Harry, closing his eyes in intense horror.

"Mere talk," said Fred, cheerily.

At this moment another shout arose and eight men entered with something slung on poles.

Each two carried a small barrel of rum, which they had found in the pirate village.

A terrific shout of joy arose.

Rum and whisky are the weakness of all savages.

Harry and Fred crept together under shelter of some bushes.

In the universal joy they were forgotten.

The savages were used to the management of such prizes, and went about their work in a scientific way.

The barrels were placed on end and the heads knocked out.

Then each man dipped in the cocoanut cup, which he carried at his belt, and drank.

Four barrels of fiery raw rum.

They were, however, disposed of in about ten minutes.

At once the savages became frisky, and, as usual, gave vent to their feelings in a dance.

As the fiery liquid got in their heads however, they speedily became ferocious.

Of course the first thought was the prisoners.

But they were nowhere to be found.

Evening, too, had set in, and to chase them was difficult.

"We must not stop here," had said Fred, "even if we give ourselves up again —it won't do to remain with them while drunk."

Harry shuddered.

"Let us flee at once!"

"Follow," replied Fred.

And without the slightest hesitation they dived into the bushes and fled.

Naturally enough they made towards the sea.

It was to English boys the only hope of escape.

"If we could only find Ned," whispered Harry, more to himself than to the other, "I think we might still hope for escape."

Fred sighed.

"Let us go in search of him, Harry," he replied; "but doubtless he would keep in the rear of the savages. Having escaped, rely upon it he is following our trail."

"Of course," said Harry, naively.

"Then we must make for the interior of the island," added Fred.

"If Ned cannot find us," said Harry, "I know what he will do—that is, if he finds we have escaped."

"Let's have your notion, Harry."

"He will go to the castle, my beautiful castle in the hills," he cried.

"You are right—we must find a place where to hide for the night, and then at daybreak we can reconnoitre," said Fred.

They retreated through a dense wood towards the interior of the island, in a direction which, as far as they could judge, would take them to the summit of a hill whence they could make out pretty clearly the topography of the island.

At length they reached a spot where some tamarind trees gave shelter even against the most poisonous dews of the island.

"It ain't a upas tree," said Harry Thornton, half seriously, half joking.

"The upas tree is a fiction."

"So I've heard my father say," replied Harry Thornton with a sigh, "but my native servant used to tell me, when we lived in Java, that it was poisonous."*

"It may be poisonous, that is, contain poisonous juices," said Fred, "and yet not kill those who sleep under it. This, however, is a tamarind."

And he tore down some of the ripe fruit, which was very savoury and welcome to their feelings.

They had scarcely tasted food for many hours.

---

* In a *London Magazine* of 1773, we find—" The existence of the upas tree, in Java, and the noxious powers of its gums and vapours, are certain. Travellers and naturalists have mentioned trees of the same destructive nature in other places." The whole affair turned out to be an invention of one Foersh, a Dutch surgeon.

Then Harry went and nestled under a tree, and Fred kept careful watch for a time.

What were his thoughts?

They were never known to any save himself and his conscience.

But that night, to his mind, was one of the darkest he ever knew.

For a time his feelings towards Ned were certainly not of the most cordial description.

Why, we cannot say.

But the nobility of his heart triumphed, and Fred was himself again before daylight.

Then, their parched lips cooled by the tamarinds, and their hunger faintly appeased by a ripe cocoa-nut which had fallen close at hand, they commenced their weary walk into the interior of the island.

They kept the level ground for some little time, and then began creeping up a steep hill.

Both were silent and hopeful.

The island, though of varied conformation, was not very large, and could they but keep from the track of the Indians, Ned would surely be found.

Presently they reached the bed of a mountain torrent and proceeded to cross it.

"How, how, why run away?" said the voice of the Anglo-nigger, appearing before them with two others.

"Afraid of the rum," replied Fred, with wonderful presence of mind.

"Ha, ha, ha!" laughed the other, "lum very goot—find more—warm black man's heart—come!"

Resistance was wholly useless, and they knew it.

The savages were armed with heavy war clubs, and would slay them on the spot if they did not yield.

Utterly overcome, and wholly despairing now, they followed in the track of their captors.

They did not return in the direction of the valley, but took their way to the opposite side of the island.

This they reached before evening, and camped with their three captors.

But the others came not.

The three grew anxious, when suddenly the whole fleet of canoes came sweeping round a promontory.

With loud cries they took the prisoners on board, and started just as Sam Petworth came up and stood for hours frantic upon the shore.

What happened after this the reader knows.

The prisoners soon found, through the negro, who spoke a smattering of English, that a big war canoe of the English was in sight, and that Ned had escaped their vengeance.

"Ned on board an English man-of-war," said Harry, in a low whisper, "then we are saved."

"A man-of-war will scarcely go so much out of her way to save two lads," said Fred, drily.

"She will never desert us."

"Boys arn't much account on board of men-of-war," continued Fred.

But a fierce and threatening gesture cut short all further discussion.

They reached the island of the secret channel, and here the natives, who were in great dread of the English man-of-war, held council.

Some were for murdering the prisoners in cold blood, and then scattering over the group of islands until the dreaded foe had retired.

The others were for keeping them securely prisoners, and using them as hostages.

This resolve obtained, and Fred and Harry were taken into a deep and dreary cave, which had evidently often been used as a habitation.

The two prisoners were securely fastened to logs by the ankles, and left to the guardianship of one old woman, while the cunning savages betook themselves to their various villages, there to assume, as they had done so many times before, the air of peaceful traders.

Many an English ship had been thus deceived.

The crone was middle-aged, but fierce, angry, and vindictive. She hated the whites, and was left with them for this reason.

But she was to be cruelly put to death if she did them any bodily harm.

Lighting a fire, and filling a bowl full of semi-poisonous tobacco, that sent both Fred and Harry off choking, she seated herself near the fire, with her back to the entrance of the cave.

The prisoners were about six feet apart, and as helpless as if they had been in their coffins.

They had some tough, half-raw meat and a small calabash of water—but no more.

They, however, could converse.

The old crone, on more than one occasion, checked them, but as she dared not use physical force, they did not obey very much.

So passed the miserable, weary hours away.

A day and half a night, and still the old woman, with an occasional forty winks, watched them narrowly.

"I am faint and sick," said Harry; "if this lasts much longer I shall die."

"Who comes?" cried Fred.

With a savage yell the woman rose to face the intruder.

It was Sam Petworth, who, without the slightest remorse or compunction, brained her on the spot.

He then, waving a knife over his head, rushed upon Harry Thornton, cut the cord which bound him, snatched up his slight form, and fled.

"Wretch, release me," stormed Fred.

But with a demoniacal yell the savage midshipman fled.

But he cast away his knife, and after a quarter of an hour of dragging himself by main force along the floor of the cave, Fred succeeded in reaching it.

He cut himself loose, and then, with a hoarse, repressed cry, like that of a famished wolf, made after the infuriated midshipman and his unfortunate victim, Harry.

He was far too late to do any good, but he was at all events able to explain the true state of affairs to Ned.

When we say explain the true state of affairs, he did so with a slight reservation.

Fred Blount, though only a boy, had the high soul of a gentleman, and could keep a secret, however important and delicate.

As soon as the painful explanations had been exchanged, they slowly returned to where the lieutenant awaited them with deep anxiety.

The men were all afoot and ready for starting.

"What has been the matter?" said Mr. Titcomb. "Where have you and the dog been?"

Ned briefly explained.

"My lad, cheer up. We won't go away without your friend—now for the pirates' lair, and then for the savages," he said.

It was no use fretting, so the two brave boys clambered into the boats, and prepared to act in the dangerous expedition.

CHAPTER XXXIV.

THE PIRATES' LAIR.

TATTOO BLOCK had explained to the brave lieutenant that the pirates were a desperate and powerful gang.

Even when the ship was away over one of their accursed expeditions, a very strong body was left to guard the treasure and the cave.

The latter was thought to be invulnerable.

Unless someone had the clue, it was exceedingly difficult to get at.

But Tattoo Block, who lived in constant hope of escaping from the claws of these ruffians, had studied everything in connection with the secret cavern with great minuteness.

He held the clue of the labyrinth.

Any person knowing nothing of the place world have passed it by unnoticed.

Many a cruiser had done so.

Lieutenant Titcomb had, in the days gone by, when he was second in command of a gun brig, been tricked more than once by the consummate scoundrels.

They had vanished into thin air like the phantom schooner of the Malays.

Now he had hopes of turning the tables, the first officer of the frigate was quite jubilant.

The strictest silence was enjoined.

The word had been passed that victory meant a large sum of prize money.

Jack is always ready for anything in that way.

It means glorification at home with many, with some happiness for parents, wives, and children.

A pale, sickly moon looked down upon this desperate forlorn hope, moving into the jaws of the lion.

Meanwhile the pirates slept in fancied security.

Long immunity from punishment had made them so daring that they had forgotten how long at times is the arm of offended justice.

We say slept, but not all.

The pirates' stronghold was a cavern, situated up a creek, overgrown on both sides with dwarf trees and shrubs.

In front of the mouth was a coral reef, over which, during rough weather, the water rushed in heavy breakers, completely concealing the dangerous reef.

When the weather was calm the coral, being wholly under water, was even more dangerous.

No one but a pilot of the coast would have ventured to approach at any time.

Besides, there could be no motive.

No vessel could, under any circumstances, have been concealed there.

The only channel was twelve feet wide, and could only be navigated lead line in hand.

Consequently these desperadoes were quite satisfied that, if danger came to them, it would not be that way.

Still there were those among them whose evil consciences would not let them sleep.

About an hour before dawn two men emerged from the entrance of the cave, and approached the mouth, where the quiet waters laved the white sand.

One was a handsome, saturnine-looking man of about thirty, the other a weather-beaten sailor of about forty-five.

"Yo—oh! hoy—y!" began the latter, squirting the tobacco juice about, "what now?"

"Jacobs," said the younger man.

"Well, sir—Jake to you—ahoy! hoy! yer—hup—hoop!"

"Do be good enough to forget your fall, stamp, and haul business," said the younger man, "and listen to me."

"I am all ears."

"THEY CLAMBERED TO THE FOOT OF THE FALLS."

"There's many a true word spoken in jest," said Lieutenant Jake, "but I'm weary of this life. Captain Brand, since he has taken to drinking so much rum, is unbearable."

"He is just so—yo! hauly yo! hoy —y!"

"And I cannot understand how a set of brave and gallant men can bear his tyranny."

"It is not pleasant."

"I am resolved either to bring about a change of affairs or to cut it."

"Unless you cut his throat first, you'd better hang yourself," said Jacobs.

"There have been worse alternatives than that," continued Captain Jake.

"Cheerily, men—ho—who's to do it?"

"Jacobs, I know I can trust you. Ever since I entered upon this fatal career, now twelve years ago, you have been my friend."

"I have so, and means to stick by you."

"The men like you. They would follow me to the world's end. Why not, then, depose Brand, get rid of his ferocious gang, and sail away with the vast treasure of this cavern to some part of Southern America, where, as privateers, we might continue our dashing life, and live like *gloriosos*."

"It's fine. The wine and the lassies down yonder are tempting," said Jacobs, "and I'm willing, but if you don't take Brand in the nick of time, he'll tar, feather, and keelhaul us."

"He's brave enough, if he were not so brutal and so cruel," mused Jake.

"Brave! I should think he was. I knowed him once in a storm when the lubberly crew were on their knees, never leave the deck for a fortnight."

"He's all that," continued the pirate officer.

"Sails were blown onter the bolt ropes, bulwarks swept away, boats went, and the fellows was ready to give up, but d'yer think he would? No."

"I knew all that. You speak of years ago. What I want to know is if we are going to become mere dealers in blackbirds instead of rovers of the seas."

"I hate your blackbirds, and this here last expedition will do him no good. A lot of men were lost, and no use."

"Yes. He will be back to-morrow. Between this and then we must decide."

"Captain Jake," said the sailor, doggedly, "I've not stuck to you twelve years for nothing. Whatever you command shall be done."

"Then it is settled. How goes the night?"

"It wants an hour of dawn. Let's have one pipe and one glass. Because Brand makes a beast of himself, that's no reason we shouldn't enjoy ourselves, mate."

Nothing loth, the young desperado, once an open and generous-hearted youth —with quick passions which led him to evil—seated himself at a table, and the rum and tobacco being produced, they were presently conversing as jovially as any pirate of them all.

Suddenly a whistle was heard, and Jacobs retired to see what was the matter.

"What cheer?" said Jake, whose real name was Davidge, as the other returned.

"The 'Black Snake' being chased by a rascally English frigate," replied Jacobs.

"And how is she running?"

"For the black gut. In an hour we shall have old Brand with us. No man-of-war can follow him there," cried Jacobs.

"Except in boats, and with a pilot."

"Yes, but this highflyer can have none," said Jacobs, musing. "A pretty wind-up that would be."

"I will go out and look."

And the young pirate officer ascended a kind of shaft, in company with his faithful follower.

Faithful in all things, for together they had run away from their ship, as officer and man, after half killing the captain's clerk and rifling the money chest.

The well-like shaft led to the summit of the rock in the hollow of which was the cave.

It overlooked the lower part of the island, and above all, that coral reef, between which and the land was the only channel by which the pirate cave could be reached.

Had Tattoo Block only known, he would have shivered in his shoes.

But they were too much occupied in watching the chase.

The frigate and the pirate brigantine were about a mile apart, or not quite so much, the latter crowding on all sail to escape, the frigate majestically pursuing.

She had not all her sail set, as in that narrow channel, without a pilot, she had to keep her weather eye about her.

"Smart frigate that," sighed Jake.

"Puts you in mind of old times, don't it?" said the sailor, pulling away at his pipe.

"Jacobs, I'll cut your throat if you talk to me like that again," said the renegade seaman.

"I'll swear—so help me Bob," suddenly cried Jacobs, "it's the old 'Sultana'!"

"How can you tell?"

"Does a mother know her own kid? Ain't it only four months ago we were in Bombay on the mouch, and didn't I tell you she was there?"

"You did," sighed Jake.

"There she goes; how she blows," cried Jacobs, clapping his hands as two bow chasers were fired; "if them pills touches old Brand, it's up with his fleshings."

But the pirate kept on his way.

He was evidently making for a small promontory at the east end of the island.

"Don't old Brand sail her fine," cried the sailor, with genuine admiration. "Yo! ho! hup!"

As he spoke the brigantine went round more in the face of the frigate, and came rushing dead towards the shore.

In another minute the sails were being taken in, and then the spars, rigging, and masts were blended with the cocoanut trees.

"Neatly done," said Jake, involuntarily.

"He's clever, he is, if he is a swab—and then bang," cried the eccentric sailor.

"We shall soon have to face him," replied the younger man, coolly.

"Well, here goes," said Jacobs, heaving up the slack of his breeches.

And the two men moved down the shaft without ever turning their heads towards the southward.

Had they done so, their fates, and those of a good many others, would in all probability have been very different.

CHAPTER XXXV.

THE PIRATES' GAME IS INTERRUPTED.

WHEN they got down into the cave, they got an inkling that something was afloat, for the men were up and busy in the grey dawn, getting breakfast.

"The skipper's run aground," said one.

"He's safe enough," cried Jake.

"No thanks to you, you lubberly cuss," said Brand, entering the cavern.

Dead silence fell upon all. The cavern presented a singular appearance, half lighted, as it was, by flaring torches.

Brand was a stout, red-faced Yankee as a rule, but now he was white with passion.

"Captain Brand," cried Jake, putting his hand to his breast, "what do you mean by this insult?"

"Why, you white-livered coon, do you mean to tell me it ain't your work bringing that tarnal death of a frigate 'Sultana' down upon us?" roared Brand.

"It's a lie," said Jake, calmly; "I know no more of the matter than you."

Brand stood powerless to speak from rage.

"I tell you this tyranny is getting too hot," cried Jake, "and I won't stand it. Let us divide plunder and part."

"Thunderation!" cried Brand, "is that your little game? Yes, we'll divide plunder and part, but not as you propose, my lively joker."

And, at a signal from the pirate, four men seized Jake, and disarmed him.

Jacobs tried to interfere, and was knocked down for his pains.

"Tie them up—they shall be tried after breakfast," said the captain, coldly.

His orders were obeyed, and both Jake and Jacobs were fastened to some upright posts which supported a portion of the cavern roof.

Now began one of those festive orgies in which the pirates were apt to indulge when returning from a journey.

Brand and most of his party were already pretty advanced in liquor.

Some dozen only had accompanied him, the rest being in ambush near the ship.

"Give me a beaker," cried the pirate,

and receiving a huge tankard filled with some steaming hot decoction, he drank it slowly. "Lieutenant Jake, I looks towards you."

"Coward, set me free—give me a cutlass and face me man to man," replied Jake.

"All in good time," coolly said Brand, whose choler was getting up, and who began to mutter sundry objurgations to himself, which he followed by crowing like a cock, declaring he was the sea-horse of the mountain, a bear with a sore head, and calling himself several zoological curiosities, even to a lion with a mangy tail.

His men took up the fun, and as the liquor passed round, became uproarious.

"Let's have Bingo," shouted one of the men, throwing, in his cowardly rage, a glass in the lieutenant's face.

"Mark me, I'll remember you, Broan," cried the prisoner, in a voice of deep but suppressed passion.

"Huzza for Bingo!" roared the drunken crew.

The pirate chief here waved his hand for silence.

He was a man accustomed to be obeyed, and despite the drink that was in them, all were silent.

"Huzza for Bingo!" he said, with semi-drunken gravity, "but let's have it proper. Hy, darkies!"

Several of this suffering race appeared and brought in several gallons of whisky, which they placed in a tub, adding Malaga wine instead of water, and a variety of spice.

The pirate Brand took the chair, and the well-known Yankee sailors' game began.

"All ready?" said Brand, waving his pipe.

"Ready, sir," repeated the men in chorus.

"A farmer's dog sat on the barn door, and Bingo was his name, O!" began the captain.

Then one and all shouted in chorus—

"And Bingo was his name, O!" making the welkin ring with their hoarse voices.

Again the chief waved for silence.

"B," said the pirate.

"I," said the next man to him.

"N," cried the third.

"G," added the fourth.

"O," screamed the fifth.

Then the chorus, taking up the letter "O" again, shouted out—

"And Bingo was his name, O!"

The fun of the matter was that if any one missed a letter, or said "n," for example, when he should have said "i," his penalty was to take a drink, and the company, as a privilege, drank with him.

"Jacobs," whispered Jake, "while those drunken lunatics are making that beastly noise, cannot we give them the slip?"

"Hush! I tell you what," replied Jacob, "I think that we are safer as prisoners."

"What mean you?"

"And Bingo was his name, O!" shouted the ferocious pirates.

"SURRENDER!" roared an excited voice; "down with your arms, every mother's son of you!"

As these words were spoken, in rushed a number of British tars and marines.

"Take that, you infernal hangdog traitor!" screamed the pirate, shooting at Jake.

"Down with your arms——"

The surprise was so complete, the men were so excited with drink, that though many seized their weapons and made a feeble defence, the pirates were easily overcome.

Several were wounded, one or two were killed, and then the fight was over.

"Which is your chief?" asked Lieutenant Titcomb, when the first uproar had subsided.

"He has slided," said Jacobs, "but cut us down—one of us is done for."

"Ah, my jokers!—prisoners—how's this?" asked the lieutenant of the "Sultana."

"Pirates," muttered the wounded man, who was bleeding freely, "pirates all the same."

Jake and Jacobs were cut down, and the former's wound dressed hastily.

"Where did the villain go?"

"My God, be merciful to me," muttered Jake, who knew he was wounded unto death, "is that Titcomb?"

"Yes—who speaks?" cried the lieutenant.

"Your once pet middy, Louis Davidge," groaned the wretched man.

"Great Heaven! —miserable man—and is this the end of your follies?" exclaimed the other.

"Waste no time on me, the pirate is escaping—let not the wretched blood-sucker escape. Jacobs here will guide you."

"Guard the prisoners well," said the lieutenant, coldly, and placing Jacobs between two men, he hurried through the cavern of darkness, gloom, and mystery.

The island was doubtless a portion detached at no distant period from the continent.

Its huge trees seemed immortal; the roots looked as if they struck the centre of the earth, while the gnarled limbs seemed to reach out to the clouds.

Here and there might be seen one of these lordly specimens of vegetation furrowed by the lightning.

From its top to the base you could trace the electric fluid in its descent, and see where it had shattered off the limb, larger than a man's body, or had been turned away by some inequality in the bark.

These stricken trees, no longer able to repel the parasites that surrounded them, had become festooned with wreaths and flowers, while the damp air engendered on living tree and dead, like funeral drapery, the pendant moss, that waved in every breeze, and seemed to cover the whole scene with the gloom of the grave.

Jacobs led them through this extraordinary forest towards a dense cane brake.

"We call it, sir," he said, "the devil's summer retreat—saving your presence."

"Not badly named," replied the officer, drily.

It was a strange place. Here the reed grew to a delicate mast, springing from the rich alluvium that gives it sustenance with the prodigality of grass, and tapering from its roots to the height of twenty or thirty feet.

The vines were so interwoven as to make the place as impenetrable as a mountain, but for the guide.

A winding path had been cut by the pirates.

Presently Jacobs raised his hand for them to halt, and pointed through an opening.

They could see the water, in the dis-

tance the frigate, and in the foreground the brigantine.

The men were busy transferring necessaries to the boats, in order to escape.

"Now, sir, you have them. Give me a sword, and I'll fight like a black bear."

"Dash in; give them a volley," said the lieutenant, "and then bayonet them, skewer them—do what you like with those who do not surrender."

The jolly tars and marines needed no twice telling; they rushed in quietly first, but soon, discovering their presence known, gave at the same time a thundering cheer and a deadly volley.

"Down with the rapparees!" shouted an Irishman.

"Slay the thieves!" said a Scotchman.

"Give 'em goss!" roared a Yankee.

The pirates fought with the desperation of men with halters round their necks.

But it was in vain.

Valour, discipline, and the right prevailed.

Jitcomb found himself face to face with the pirate, who was infuriated by drink and the sense of coming defeat.

Like many another evil doer, he had made up his mind that this should be his last cruise, and that he would retire to his native land, and devote himself for the rest of his days to the cultivation of his native cabbages, an occasional buffalo hunt, but above all to the attainment of a position as a "big man."

With millions actually in his possession, with treasure enough to have started a government loan, he was brought to bay by a beggarly lieutenant.

"Have at you!" he roared; "lay down that thar shootin' iron, and let's go in for knives."

"My sword is my weapon, fellow," cried Titcomb, proudly, "and I do you honour to cross swords with you."

"How fine we are," spluttered Brand; "'spect you's gin many a hog the ear-ache."

The lieutenant knew enough of Yankee slang to be aware that he meant to insinuate he was a pig-stealer.

"Fool, cease this madness. Surrender, and trust to the mercy of outraged justice."

"Now, then, shut pass, old fellow," said the pirate, defending himself with an ability acquired once in the most elegant and polite of New York saloons, "or you'll get sweetened."

He almost took Titcomb unawares as he spoke, aiming a terrific blow at his head, which the other, however, met with vigour, and then—his sword passed through the sea robber's breast, and he fell to the ground a dying man.

"Thar, you is sweetened!" said a Yankee sailor, who served on board the "Sultana."

"Right you are," replied the pirate, with a fierce and savage grin, "but with me dies the secret of the treasure."

CHAPTER XXXVI.

THE SECRET OF THE TREASURE.

NOTHING is more satisfactory to the feelings of an Englishman than to do his duty, slaughter pirates, kill insolent Abyssinians, cut up, root and branch, sanguinary-minded Ashantees, and so forth, but when the din and smoke are over, other considerations arise.

Loot, prize money, extra pay, are matters not to be despised in this sublunary world.

It may, therefore, be readily imagined that the words uttered by the pirate were not very tasteful to the feelings of those who heard them.

As, however, the man was dead, there was no remedy.

Every pirate who remained alive was made prisoner and fastened securely.

Then the brigantine was gutted.

In addition to plenty of food, excellent wine, and other luxuries, a considerable amount of money and plate was found.

Silver lamps, church candlesticks, flagons—even cups of gold—which were placed in a heap.

Then the vessel was fired.

Parcels then were made of the plunder, and under the guidance of Jacobs, the whole party prepared for the return march.

Just, however, as they were about to take their departure, the captain's gig touched the shore, and a midshipman touched his hat.

"Well, Willis, what's the news?"

"Captain, sir, sent me to learn how the fighting was getting on."

"Well, you see, pretty well. We've had a hard scrimmage, and a good many are hurt, but not one has lost the number of his mess."

"Glad to hear it, sir."

"Just wait one moment, and I will write a few lines," continued the lieutenant, tearing a leaf out of his tablets.

Having written a few lines, he handed it to the midshipman.

"Take that on board. Remember, three rockets will show all is right—two that we are victorious, but that the reward is not achieved."

"All right, sir," said the middy, and at once took his departure.

The dead pirates were hastily buried, and the rest liberated.

Their arms were cast into the seething furnace of the burning ship—without which they were utterly helpless.

They had no resource but to flee to the mainland before the savages found out their helplessness.

Then Jacobs, who was deeply anxious about his young master, placed himself at the head of the party, beside Lieutenant Titcomb.

"I want to get back and see how Jake is."

"By Jake, I presume you mean Mr. Davidge," said the lieutenant, drily.

"Well, sir—yes, sir," he replied.

"Best thing he can do is to die," answered the officer, in a suggestive tone.

"Why, sir?"

"Desertion, after striking a superior officer, and piracy on the high seas, carried on for several years, are usually punished by hanging."

"Hang poor Davidge?" cried Jacobs.

"And you too, my fine fellow," added Titcomb.

"That I don't care a button about," replied Jacobs, "but my poor master!"

"He has brought it on himself."

"And yet if you knew all you wouldn't hang him," said Jacobs, with something like a chuckle.

"I should like you to show me any reason."

"He's the only man left who knows

the secret of the treasure," replied Jacobs, drily.

Titcomb was taken aback a little, but he was too much of a general to show his cards at once.

"But, you know, my fine fellow, is there such a thing as this so-talked-of treasure?"

"Well, sir, we were a hundred and fifty of us, and next Christmas was to be division day. I fancy the man who didn't get five thousand quid would have felt himself robbed."

Titcomb started.

"So much," he mused.

"I will speak fair and straight, captain," said Jacobs, emboldened by his manner.

"Out with it; you can trust me."

"The treasure is *said* to be two millions sterling—that's what Brand owns to—the accumulation of twenty-one years, during which the band of brotherhood has worked."

"A pretty sum; a pretty band of brotherhood," cried Titcomb, excitedly.

"I *know* it to be five millions in value. Old Brand wants to chisel us. Now, give me the captain and a canoe, and enough 'shiners' to take us safe to Ameriky, and the dollup is yourn. I can't say fairer."

The lieutenant tried to look stern. But in those days promotion was slow, prize money not to be had every day, and the share of officers and men would simply be stupendous.

"Jacobs," he said at length, "you are a faithful fellow, and shall have your captain, and as much gold as you can conveniently carry off."

"But you must give us a few hours' law. If the other beggars only 'sniff,' we're dead men."

"You shall have every chance. If you reach the States in safety, drop this life."

"Rely upon that, your honour," said Jacobs, gaily.

All this while they were walking through the cane brake on their way to the cavern.

They reached it about nightfall.

All this time Ned Summers and Fred Blount had been active and brave.

Much as they regretted the loss of time, much as both gave their thoughts to poor Harry, they knew that the destruction of the pirate gang was an imperative duty.

"Poor Harry will think he is forgotten," sighed Ned, "if he thinks at all by this time."

"I have no fear for his life," observed Fred.

"Have you any reason for hoping?"

"Samuel Petworth will not kill him," said Fred, in a hearty tone, trying to cheer Ned.

"Well, that's something. But he's a rare brute," retorted Ned.

"He is all that, but Harry's life is safe."

And with this oracular statement the subject for the moment dropped.

When the victorious expedition re-entered the cave, they found the pirate Jake asleep.

The lieutenant exchanged a few words with the young officer in charge of the prisoners.

All their weapons were collected, and broken up in pieces.

"Now, you fellows, be off. In an hour my ship will be here, and if Captain Dumer catches any of you rascals, he'll skin you alive."

The pirates required no twice telling, and rushed away to hide themselves until the ship had taken its departure.

In the mean time Jacobs had a conference with Jake, *alias* Davidge.

The wretched man was better. His wound had been cared for, and there was every sign of his recovering.

"I will give up the secret of the treasure," he said to Lieutenant Titcomb, "without conditions, but you shall keep your word to Jacobs."

"And, Davidge," replied the officer, "quit this life. Get over this, and follow a better course."

"I will. Never has my heart been in it. Jacobs here knows what I have done to save life, and how my soul has often revolted at the existence."

"I am glad to hear it," replied Titcomb.

"But all this is waste of time," said the pirate, "Jacobs knows. I will remain here, and then you can have me helped into the boat."

Titcomb nodded and followed Jacobs.

Four sailors carried torches and crowbars, which Jacobs gave them.

They went down a narrow passage, and halted in what looked like a blind alley.

A solid lump of rock stopped the way.

Jacobs pointed out, after using his knife, some small holes.

The sailors went to work, and in ten minutes had demolished the wall.

"That is the secret," said Jacobs, as he leaped over the *débris* and held up a torch.

A circular chamber was revealed, piled up with bags, barrels, and other receptacles for cash, silver in bars, silver in mugs, flagons, and every conceivable shape known to the goldsmith.

"It is all yours, sir," said Jacobs; "there are no owners left."

It was amazing, stupendous, tremendous.

When Titcomb gazed at it, piled up in the outer cave, he could not believe it real.

He, however, sent out a midshipman to send up the three rockets.

"And now, Davidge, farewell," he said. "I have acted on my own responsibility—go."

"With thanks," replied Davidge, who, aided by the two men, was carried to a boat, followed by Jacobs with his sack of gold and other valuables.

They were never seen again.

But somewhere in the Green Mountains is a wild and saturnine man, with an aged servant, who, though tolerably rich, lives hardly, hunts nearly all his time, and is good to the poor.

Two hours later, guided by Tattoo Block, the exiled captain entered the cavern.

The report nearly took away his breath.

"Titcomb, we're made men," he said, "thanks to you."

"Thanks to this boy, our gallant leader," replied Titcomb, without mentioning names.

And he explained.

"He wants to find his lost comrade."

"By all means. Take the pinnace, and, if needed, I will wait a week."

"Thank you, sir," replied Ned, warmly.

"We shall want the long boat and the pinnace," said the lieutenant.

"My dear Titcomb," cried the delighted captain, who was devouring the treasure with eager eyes, "take what you like. I will carry all this precious stuff on board and make an inventory while waiting."

The lieutenant bowed, saluted his crew, and, with Tattoo Block for a guide, started in search of poor Harry Thornton.

But it was only a start. As soon as they were free of the cavern reef, they took up a position for the night.

The men were weary and exhausted, and wanted both refreshment and sleep.

CHAPTER XXXVII.

THE ISLAND HOME.

WHEN the infuriated madman entered the camp, and carried off Harry Thornton into a kind of slavery, he had, with that cunning which marks the partially aberrated, made his preparations.

The boat was ready with provisions at no distance from the shore.

He pushed it away with a vigour which sent it spinning over the waves almost like a flat stone when thrown by a schoolboy.

Harry Thornton, after the struggle was over, and his last despairing cry, sank in the bottom of the boat like an inanimate log.

The madman kept paddling for two hours, and then reached a large island, which he was supposed to have once before visited in a futile attempt to escape.

Hiding the boat, he made for the interior, which, by the light of the moon, he made out to be a fine country, heavily stocked with timber, and sprinkled with occasional swamps and thickets.

Having reached a small clearing, Sam set Harry down, and himself, exhausted and weary, sank beside him.

Harry had no weapon save a small, concealed life preserver, while Sam was wholly unarmed.

This he considered a blessing.

But Sam took no further notice of him that night except securing his feet by a rope.

When he awoke this was loosened, and Sam, opening his wallet, placed food before him.

He then filled a calabash from a spring close by, picked some fruit, and indulged in a hearty meal.

Sam was gentle and deferential, which made Harry still more wary and cautious.

When breakfast was over, the semimaniac turned to Harry with a glare of strange significance.

"Now, my joker," he said, "you've done with your friend Ned, and shall be my——"

What he meant to say cannot be known, as there came the heavy report of a musket not twenty yards distant, just within the confines of a thick swamp, and at the same moment an arrow, aimed with more precision than the bullet, almost scraped Harry's arm and buried itself in the tree.

With a wild howl Sam arose, and snatching up Harry, took to his heels.

From much practice he was now a splendid runner.

Then there came a crashing through the bushes, and such a hideous yelling as defies description.

Had a regiment of imps been let loose, they could not have made more awful sounds.

Sam never stopped until he was in the swamp, when he skulked low, keeping still on his way, until, after many twists and turns, he turned into a thick clump of bushes.

This, however, was only a respite, as the rascally savages now ceased their yelling, and commenced a game of still hunting.

Harry was apathetic and dull. He appeared to care little for the result.

Indian savages or Sam Petworth were very much the same to him, though probably, had he known the truth, he would have preferred the savages.

After keeping quiet a few minutes, Sam led the way across the swamp.

After toiling through the mud and briars for more than an hour, they halted by a pool of water.

Sam pushed Harry behind a tree, and pointed to a small fire, near which lay three white men.

They had evidently been feeding heartily, and then laid down to sleep.

Half a deer and an empty flask indicated the nature of the meal.

Making sure that they slept, Sam crept up to the camp-fire and seized a couple of muskets, ammunition, and a bag.

He then clutched the meat and returned to Harry.

Aware of the deadly fury which would be aroused in the defrauded, he immediately started off to some more secure retreat.

Despite his wild state of mind, there was a cunning method in his madness which amazed Harry.

But what amazed the lad most was the absence of brutality in word or deed.

At last he found himself once more in an almost impenetrable swamp.

To go on was impossible, to retreat equally so, as night had come.

It was, as Fred Blount would have said, at least three shades darker than midnight in a coal pit.

Harry shuddered as night fell, for it was the signal for such a concert of vocal music as he had never heard before.

Everything seemed represented, from the annoying buzz of the mosquito to the melodious notes of alligators and panthers, who made night hideous with discordant revelries.

Sam chuckled to himself, though not fool enough to attract attention by making a noise.

"My poor head!" he presently whispered, putting his hand to his forehead, "it aches."

Harry was too terrified to speak.

Sam moaned as if in pain, and then, taking up the horn which he had stolen, drank off a considerable allowance of whisky.

He then proceeded, in a hollow, overgrown tree, to make a fire, which would scare the beasts and enable them to cook their food.

By the light of this Harry grew braver, and even forced himself to eat a little.

"I don't seem to recollect," muttered Sam to himself, "what has happened."

One of his lucid intervals was coming on.

Harry looked keenly at him.

"Do you feel better?" asked Harry, timidly.

"I don't know—my head! Here, take the gun and keep watch," was the rather surly reply, and casting himself on the ground, he was soon performing bass to the "other varmints."

Harry, who never fired a gun except with deep reluctance, placed it on his knee, and determined to watch, and awaken Sam if anything went wrong.

But fatigue overcame his better judgment.

Drowsiness came upon him, and he slept.

How long he slept he was never able to say, but suddenly he had a confused sense of having been engaged in a panther hunt.

When he rubbed his eyes and sat up, he heard the unmistakable voice of a panther within a few yards of him.

He trembled violently, but instinctively grasped his gun.

To awake Sam from a sound slumber, brought on by fatigue and whisky, was impossible.

He looked in the direction of the sound, and shivered as he looked.

His eyes were open enough now, and he saw a pair of the largest, brightest eyes that ever he had seen on a dark night.

They glared at him with all the brilliancy of gaslights, though, unfortunately, without lighting up the surrounding darkness.

There was no help for it. Harry lifted the gun to his shoulder, levelled it at his glaring eyeballs, and, with a convulsive shudder, fired.

A half-smothered howl followed the discharge, and Sam, springing up, darted away into a mud-hole up to his arm-pits.

"Where's the red devils—where's my gun? Bear a hand, Harry, and lift me out of this mud-hole!"

But Harry had fainted, and when he scrambled out his astonishment may be conceived to find a huge panther lying in the agonies of death, not ten feet off.

"What an escape!" said the wretched midshipman, who was now to all appearance in full possession of his faculties.

"Brave as a lion heart!" he muttered, as he threw water over the other's face,

forced him to drink some whisky, and then began to unfasten his tunic.

"I'm quite well now," said Harry, sitting up, and speaking in a dreamy, terrified way. "Is he dead?"

"Dead as Wat Tyler," replied Sam. "I never was so scared before."

No more sleep was attempted that night, both watching with their fingers on the triggers.

As soon as morning came Sam led the way out of the swamp, and began climbing up the side of a pleasant slope, well wooded, and where they were likely to discover some fissure or cavern where to repose out of reach of the Indians.

The summit of the hill was nearly reached, however, before they came to a kind of terrace, overgrown by trees and shrubbery.

It was not easy to approach the spot without being seen.

Suddenly Harry gave a great cry.

"What is the matter?" said Sam, sulkily, the fire of semi-insanity again glaring in his eyes.

"The ship! the ship! we are free!"

Sam looked, and saw the tall masts and bellying sails of the frigate not three miles distant.

"Quick! let us to the shore," cried Harry.

"Never!" said Sam, clutching the other by the arm, "never!"

And he whispered one sentence in his ear.

Then Harry understood it all, and shivered from head to foot at the meaning of the cunning madman.

"We will live here for ever," continued Sam, with an hysterical laugh, as he shouldered his gun and handed one to Harry. "Come along. I will have no signalling. Sam Petworth is no silly fool to be caught in a trap."

He had let Harry go, and was shaking his fist at the distant ship.

Harry made one bound into the bushes, and darted down the side of the hill.

The action was so sudden that, before Sam could follow, he was out of sight.

Wild and frantic curses were heard in his rear, and then the noise of a heavy body crashing through the bushes.

Harry, with a set and resolute look on his face, such as had never been seen there before, stood still.

He loosed his knife from its sheath, and keenly examined the priming of his gun.

Some stern purpose was evidently passing through his mind.

Separate from Sam he determined to.

"Never will I submit to him," he muttered aloud, "and, please Heaven, I will reach the ship."

He sighed.

"Poor Ned! If I cannot find him, at least I may console my poor father and mother."

He crouched now behind a prickly pear bush, and listened.

Sam was not twenty yards away, blaspheming horribly, and cutting and slashing the bushes with a stick.

"Come back!" he then whined; "I won't be cruel. You shall be master and I will be slave."

But Harry simply waited until he was out of sight, and then struck out for the shore.

If he could only reach that, he relied on making some signal which would be seen by the ship.

But the woods were confusing.

Harry was not much accustomed to prairie or forest travelling, so that though he pressed on for hours, he came no nearer to the much-wished-for goal.

At length, weary and footsore, Harry selected a sheltered clump of cocoanuts and reposed.

He easily opened some of the ripe fruit with his knife, and drank some of the milk.

But still he was too fatigued to walk.

Harry, however, determined to rest only one hour, and then resolutely resumed his march.

Night was approaching.

Terrors unnamable were in his heart, and yet the frail, delicate, but plump little fellow walked along, with his gun on his shoulder, towards the sea.

With what inexpressible delight he suddenly heard the dashing of the waves.

He took to his heels and ran.

The ocean lay before him.

And there was the tall ship, heading leisurely to the breeze as it made for the pirate's cavern.

What could Harry Thornton do?

He rushed down to the rocky shore and fired his gun, then he raised his voice, waved his cap, and uttered frenzied cries.

A blank horror fell upon him as his cries were unexpectedly answered.

"So, my little bantam, I've got you again," said the harsh voice of Sam. "I've a great mind to give you a good flogging."

"What for?" gasped Harry, clutching his empty gun. "How dare you?"

"Well, I won't this time, so shoulder arms, march," he said, in a menacing tone.

There was no resource but to obey. His gun was empty, and in brute force he was no match for the young ruffian.

They reached the wood, and were about to conceal themselves beneath its leafy shadows, when, with a savage howl, a number of Indians rushed forth and made them prisoners.

Resistance was madness and folly.

Both were disarmed, though Harry's knife was so concealed that they did not notice it.

"We'll escape," muttered Sam.

"I'd rather be an Indian drudge all my life than be your slave," said Harry.

Sam gave him a fearful scowl.

"Wait till I tell the savages all."

Harry scorned a reply, and the two walked on in silence.

They were placed in separate huts, to the great satisfaction of Harry, whose fear of Sam was now something terrible.

Both were secured by withes, and left to pass the weary night as they liked.

It was a long, miserable one for both.

Harry almost sobbed himself to sleep, while Sam gnawed his hands in his endeavours after liberty.

Then morning broke, and the prisoners were led forth.

The savages were now reinforced by a number of the escaped pirates.

With a savage grin the prisoners were led to two upright posts and secured.

"Now then, you rascals," said one of the pirates, "we're about to pay you out for all."

"What have we done?" asked Harry, shivering.

"You belong to the darned lot," answered the pirate, "and we're going to roast you alive. Give it to them, redskins."

They began to cast the faggots around the wretched victims, when a cheer was heard, and in dashed the "Sultanas," firing a volley as they came.

"THE DOG HAD PINNED SAMUEL BY THE BACK OF THE NECK."

CHAPTER XXXVIII.

A HOT FIGHT.

A SINGULAR result followed. One of the pirates on duty as sentinel had seen the sailors coming.

In the terrible hurly burly which was going on he was not heard.

But he determined that the prisoners should not be rescued.

He cut the withes which bound them, and while the great majority of the redskins and pirates turned to defend themselves against an attack which was as unexpected as it was unpleasant, he and some others of them made off with the prisoners.

Sam was simply driven before them by the stern argument of blows, while one of the stouter and taller pirates carried Harry Thornton in his arms.

He had fainted and was insensible to all around.

But the fight was short. The dash and valour of the sailors overwhelmed all else, and the ill-assorted allies fled.

"Victory!" cried the lieutenant.

"No," answered Ned—"for where is Harry?"

"I saw a big fellow carrying him off in his arms," replied Fred.

The naval officer hesitated for a moment.

"I tell you what it is, my lad," he cried, after some moments of reflection, "we owe you so much that whatever you wish us to do shall be done."

"Follow, then," answered Ned, earnestly.

Immediate orders were now given for the men to reload and prepare for a second march.

A short rest and some refreshment were however, absolutely necessary, and the word was passed.

The men seated themselves on the grass, under trees and in various convenient positions, and began eating their rations with gusto.

A keg of very excellent wine, and some brandy, the spoil of the pirates, was an excellent supplement.

Then orders were given to advance.

The black man, who was such an experienced guide, volunteered to go in advance.

He would keep in sight of just two of the sailors, and they were to act on his signs.

Tattoo Block was as good a scout as any American Indian.

His ear drank in every sound, he trod the woods with the lightness of a fawn, his feet scarcely stirred the leaves and twigs that covered the ground, and his weapon was so held as to avoid all chance of contact with the trees.

There was something singularly solemn in the aspect of the forest through which the black glided noiselessly, stealthily, as a snake does through the tall prairie grass or the thick underbrush.

The trail of the flying savages and pirates was plain enough for some considerable distance.

Then it wholly disappeared on the banks of a stream.

But after a short pause the black crossed the stream and continued on his way.

But night approached without his making out the foe.

The naval officer ordered a halt.

"I say, Block, this seems a blind sort of navigation. Are you really going right?"

"Ees, massa. Know whar 'em go. To de valley ob de Debble's Thumb," said the guide, with a broad grin.

"Rum place that. Is it far?"

"Two more hours' march, massa."

"Very well. But the men are tired and must rest. Can you find your way in the dark?"

"Ees, massa. Yah! yah! you see."

"Will this suspense never end?" said Ned to his friend Fred. "I cannot rest."

"And yet, my dear fellow, when we get up to these reptiles, we shall want all our strength. They will be prepared now to make a hard fight for it," urged Fred.

With great difficulty Ned was persuaded to take food and drink, but his impatience was terrible. He was pale, haggard, and restless.

"Ned Summers," said the lieutenant, "don't think I blame you, but men cannot act like machines, and, unless restored, will be poor hands at fighting."

"I know it, sir," replied Ned. "But Harry and I are more than brothers."

The lieutenant smiled. He had not wholly forgotten his days of boyish enthusiasm.

At length the men of their own accord declared themselves ready.

Tattoo Block at once rose and took the lead of the column.

They now marched in Indian file.

Everybody kept close to his front rank man, as the best guide.

All was darkness, gloom, and night.

There was not a sound to tell that nature was not dead.

Not an owl hooted, not a wild beast was heard to roar.

Still the black moved along with the unerring instinct of a woodsman. Ned, who walked beside him, wondered at the trifles which guided him.

There were no obvious marks.

But the moss on the trees, the pebbles on the path, the colour of the bark, the twinkling of a star, the point of a rock, were indications to the guide as good as any sign post.

Presently Tattoo Block slackened his pace, and coolly seated himself at the foot of a tree.

"Why do you halt?" asked Ned.

"Dis chile listen."

He laid himself flat on his face, his ear to the ground, and remained in that position a minute.

"I hear 'em," he said.

"Let us advance," cried the lieutenant.

"Dey all active as bees now; soon rest. Most best surprise 'em by-and-bye."

Tattoo Block offered to advance and reconnoitre. A loud, thrice-repeated hoot of an owl would be the signal to advance.

The officer signified his assent, and the black slipped away, closely followed by Ned.

Passing under the trees, they soon came to a small piece of arid soil, which was bare of any vegetation.

Beyond this lay a gloomy pile of rock, which rose to an elevation of two hundred feet.

"What dat?" suddenly cried Tattoo Block, turning sharp round, and facing Ned.

"All right," replied the boy.

"Golly! but you give me powerful scare," said the negro; "keep back; dem debbles see us; dey make cullender of your body."

And he skirted the wood, until he faced the entrance to the valley known by the euphonious name of the Devil's Thumb.

They became spectators of a singular scene.

A high barrier was constructed across the entrance to the valley, on which stood sentries, their figures brought out in bold relief by the fires within the valley.

"Dem beggahs means fighting," muttered Tattoo Block, "well, nebbah mind."

Ned stared. He could hear them talking, laughing, chattering, like peaceful citizens, when they knew how near they were to destruction.

"Come," said Tattoo Block.

He once more retreated into the wood, and turning his back on the pirate entrenchment, put his hands to his mouth and gave them the well-known hoot of the screech owl.

Then he waited.

In ten minutes the lieutenant, guided by the sound, came up and joined them.

Tattoo Block explained that the enemy had made a strong barricade and were prepared to defend it with determination.

"I'm sorry for it," said the lieutenant, quietly, "but our duty is clear. We must on."

"But, sah, 'spose we circumwent de warmints, as de Yankees say."

"Can we do it?"

"Yes, sah. Me take just six men, and we get inside. Den we fire and you charge—de ting is done."

The negro explained that there was a rift, or fissure, leading into the valley of the Devil's Thumb, by which a stream poured out, by means of which men, wading to their waists, could enter the valley.

It was a wild path, but would serve them well.

"I will make one of the six," said the lieutenant, who, having selected five stout fellows, gave the command of the others, with instructions, to a quartermaster.

Once more Tattoo Block led the way, until they reached a perpendicular rock, through a narrow fissure of which ran the water.

Dark as the night was, they could just make out that the sides of the fissure rose, to all appearance, fifty feet.

They were in a moment up to their knees in water, the stream rushing swiftly by.

Tattoo Block walked steadily on, until at last the rocky torrent bed began to ascend.

In ten minutes they were on a platform overlooking the camp of desperadoes.

They were feasting, smoking, playing dice or cards, and otherwise employed in pursuits of peace, though every man had his weapon by him.

Ned peered around. Nowhere could he see either Harry or Sam.

"What is to be done now?" said the lieutenant, who observed that the platform went sheer down to the camp below, forty feet.

"Golly, dis niggah show you," he replied, presently, after gazing around as if to refresh his memory.

He moved along the platform until he came to a slope, going down at an angle of about forty-five degrees.

It was overgrown with brushwood, and it was therefore possible to creep down unperceived.

It was a daring deed to do, and the only hope was in the utter surprise.

They began the descent.

In the meantime the sufferings of Harry Thornton had been great.

The brawny pirate no sooner found the poor boy reviving from his fainting fit, than he put him on the ground, and, threatening him with a knife, urged him forward.

Trembling as with the ague, Harry obeyed, though scarcely able to crawl.

When the bed of the river was reached a halt was declared.

Tattoo Block, during his sojourn with the pirates, had not learned all their secrets.

Going up the stream, the numerous band of fugitives hit upon a beaten trail, which shortened the distance to the valley some hours.

They followed this leisurely.

As soon as the valley was reached—it was near the shore—they thrust Sam and Harry into a gloomy cavern, and rested.

When their fatigues were past, they rose and began to feast.

A woman then entered the cavern with a light, and gave the wretched prisoners some food and water. She left a torch burning. Both looked haggard.

Sam was suffering from a kind of epileptic fit, from which he slowly recovered.

"Where are we?" he said, in a low, hushed voice, feeble as a child's.

"We are again prisoners of the pirates and savages," replied Harry, painfully raising the gourd of water.

"Ah! but we will circumvent them," said Sam, in a low whisper; "we will get away from them, and we will escape from Ned Summers—how I hate him!"

"Don't say a word against that noble and generous fellow," cried Harry.

Sam laughed a maniacal laugh.

"Rather than he should take you from me," said Sam, "I would die."

"What do you mean to do?" asked Harry, timidly.

"Hide. When the pirates have gone, and the sailors are tired, they will go away. Then we will go to your palace, and live—oh, so happily."

Harry did not know what to say. His hatred and abhorrence of Sam was something fearful.

"I must go. I will not stay here; I have dear friends in England."

"I have none anywhere," said Sam, who all this time was eating ravenously.

"It is your own fault."

"Dare say that again, and I will strangle you," said Samuel Petworth.

And rising, he approached the mouth of the cavern.

Two savages were seated at no great distance, on the watch.

Sam retreated with a fearful imprecation.

He was unarmed and helpless.

"We must away from here," he said, wildly. "Can you—will you run?"

"No," said Harry, coldly. "I will rather remain with the savages and pirates than go with you."

"Why?" sighed Sam, hotly.

"You know," was the expressive but inexplicable reply; "and if you approach any nearer, I will stab both you and myself."

He held up a short, bright blade, which ever since he had gone down into the cabin to dress, during the shipwreck, had never left him.

Sam stared wildly.

"I won't hurt you," he said, humbly.

"Keep off," was the stern reply. "I know you too well to trust your word."

Sam rapped out a great oath and stood back a little.

At this moment a volley of musketry was fired close at hand.

Furious cries, imprecations, and ejaculations arose on all sides.

Then there was a crack of musketry from every side.

Harry Thornton kneeled in prayer, while Sam cautiously advanced to the mouth of the cave and peered out.

The pirates and their new allies had been surprised, but were fighting desperately.

They were taken between two fires.

Sam Petworth howled with rage, and gnashed his teeth in his impotency.

He returned towards Harry, but the boy held his knife menacingly.

"Let us escape during the hubbub," he cried.

"No," said Harry.

"Do not be foolish. Now is our only chance," urged Sam, wildly.

Again a terrific hurrah is heard, as the pirates and savages are driven from their posts.

On come the blue jackets, the marines, Tattoo Block, and the two boys.

Foremost was Ned, who soon secured Harry, and led him out of the conflict.

Sam Petworth was dead, slain by a stray shot.

The savages made a slight defence, and then pirates and redskins fled.

The victory was quite complete this time.

The enemy hid in holes, in various places known to themselves, and finally scattered over the island.

They all camped where they stood, and never were two boys happier than Ned and Harry.

"I thought you were lost for ever," said Ned; "if you had been I should have died."

Harry could not speak. The tears actually came into his eyes.

At daybreak the march was recommenced, and at midday the place was reached where they had left their boats.

CHAPTER XXXIX.

CONCLUSION—AND A WONDERFUL DISCOVERY.

THE sailors were at once drafted to their several boats, the three Crusoes accompanying the delighted young lieutenant—he was a third, and his name was Cromer—who saw in this adventure a source of great personal advantage to himself.

The "Sultana" frigate was on her return voyage from India, with several passengers, male and female, of high rank under government, and there was a certain Miss Marchmont, who had wonderfully pleased him.

As they approached the vessel, they saw that the poop deck was crowded.

The captain was there, surrounded by gold bands, men in private clothes, and ladies.

His glass was fixed on the three boys dressed in deer skins, and with such dark visages.

Suddenly the telescope fell to his side, but it was observable he spoke not.

The lieutenant and his charges were the first to come on deck.

Cromer led them direct to the quarter-deck.

"Ned Summers is safe and sound with his comrades," he said.

The confusion was intense; but waving his hand, the captain commanded silence in a firm but husky voice.

"Ned Summers alive!—and Petworth?"

"Dead! and so much the better. All that has happened was owing to his villany," continued the lieutenant.

"Ned, my boy, your hand. I can see from Cromer's manner that you were no willing deserter, and are worthy of your noble father. Take him."

And Ned Summers was clasped to the beating heart of a bronzed, bearded-faced man, for whose sake the commander of the "Sultana" had come out of his way.

In a brief sentence or two Ned told the assembled company his story, which was heard in hushed and solemn silence.

Suddenly a pale lady, leaning on the arm of an aristocratic-looking gentleman, screamed, and, rushing across the deck, caught Harry Thornton round the neck, embraced him frantically, and dragged him away with her husband to their state cabin.

It was Mr. and Mrs. Thornton, who were invalided home, broken-hearted at the loss of their only child.

In about an hour silence was restored, and then it was agreed to pass the night in the bay, and on the next day pay a visit to the scene of such wonderful adventures.

Ned and Fred were handed over to the midshipmen's berth for a rig-out, and told to be ready in the saloon for dinner in half an hour.

They were ready, and the whole company were collected ready for the meal.

All save Mr. and Mrs. Thornton, and their child.

Ned, though with his proud father beside him, was anxious.

Was Harry about to cut him?

Suddenly a door opened, and the steward, in a very significant tone, announced Mr. and Mrs. and Miss Harriet Thornton.

Ned turned pale as death.

Yes; there was no mistaking it; his Harry, his chum, the boy he had loved so well, was after all—a girl!

He advanced trembling, as if to bow, but Harriet, more agitated than himself, ran forward and caught him in her arms.

"Ned, Ned," she cried, "my own noble friend, can you forgive Harry now for being such a sad coward?"

Ned could not speak for a minute or two, and then his words were strange.

"Did Sam know you were a girl?"

"Yes."

"Then I forgive him. No wonder he wanted to steal you."

The ladies laughed, and Mr. and Mrs. Thornton coming forward, in deeply agitated tones, thanked him for all he had done.

"Never, never can we repay you for saving our daughter from shame, and misery, and death," said Mr. Thornton, a civilian of high rank.

Ned took Harriet's hand gently in his.

"I loved Harry with all my heart and soul, and would have died for him, and now, if parted from Harriet, I think I should die," he said, gravely.

No answer was made as the dinner-bell rang, and Ned and Harriet walked arm-in-arm to their seats.

Fred Blount followed them with his soft, grey eyes.

Harriet's sex had been no secret to him from the first, but he also saw through the utter devotion and love of the supposed boy for Ned Summers.

All that evening the cabin passengers sat in silence, while Ned told his story.

Next day, the Indians having moved off in the night, with their dead and wounded in the canoes, all the passengers landed, under an escort, and visited the principal scene of their adventures.

Their fort, their tame goats, were a marvel, and the choicest were taken on board to be transplanted to England.

Fruits, fresh meat and water having been procured in abundance, the vessel, after a week's stay, took its departure.

The three friends saw its shores fade away with some regret.

Sam was buried in the centre of the Indian village.

Ned resumed his rank on board, but, on reaching England, Mr. and Mrs. Thornton announcing their intention of settling their whole large fortune on Harriet as soon as the young people were married, Ned retired from the service and took to agriculture.

As heir of his grandfather's Norfolk estates, he was not poor.

The end of all was—that, one year from their arrival in Old England, the Rival Crusoes were married; and of an evening for many and many years, it was the delight of the children to hear from papa, when in a particularly good humour, how he met their ma all by herself on a desert island, for all the world like Alexander Selkirk—monarch of all he surveyed.

THE END.